DOC HOLLIDAY'S GONE
A Western Duo

DOC HOLLIDAY'S GONE
A Western Duo

Jane Candia Coleman

Five Star
Unity, Maine

Five Star Western
Published in conjunction with
Golden West Literary Agency.

Cover photograph of Kate Elder courtesy of
Glenn G. Boyer
Cover photograph of Viola Slaughter courtesy of
Arizona Historical Society

December, 1999

First Edition, Second Printing.

Five Star Standard Print Western Series.

The text of this edition is unabridged.

Set in 11 pt. Plantin.

Printed in the United States on permanent paper.

Library of Congress Cataloging-in-Publication Data

Coleman, Jane Candia.
    Doc Holliday's gone : a western duo / by Jane
Candia Coleman. — 1st ed.
        p.   cm.
        Contents: Doc Holliday's gone — Mrs. Slaughter.
    ISBN 0-7862-1841-X (hc : alk. paper)
        1. Fontier and pioneer life — West (U.S.) Fiction.
    2. Western stories.   I. Coleman, Jane Candia.   Mrs.
    Slaughter.   II. Title.   III. Title: Mrs. Slaughter.
    PS3553.O47427A6 1999
        813'.54—dc21   99-41705

DOC HOLLIDAY'S GONE

My thanks to Michael Horony and the entire Horony family for sharing with me new information about their famous relative and for inviting me to a spectacular Horony family reunion in June, 1997. Also to Wilbur and Charles White who walked me over the old town of Dos Cabesas and who provided their personal memories of Kate and Jack Howard. And to Karen Holliday Tanner, author of DOC HOLLIDAY, A FAMILY PORTRAIT, for her invaluable insights into Doc and his early life.

Jane Candia Coleman
February 1999

Table of Contents

Part One

Prologue

Dos Cabezas, March, 1930

Doc Holliday's gone. And Wyatt Earp. George Cummings, my second husband is dead, and now Jack Howard, who gave me thirty years and a different kind of love, different from all the rest.

The lantern flickers. It's early April and windy, and the night is cold. I put more wood in the stove, pour myself coffee from the big enamel pot. I suppose if I stay here I'll have to cut down on luxuries like firewood and coffee, but that is to think about later. Tonight I'll be warm, comforted, if comfort there is, by the heat of the stove, the quilt around my shoulders, memories.

Tonight I'll sit with Jack as we have sat every night for so long—the happiest years of my life. I won't pull the sheet over his face just yet. I want to watch him a while, to say good bye and thanks.

In the morning I'll walk the three miles to town and ask the Whites for help with the burying. But tonight is mine, and I'll use it to remember, because memories, at least to me, are prayers.

I

Glenwood Springs, 1887

Doc Holliday fought a long and futile battle, and I was with him at the last, unable to help or to give him breath. After the funeral I packed his things. Such a few things he had to show for his thirty-six years! Some clothes, his razor, the diamond stickpin he'd brought with him from Georgia, minus the diamond that he'd pawned in Leadville when his luck at the tables ran out. I wanted to put a letter in the trunk. A note saying that he hadn't died alone or unloved. That I'd been with him whenever he needed me for over ten years and had done my best that, in the long run, wasn't good enough.

But I knew his family, and the nun to whom I was sending the trunk wouldn't appreciate any words from me—mistress, fallen woman. No matter that I couldn't help my past, relive it, change it, make of myself anything other than who I was—Mary Katherine Horony, Kate Fisher, Mary May, Big Nose Kate, Kate Elder, a different name for every place I'd been and left, sometimes with the law on my heels.

So I wrote nothing, and, standing in the bitter cold that gray November day, I closed the door to my heart and made a vow never to look back, a futile promise as it turned out, for my past has shaped my present. What I was is what I am.

"We'll go on home." My brother, Alex, helped me into the wagon and handed me a robe to wrap around myself.

"Yes," I said, though his words sounded out of place. What did it mean to have a home? I'd never stayed anywhere long enough to put down roots and find out.

"Eva and I want you to stay with us," he added, picking up the reins.

"Yes," I said again. "For a while anyhow."

"As long as you like. The children love you. *We* love you."

Frankly, all love scared me. What had it gotten me but loneliness?

As if he'd read my thoughts, he said: "Doc had his own way to make, Mary. You did the best you could."

Anger replaced grief. "If I could have gotten him out of Tombstone. If I could have gotten him away from those Earps so we could've stopped running and fighting. But they always came first with him. I hardly counted."

"That's not true."

I shrugged and looked out at the Roaring Fork. It reminded me of myself, running madly to nowhere. "We really didn't suit except we were both two black sheep on the lam."

"You weren't the first woman to do what you had to."

"But the fact is . . . I did. I'm not the kind a man like Doc takes to meet his family."

He clucked to the team and turned up the trail by the Crystal River. "Like I said, you aren't the first. And you're a Horony. That counts for something, even if we're the only ones who care or know what that means."

He was right. The West was filled with whores who'd married and turned respectable, their pasts swept under the carpet. I supposed he was hinting that I could do the same.

"Mama wouldn't know me," I said.

His smile was wry. "She wouldn't know me, either. Chopping wood, digging holes in mountains. Her life wasn't ours. It was another world, face it."

I didn't want to face any of it. In a few short years, I'd gone from being the pampered daughter of Hungarian aristocrats, to the wife of a St. Louis businessman, to prostitution, simply to stay alive. That was my excuse, and it was, to me, a good one. Faced with the prospect of starving, I'd sold myself as had a good many others.

And then I met Doc, and that made all the difference. For a long time we were happy—alone and carefree—before the Tombstone years and disaster.

I said: "There's probably still a warrant out for me in Texas. For arson."—and Alex looked at me with an expression that was part amazement, part devil-may-care Horony.

"Best tell me what else you've been up to," he said with a grin.

I closed my eyes against the stark winter mountains, the naked trees, and was back in Griffin in the spring of 1876.

"It was one of those crazy things you do without thinking too much. Doc was in jail, and they were going to hang him, and I wasn't about to sit there and let it happen."

Alex's grin widened. "Even when you were little you were always in trouble."

"I wasn't!" What I remembered was tiptoeing around the house, taking care of Mama and the little ones.

"I remember, if you don't," he said. "You should've been a boy."

"Well, that's what I did in Texas. Dressed up in pants and started a fire in a stable to distract everybody so I could get Doc out. It worked, too." I stopped, seeing it, hearing Doc's voice as plain as if he sat beside me. *"By Christ, Kate! You set the whole damn' town on fire!"*

Looking back, the whole plan had been crazy, but it had worked. Doc was free, and I'd saved him. All we had had to do was get out of Texas.

We had good horses and the rest of our lives ahead of us. We were young, and the West was a different place from what it is now. There weren't any roads or fences. We had only the stars and the sun to go by—and the cattle trails that gouged out the prairie, stripped the grass, left a map anyone could follow.

If ever Doc loved me, it was then, unencumbered by past or future, two fugitives with a single purpose and a passion for life that tinged our love-making with a kind of glory.

Each time we kissed, touched, it seemed it might be the last time for us. We threw ourselves at one another with a sense of desperation, the knowledge that the law was on our heels, that time was running out. Death lurked everywhere—on the plains, in the sky, in our own poor bodies. Especially Doc's.

Sometimes, with his arms around me, my head against his chest, I could hear the faint rattle of the disease that had ruined his life, his hopes—hear it and taste my own fury because I was helpless, a pawn in a game we were both bound to lose.

Funny that, for all our intimacy, I never caught it from him, that I should be the strong one. But why? Here I was, thirty six years old, the past buried in a grave in Glenwood, and a future that held no promise.

Behind my closed eyes I saw the plains spreading out like a painting by an artist gone wild—bluebonnets, white poppies with petals like tissue, the brilliant, color-streaked faces of galliardias, and the grass rippling like a scarf of green silk in the never-ending wind. Far away, where the heat waves made illusions against the horizon, Doc and I were riding north, the wind making music in our ears.

Tears I'd held in started then, slipping down my cheeks and turning to ice. Alex leaned over and took my hand.

"I thought you were never going to let it out," he said.

I reached for my handkerchief. "I thought I didn't have any tears left."

Crying doesn't do anybody any good. Tears can't raise the

dead, and, if they go on long enough, people avoid you. So I stopped crying and tried to think of something to say so Alex wouldn't blame himself for what he hadn't done.

"It was a good life for a while."

He looked straight ahead. "You're still young. You'll marry again."

"No." I shook my head, determined, then thought better of it. "Maybe. But not soon."

Still, who wanted to be the unmarried sister or aunt? I'd seen enough of those—living off their relatives, always in the way, humbling themselves in thanks for their keep. I wasn't one to be humble, even on my worst days.

"I'll stay the winter," I said. "Then I'll figure something."

I still had some money from the sale of my hotel in Globe and more energy than two people. Cooking was what I did best; everyone said so, even Doc who was hard to please. Perhaps I could open a restaurant—a small one, with a room for myself in the back.

"Just so you know you're welcome." Alex pulled up at the door of the cabin, and Eva came out, her arms open wide.

"Ah, Mary, poor child," she said.

I took offense, though her motive was kind. I wasn't anybody's child but a woman who'd seen enough death for ten, who'd slept with more men than Eva had ever met.

"Don't!" I said, avoiding her embrace, fearful that tears would start again, and I'd be unable to stop them.

She looked behind me at Alex, her eyes questioning him. I went inside, taking off my bonnet and going to the fire to warm my hands. The house was comforting, cheerful, but I didn't belong. A person gets used to making decisions, being on her own. Here, I was a cipher. Aunt Mary or poor child fallen on hard times. At that thought I laughed to myself. Since leaving home, it seemed I'd had nothing but hard times, but I'd survived, and would again. I'd make do or die.

II

The dream is always the same. It's Tombstone in October, 1881, and the trouble that's been festering between the Earps and Doc and the cowboy gang is about to boil over. It's serious trouble, good against evil, and I'm in the middle of it though I never wanted to be.

Ike Clanton comes into Fly's boarding house looking like a gargoyle, and I want to run away, but my feet are stuck to the floor so all I can do is wrap my arms around myself for protection. Not that Ike is going to rape me. Ike doesn't much care for women. I'm simply trying to keep my distance.

"Where's Holliday?" He has a high, squeaky voice like a young girl's. It's at odds with his face, his pale, cruel eyes.

I shake my head. No words come. I run then, back to Doc who straps on his pistol and goes quickly out the door. A few minutes later the shooting starts. They are all there—Wyatt, Morg, Virge, and Doc; the McLaurys, Billy Clanton, Ike, Johnny Behan in that big, white hat you can see a mile off.

The shots come in two bursts and sound like cannon fire. A bullet comes through the window over my head, covering me with splinters of glass. I see Morg spin around and go down, see Doc fall, and my own face and hands blood-covered so it seems I've been shot, too. But I can run. I'm running out onto the street toward Doc who's alive and cussing. There's dirt on his face, but his eyes shine, blue and hard, like jewels.

"That's three less of the murdering bastards."

The women are there—Allie, Lou, and Josie Marcus, hatless, her face carved out of ivory, her hands stretched out toward Wyatt who's standing grim as death, who's done what he meant to do all along.

Except he hasn't finished. The killing will go on, and Doc will go with him, ignoring my pleas, shaking me off like I'm an annoyance, a clinging vine of a woman who only wants peace and her man home with her instead of out somewhere, a target for the rustlers and con-men who run Cochise County.

There's the taste of blood in my mouth. My lip is cut. I lick it, spit out blood like I'd like to spit out my anger. I'm a victim, too—caught like we're all caught in this nasty little town that has no reason to exist but greed.

I wake up whimpering. It's dark, and the house is cold. Outside, the moon reflects off fresh snow. The mountains hold up the sky on massive white shoulders. I miss the desert. Cloud shadows riding purple over those endless valleys, the fragrance of secret bloomings. I miss Doc with an ache in my heart, my loins. For all our anger, bitter words, foolish betrayals, I miss him.

Maybe someday I'll get over this; stop dreaming, stop wanting. Maybe.

Spring came slowly that year, as it always does in the high Rockies, and I was impatient to be gone. "Cabin fever," they call what I had, the feeling of being locked in, locked out, every crack in the walls, every bump in the floor memorized until I could find my way blindfolded.

In spite of the deep snow, I went down to the river and watched the magpies arguing in the trees. In Hungary, magpies were considered pests, and there was a bounty on them. Here they were simply winged jewels flashing against snow and sky.

Somewhere I'd heard that, if you could catch a young one,

it would learn to talk, like a parrot, and I wondered what it would be like to have a magpie as a companion, one that, unlike humans, said only what it had been taught and sat on your shoulder, preening its iridescent blue and white feathers.

Only a few months before, Doc had sat here and watched them with me. Now, in his place, was a space I couldn't fill. Even the splendor of the day—the brilliant snow, the sweeping flight of birds—had no meaning. It wasn't only cabin fever that had me by the throat. Sorrow had turned me numb, stitched me into myself as if I, too, was wrapped in a shroud and buried.

I said—"Doc!"—and the hills caught the word, sent it back in echoes, and the magpies, startled, flew toward the mountains and left me lonelier than before.

Slowly I trudged toward the cabin, leaning into my own shadow, blue on the snow in front of me. Eva was outside doing a wash, and she waved.

"I decided to hang the clothes out since the sun's shining," she said.

"What can I do?"

She pointed at a tub of freshly rinsed sheets. "Hang those, if you would."

I set to work pinning them to the line, smelling the sweetness of soap, the mountain air. Unconsciously I must have sighed, because Eva turned and watched me a minute.

"I wish I could make you happy," she said.

How could she erase the past, bring Doc back? Everything seemed hopeless, but I couldn't tell her so. "Nobody's happy all the time," I said.

She stirred the clothes in the wash tub with a wooden paddle. "What I mean is . . . you're not happy with us."

She didn't understand. How could she, with her home,

her husband, her children to keep her warm?

"It's not you," I said. "I love you all. But Doc's here. His ghost, his memory. I've been thinking about everything, and I decided I'll go into Aspen when the snow melts. Maybe open another restaurant."

She came closer and patted me on the arm. "I think that's a good idea. Maybe you'll meet somebody."

When I started to protest, she silenced me. "Let me say it. You're the kind of woman who gets along better with men than with women. Men like you. Alex and I both think you'd be happier if you had someone."

She was right. Whether I'd been born that way or experience had molded me, I wasn't made to be a hen in a hen house. My stay in the convent, even my months at Bessie Earp's, had been proof of that.

"Nobody can take Doc's place," I said, though I agreed with her premise.

"Of course not! But life goes on, and you're still young."

In my heart I was old. The heart can only break so much, and then it atrophies, turns into a mockery of itself.

"I'm thinking about Aspen," I said.

Colorado was booming. The treasure trove of gold and silver that lay buried in the mountains was luring miners from all over the world. In the big camps—Aspen, Leadville, Silverton—you could hear a dozen languages spoken at once, and many prospectors paid their way with a bag of gold dust, a handful of nuggets. There was money to be made, and, though I was grieving, I knew I had to earn my own way.

Eva pulled me into her arms and hugged me. "Don't think I'm trying to get rid of you. I just hate seeing the shadows in your eyes."

I submitted to her embrace. She was a warm, motherly soul, and I'd been motherless for longer than I cared to remember. "I'll come back and visit. And you can bring the children for a day or two. Aspen isn't far."

Aspen had another point in its favor, one I didn't mention. Aspen wasn't Glenwood Springs or Leadville, those places haunted by ghosts. I'd never figured why Doc stayed in Leadville even though he knew it was hurrying his death. Sometimes I thought he'd simply decided to die.

III

Leadville, 1885

"You start out with a dream. Then it all goes to hell," Doc said, and coughed until I thought he'd die right then.

He had pneumonia. Leadville wasn't the place for a man with his lungs as he had to have known.

I wanted to shake him but didn't dare. "Listen to me. Let's get out of here. You beat this before, you can do it again. I know you can. We'll go to California, change our names, and you can sit in the sun and breathe real air and get well. We'll be happy there like we used to be."

He didn't answer, just turned away and looked out the window. It was snowing. It seemed it was always snowing in Leadville.

"Go ahead and die then," I said. "Go ahead and leave me."

He hunched his shoulders and coughed again. "You'll find somebody else to boss around soon enough."

"You're a quitter!" I stomped across the room.

His smile shivered across the bones of his face that were so prominent they seemed ready to break through the skin. "Go away, Kate. I'm a realist, and you're the kind of female I hate."

"So hate me!"

A sigh shook him. "Go next door and get me a drink."

"No."

"That's you. Always telling me what's good for me. Who in hell do you think you are?"

I straightened up and looked down my nose at him, a look I'd learned in my cradle from my mother and that never failed to intimidate. "I'm a Horony. My family's been in Hungary since Arpad, and don't you forget it."

He snorted, then laughed, and I felt better. Putting him in a good mood had become an almost impossible challenge. "Kate, Kate," he said, "I'll bet you can't even tell me who Arpad was, but that's all right. I don't feel up to a history lesson. And anyway, I agree. There's not a one like you. Not a whore in five states."

It hurt. He had the power to hurt because I loved him and wished I didn't. We were bound together by our upbringing and by a passion to conquer one another. Except now I had the upper hand. I was young and healthy. Still, the nasty words spilled out.

"I hope you die tonight. I hope you go straight to hell where you belong."

He looked at me with those incredible blue eyes, and I saw what he would have been without trouble and disease. "You believe everything I say. Won't you ever learn I love to tease you?"

"You love torturing me."

He reached out a hand that trembled. "No, sweetheart. It's just you take it all so seriously."

What other way was there? I said: "I'm going back to Globe."

"Good. Then I can die drunk and in peace."

I kicked a chair and wished it was him. "If you hadn't followed Wyatt, if you hadn't gone off with him and killed those cowboys, there wouldn't be a warrant out on you. You could come with me. But you wouldn't listen. You never do."

He shut his eyes. "It was a matter of honor. Something you obviously can't understand."

I snickered, misrepresenting what had happened to suit my own purpose. "A bunch of big city gunmen with pistols killing a bunch of no-good cowboy rustlers who couldn't shoot their way out of a barn. That's not honor."

He didn't answer, and I saw that he'd fallen asleep. I covered him, lowered the lamp, and went out and down the stairs. Outside it was still snowing, and the thin air had a bite to it that made my eyes water. How had we come to such a brutal parting?

"Fool, fool," I said, and didn't know if I meant Doc or myself.

Prescott, Arizona, 1880

"What is it now?" Doc was pacing the floor of the room we'd rented. It was the spring of 1880, and we were bound for Tombstone at the urging of Wyatt Earp, except I didn't want to go.

That morning I'd gotten a letter from my brother, Alexander, who was homesteading in Colorado. He was urging me to come for a visit to Leadville, where he and my younger brother, Louis, had staked a mining claim and were hoping to strike it rich.

"You always want what you can't have," Doc said, when I showed him the invitation. "Nobody can satisfy you. I give you a week before you come running back."

He was right. I wanted him, but on my terms, and I wanted my family that I hadn't seen since I'd run away at age sixteen. I felt like one of those tumbleweeds that were beginning to become a nuisance on the plains, blowing here, touching down there, sailing on at the whimsy of the wind. And I was sick of the Earps, all of them, but Wyatt in particular. It seemed that all he had to do was snap his fingers and Doc jumped, while I had to beg, plead, argue even to be listened to.

For Doc, the Earps took the place of his family. I came sec-ond—or last—and the fact rankled. At least Doc and I shared sim-

ilar backgrounds, while the Earps were a tough, noisy bunch, always on the move, always looking for the main chance, dragging their women along like so much baggage.

Again, though I loved those women, I hated being classed as one of them, and I hated Wyatt's Mattie on principle. After all, in my mind, I'd had him first, and I never could understand what he saw in her with her violent temper, her country ways, and how, when that temper flared, she'd get drunk and smart-mouthed, ripping into Wyatt and the rest of us without a care. She and I avoided each other, though sometimes that was hard to do, traveling together as we were.

"Go if you want," Doc said. "Just don't expect to find me when you come back."

"I'm not going to this Tombstone place with you and them. That's final."

"Suit yourself. Do you have enough money?"

I didn't, and it riled me. I hated taking money from him, being dependent for every little necessity.

"I'll pay you back," I said.

He came closer and cupped my face in his hands. "No need. Just take care of yourself. Those mining camps can get pretty rough."

When he was gentle like that, I was willing to do anything. "I don't have to go," I said.

"Yes, you do. You miss your family. God knows I can understand that." His eyes took on that look of longing they always did when he thought of his own family and the life he'd been forced to leave. "I'll miss you," he said.

I stared at him. "You will?"

He smiled. "You're like a toothache. Pull the tooth and it leaves a hole."

It wasn't flattering, but I didn't get mad as I usually did. "I'll miss you, too." I kissed him, and he returned it with passion, hold-

ing me a long time.

Then he said: "What a strange business life is."

"At least, we found each other. At least, there's that."

As usual, he reversed himself. "Yes. And now you're off some place. Talk's cheap, Kate. And don't expect me to come after you."

I pushed him away. "I don't expect anything. You taught me not to."

He went out, and I packed and left for Colorado.

The Denver and South Park Railroad at that time only went as far as Buena Vista. I got out of the train, retied my bonnet, shook the soot out of my skirt, and looked around for directions to the stage dépôt. Another woman stood on the platform with me, obviously as confused and as tired as I was. When our eyes met, she gave a dazzling smile and walked over to me.

"I hope you're going to Leadville, too," she said without preamble.

"I am." I decided she had to be the wife of a mining magnate, or, at least, the mistress of one, dressed as she was in a blue suit that matched her eyes, and wearing a Tuscan straw bonnet I'd have killed for.

"Good!" A blonde curl slipped out from under one of the bonnet's ribbons and blew across her cheek. "I wasn't looking forward to going on alone with all those strange men. They stare so. My name's Elizabeth Doe, but everybody calls me Baby."

I blinked. It was a ridiculous name, one more suited to a prostitute, but then, in view of my past, I couldn't be particular. "Mary Holliday."

"Well, Mary, where do you suppose we catch the stage?"

"Just what I was wondering. But two women ought to be

able to find out anything."

She laughed at that. Not one of your muffled, lady-like sounds, but a genuine laugh like a good bell. "You're so right."

With a gesture she summoned a porter who was so taken with her beauty he could only stammer a few directions, but she seemed to understand him. "See that our trunks get there, will you please?" She opened her purse and searched for a tip, then took my arm. "We'll walk. Won't it feel good to walk after that awful train?"

And so together we boarded the stage for Leadville and settled ourselves in the most comfortable seats, if so they could be called.

"Is someone meeting you?" she asked.

"My brothers. One I haven't seen in fifteen years." As I spoke, I was shocked at how old I felt, at the things I'd seen—and done.

"A reunion!" She clapped her hands. "That's wonderful. I'm going to meet the man I love." She spoke as if there was no one else present but me, as if the other passengers, all male, weren't watching her, hanging on every word.

With some amusement, I saw their faces fall, their hopes destroyed by her obvious excitement. She, however, paid them no mind, continuing on with her story. How she'd been married to one Harvey Doe, a shiftless drunk; how she'd fallen in love with Jake Sandelowsky, lost his child, lost everything in her subsequent divorce from Doe. "So you see, I'm a fallen woman," she said, eyes sparkling. "And it doesn't matter any more, if it ever did. I'm going to meet Jake and be married, and that's an end to it."

At the mention of her dead child, I thought of little Michael, named for my father and buried in St. Louis, taken away by the yellow fever.

"What is it?" She reached out a hand in a pale blue glove and took mine.

When I told her, her eyes filled with tears. "I'm sorry. For us both. Life is so unfair sometimes."

"Especially to children. He was so little. So dear. After that, I didn't care about anything. Not for a long time." No, I hadn't cared. I'd gone from respectable married woman to Bessie Earp's brothel in Wichita in a descent so rapid I even now couldn't recall all of it.

Baby nodded. "They say that sorrow makes you tough. I think it only cuts away little pieces until there's not much left."

Neither of us could know what the rest of life had in store for us. Baby would become the mistress, then the wife of millionaire H. A. W. Tabor, a fairy tale with a bad ending. When I last heard from her, she was living alone and broke in a shed near the Matchless Mine that had made Tabor—and for a brief time Baby—rich.

And I? Well, that's my story, and I'll tell it as it comes—in fragments, scenes, like the unfolding of a flower, petal by petal, until I reach the heart.

IV

Leadville, 1880

They were Horonys. There was no way I'd have missed finding my brothers, even in the milling crowds at the dépôt. There were the blue eyes in the bony faces, the prominent ears, the long, thin noses so much like my own that had given me the name I detested. Big Nose Kate! I hated it the minute it was given me—and have spent the rest of my life trying to live it down.

Hugging my brothers, my heart beating so hard I thought I'd faint—from altitude as well as emotion—I suddenly understood Doc's attachment to the Earps. They were fellow adventurers, a warm-hearted bunch of Gypsies, and as much of a family as he could hope to have. One woman, and that one as rootless as he, couldn't supply the security he needed. I sighed and looked at Louis, now a head taller than I was.

"You grew up!"

His eyes twinkled. "And so did you, big sister. His hands were large and rough, miner's hands, hardened by shovel and pick axe. "Come on. Let's get you something to eat and catch up on things."

At that moment, over his shoulder, I saw what looked like an army marching down the street—a platoon of armed men, determined and in step.

"Is there a war?" Dim pictures of soldiers and cavalry came back and frightened me. Maximillian in Mexico on his prancing stallion; my father and Kossuth, planning freedom for the Hungary they loved.

"There's a strike," Alex said. "The mine owners cut wages. There's so many workers in town, the bosses can hire who they want at the price they want, which doesn't sit too well with the old-timers. That's one of the local militias, hoping to scare the strikers into accepting the pay cut and going back to work."

Looking around, I saw a bunch of rough men carrying clubs and in some cases pistols, their eyes following the progress of the gaily dressed militia with hatred.

"Is that them? The miners?"

"Some of them. The rest are up at the mines, hoping to organize and get more followers. Things will get violent, Mary.

In fact, we've been thinking of getting out before the whole town goes up."

"But I just got here!" I was stiff, sore, hungry. The idea of getting on another stage to nowhere held less appeal than a war.

He took my arm. "They might settle quickly. Particularly if the governor gets involved. But these men are mad. And they're right, even if no one wants to admit it. Let's get off the street, and then we'll talk."

Baby waved at me from across the street, where she stood with, I supposed, her beloved Jake. "Come see me, when you're settled!" she called.

My brothers stared at her with fascination. "Who's that?" they asked simultaneously.

I told them. Alex shook his head. "Jake's a lucky man. If he can hold her."

"Why shouldn't he?"

"She looks like a fortune-hunter, and who's to blame her with a face like that?"

I thought about other women I'd known—Blanche in St. Louis, Bessie and the girls in Wichita, Lottie Deno in Griffin. "She's not a bad woman," I said, knowing that in reality there weren't any bad women, just frightened ones down on their luck. Alex didn't know about that part of my life, what I'd done to keep body and soul together, and I wasn't about to tell him.

"Let's go eat," I said, changing the subject.

We hadn't gone a block when the madness erupted.

Someone hurled a stone that was followed by a hailstorm of them, crashing into the window of a newspaper office and into the shop windows on either side. There were shouts, more stones flying without direction, gunshots, and bodies milling and pushing like a herd of maddened longhorns. Alex lost his grip on my arm, and I was swept into the midst of the mob, fighting to stay on my feet, to get to the relative safety of the sidewalk. I felt as if I were drowning, struggling to catch my breath, flailing my arms, and trying to keep hold of my purse at the same time.

Around me were angry men fighting for their livelihood in a rebellion that had been repeated in one way or another since the beginning of history. The strong against the weak, the rich against the poor. I could smell their anger. It was tainted with the smell of fear—my own and theirs, those men who had been pushed too far.

One of them, with hard boots, stepped on my feet, and I cried out, but the sound was lost in the shouting. Like a leaf I was shunted back and forth until, by a miracle, I got shoved into a post and, panting, wrapped my arms around it.

"Mary!" Louis came toward me, dodging fists and bodies. "Hold on!"

I held on so well he had to pry my hands away. Then he dragged me into an alley between a wall of buildings. "Are you hurt?"

I flexed my toes inside my shoes and tried to find enough breath to answer. "No," I said finally.

"Come on, then." He put an arm around my waist, and in spite of myself I laughed. My little brother had, indeed, grown up. We'd all survived life in a new country, without parents or guidance or any help at all but our wits. Or maybe because of dumb luck. If it was that, I wasn't pushing it any further.

Straightening my hat I said: "Alex was right. Let's get out of here. I've seen enough. Leadville's a disaster."

How much of a disaster I'd learn a few years later.

V

Ruby, Colorado, 1880

Ruby was never a big mining camp, but there was enough gold being taken out to keep a thousand or so hopefuls burrowing into the mountains, my brothers, who had claims there, included. Louis worked the prospects, and Alexander came and went, dividing his time between his homestead and prospecting. To me it seemed paradise after the smoke and furor of Leadville, and I hadn't been there a week before I rolled up my sleeves and went into business.

Men had to eat, and there was money to be made feeding them. Besides, I've never been one to sit still and do nothing. When I broached the subject to Louis, he was baffled.

"You're supposed to be on vacation."

"I can't just sit here and look at the scenery all day," I said. "But I'll need some dishes and a few cooking pots to start. And a little extra cash."

"If you mean it, I've got credit in Leadville," he said. "You can pay me later. You'll be able to. These guys'll jump at decent cooking."

So I retraced my steps and went back to Leadville, and spent a day buying the essentials, contracting with a freighter to bring everything over the mountain, including sacks of flour, beans, potatoes, and rice.

I also mailed a letter to Doc, telling him about my plan and hoping against all hope that he'd give up his notion about Tombstone and come and find me.

When I'd finished, I stepped outside and looked up and down the street. As usual, it was bustling, but the strike had been settled and no angry mob greeted me. Instead, I came face to face with Baby Doe.

"Mary!" she exclaimed. "Where have you been? I looked all over town for you, but you disappeared."

I explained, and she listened, then said: "Come have lunch with me. The most wonderful thing has happened, and I need to tell somebody, but none of the women here will talk to me." She laughed. "Like I said, I'm a fallen woman. A second time. So I'm doubly in disgrace."

She was wearing a diamond ring as big as an egg, and her eyes were sparkling. Disgraced or not, she was making the best of it, but Jake Sands, as he now called himself, had never bought her a jewel like that one.

We settled ourselves at a table in the dining room of the Clarendon, where, she informed me, she was now living in a suite.

"Who is it?" I asked.

"It's the strangest, most romantic thing, and I have no defense. I met Horace at a ball. He asked me to dance, and, of course, I said yes. The minute he took my hand, we both felt it. Like we were meant to be. I can't explain it any other way, Mary. Who ever could explain how love happens?"

That she meant what she said, I had no doubt. Her face was radiant. She looked like a young girl in the throes of first love. Had I looked like that, I wondered, when I first met Doc, when we were making our way over the cattle trail to the safety of Dodge?

"Horace who?" I couldn't restrain my curiosity.

"Horace Tabor." She waved her hand to stop my words. "I know what you're thinking. That he's rich and I'm in love with his wallet, but it's not so, Mary. He's kind and good and . . . ."

"Married," I put in.

"To a dreadful woman who won't give him a divorce."

And she wondered why the town society women shunned her! I chose my next words carefully, knowing exactly the dilemma she'd let herself in for.

"You'll always be unacceptable to the old cats. Even if he does get a divorce and marry you. You'll never fit in, and, if that's going to eat at you, you'd better decide now. You can't have it both ways. The world isn't made like that."

"I already made up my mind." Her voice was soft, but her look was determined. "For better or worse," she added. Then, with a lift of her chin, she said: "Are you going to scorn me, too? I thought you were cut from a different bolt of cloth."

I chuckled. "I'm not in a position to criticize, believe me."

"Then you understand."

"Of course."

"And you'll be my friend?"

Millionaire's mistress or not, she seemed like a child, helpless, vulnerable, and I understood her situation only too well. And there was also a great deal to be said about having access to H. A. W. Tabor and the power of his influence. I reached across the table and took her hand. "If you'll be mine."

Dimples framed her mouth. "We make a fine pair, Mary, and I thank you."

When I went back to Prescott at the end of the short mountain summer, I had five hundred dollars squirreled away. Some I'd earned cooking at Ruby. The rest came from H. A. W. Tabor's largesse via his much-adored mistress and soon to be wife, Baby Doe, who turned out to be a very good friend, indeed.

VI

Prescott, Arizona 1880

"So you're back. Like the proverbial bad penny." Doc softened his words with a kiss. *"Have you changed your mind?"*

"About what?"

"Tombstone." He gave me a wicked look.

I felt my purse, heavy with the gold of freedom. *"No."*

"Too bad." He folded a shirt and put it in his bag. *"For you,"* he added.

"I'll go with you," I said, needing him more than I wanted to admit. *"But I won't stay."*

"Then why bother?" He turned to face me. *"What's in it for you? Or for me? What's this crazy game you play all the time? Go or stay, Kate, but don't do both. Make up your mind and stick with it."*

"I can't."

"Why not?"

A good question, and one I couldn't answer because I couldn't make him understand my hopes.

I said: *"We always end up in a fight, but it doesn't have to be like that."*

"You want a lap dog. I'm not it."

"I want you."

"As much as there is to have, you have me." He smiled, but it was a cautious smile.

"What's in Tombstone for you anyhow?" I asked, changing the subject. *"You can set up a dentist's office any place."*

"No, Kate, I can't. People are afraid of me. Of it. I'm a leper."

"You're a good dentist."

"And you're biased. Of course, I'm good. Or was." He shrugged. "But I can't just lie down and wait for the bugs to get me. I'm not built right for that. Wyatt's got some layouts going, and I'll be earning my way, such as it is, so don't try and take that from me. Let me have some pride, and there's an end to it."

It hurt me to see him fighting for some male notion of manhood, so I shut up, repacked my trunk, and went with him to that damned town that grew like an evil weed in the valley of the San Pedro River. I went, looked, and felt the wickedness with an intuition I hadn't known I possessed. I lasted a week.

"Stay if you have to. I'm going to Globe."

"With what?" He faced me across the table where we'd just finished our dinner.

"I saved my money. Don't worry, I won't ask for a loan."

His eyes burned until I thought my face would be scorched. "Don't look at me like that," I said. "I can't help it. This place . . . those people. They'll destroy you, and I won't hang around to watch."

"I didn't ask you to."

He hadn't, but just once I wished he would, wished he'd say what I wanted to hear whether it was true or not. Certainly I had other options. Colorado was full of men who were looking for a wife and not choosy about her background. I could have stayed there, dignified by a proper marriage and my connection to my family, and given up on Doc and our explosive relationship. But I didn't, and for all the trouble and sorrow that happened, I still can't say I have any regrets.

In Ruby the men had flocked to my tent restaurant where I dished out good meals. They came, they ate, they returned again, and they proposed marriage, regardless of the fact that I told them I was already taken.

Only one actually caught my eye—a tall, lean, determined

prospector, George Cummings. George had come to Colorado early, had fought off Utes, claim-jumpers, the unpredictable mountain weather, and he had fallen in love with my cooking first, then with me.

"Stay with me, Mary," he said, when I was packing up to leave before the first snow. "You'll bring me luck, and I'll buy you the biggest mansion in Aspen. You'll never be sorry."

He was handsome, I had to admit—dark-haired, muscular, with a wry twist to his mouth that appealed. But there was Doc somewhere in Arizona, and we were tied together by our strange hungers—for each other, for the need of a rough respectability. God knows I wanted to live down what I'd been. And Doc—well, he wanted what he'd been born to. The Southern aristocracy. If it hadn't been for what I'd done, I'd have filled the bill. Except I'd been a whore, and he knew it, couldn't trust me to assume the demeanor he demanded. And no matter what I said or did, he couldn't believe me.

There's the tragedy. To know one's self and to have one's lover scoff at the truth. And tragedy it was. I've spent the rest of my life attempting to figure it, wondering what I could have said or done to prove my worth.

I still don't know, and now it doesn't matter. He's gone. I'm old. For better or worse, I've lived my life, and what matters now is that I can open my eyes in the morning, look out and see the mountains, the desert, the stubborn trees whose roots go hundreds of feet into the earth. What matters is the singing of birds, the lifting of thunder clouds in late summer, the music of the senses that clutch the heart. What matters is life itself, and the fleeting moments of unadulterated joy.

VII
Globe, 1880

From Globe I watched the drama in Tombstone unfold like a play, the ending of which I knew in my bones would be disaster, and I was involved in spite of myself.

I couldn't stay away from Doc. Like an opium smoker, I was addicted, and he was the same, always writing me to come for a visit, to stay a while with him. And I went, though I feared for his life and my own, though I'd proved I could survive without him.

So I went back and forth between the towns, the outcome of my journeys always predictable. Trouble. Pain. Anguish. And at the last, the street fight in Tombstone where three badmen got what they deserved, and Doc and the Earps were branded murderers by snotty, little Sheriff Behan.

I'd had my own run-in with Behan before then. Doc and I had had a bitter fight, and I had been alone and miserable until Johnny Behan came along, all smooth-talking and oily. He had calmed me down, flattered me in that way he had, then bought me dinner and enough wine so I couldn't think straight. Back in his office, he had twisted my arm, had pulled it back, and had twisted till the pain got so bad I had cried out.

"Just sign the paper, Kate." His voice had been low in my ear. "Sign it and you'll never have to have anything to do with Doc again."

"You're hurting. . . ."

He had given another twist, and I had thought I'd pass out. "Sign it, Kate. He's no good. You know it. I know it."

There had been the pain, the haze of liquor, Behan's breath warm on my face, the blurred light of the lamp on his desk where the paper lay ready for me, and nothing had mattered but an end to the torture. Doc would understand what I was doing. He'd make it right, come morning.

Except in the morning I had found out I'd signed a paper implicating Doc in a stagecoach hold-up and the murder of Bud Philpot. Doc and Wyatt had fixed it all right, and I had had to go to court and swear I'd been drunk and forced, and that I didn't know anything at all about the hold-up or Doc's whereabouts on that night. And then I had gone back to Globe, stung by Doc's fury and Wyatt Earp's contempt.

Some years ago, I read about Johnny's funeral in the Tucson paper and said to myself: "Good riddance! A pity it didn't happen sooner." If it had, maybe things would have turned out differently. But who knows?

Certainly nobody could have stopped Wyatt from doing what he did after the cowboy gang murdered his brother Morgan. Wyatt went out for revenge, and he got it—Frank Stilwell in Tucson, Curly Bill at Iron Springs, Indian Charley in the Dragoons, and nobody ever counted or found the others. Wyatt rode through Cochise County like the devil on horseback, visiting every ranch, camp, rustler hide-out, and Doc was with him, as set on revenge as Wyatt.

Morgan had been Doc's friend, and Wyatt was the brother he never had. Call it a blood feud, call it honor, call it what you will. They rode out, and they didn't stop until they'd cleaned up the den of thieves that had been running roughshod for years. And then, with murder warrants hanging over them, they headed for Colorado.

I'd written to Baby Doe as soon as Doc told me his bad news. Baby and I had kept in touch, and I was one of the few who knew about Tabor's secret divorce and his even more secret marriage to Baby.

Governor Evans was out of the state, and Tabor was lieutenant governor of Colorado when the extradition papers got there. It was like an act of God, especially when Tabor turned down the Arizona warrant, refusing to send Doc back to Arizona. They didn't even try for Wyatt after that. So I had still another reason to bless my friendship with Baby.

Doc wrote from Colorado and told me the whole story, and urged me to come for a visit. But I was stuck in Globe with a hotel I'd bought mainly to prove my independence. Now it was a millstone around my neck, profitable though it was. I put it up for sale, but no one wanted to pay my price, and I wasn't about to cheat myself after all the work I'd put into it. So I stayed, and was there when Doc and Wyatt came back in that hot summer of 1882—came back in secret, by train and on horseback, and caught the last of the outlaw gang, John Ringo, while he was camped in a cañon near West Turkey Creek.

His body was found propped in a tree, his gun belt upside down, no boots on his feet, and a hole in his head. The coroner's verdict was suicide, but I knew better. Doc made a quick stop in Globe on his way back to Colorado.

"You haven't seen me, sweetheart." He had his arms around me, and I was crying because I was so happy to see him. "If anybody asks, tell them that."

"I'm glad you got Ringo," I said, still sniffing. "He was no good for all he tried to pretend he was a gentleman. When he was sober," I added.

Doc snorted. "He was trash like the rest of them."

"Is there going to be more of it? More killing? Or are you through?"

"We've got most of them. Except that bastard Behan. I'll drill him dead center for what he did to you that night, if I ever catch him."

"Forget him," I whispered. "He's not worth killing."

"I'll forget him for now, but only because time's running out."

He kissed me—softly at first, then harder. The fire was still there between us, the passion that was love, anger, hate, despair, all of those things. When he let me go, my legs were trembling.

"Take care, sweetheart," he said. "And remember, you haven't seen me."

Then he was gone into the first gray light of morning—gone into exile yet another time, the last.

VIII

Aspen, Colorado, 1888

Alexander went with me to Aspen. "Till I'm sure you're settled in," he said.

I smothered a smile. Settling in, as he called it, was what I'd been doing for years in one town after another, one country after another. Like the Gypsies of Hungary, I knew what to look for, how to make out, no matter what. Still, his concern touched me. It was sweet to have a brother again, someone who shared a past, however distant, someone who cared.

Aspen had grown since I'd seen it last. It had wide, well-planned streets lit by electricity, with running water and even a sewage system. And it had the mansions of the mine owners, private clubs, hotels, stores that stocked everything from bonnets and lace to musical instruments, baseball teams, and a race track. Above it all loomed the mountains, and the tunnels, shafts, mills that twenty four hours a day spit out silver—thousands of tons of it.

There was talk of telephone service, and the skeleton of what would become the opera house dwarfed the neighboring buildings. All in all, it was a splendid place to go into business, and go I did, buying out an already established restaurant named, of all things, Aunt Mary's.

"A good omen," I said to Alex, who was amazed at the determined way I'd conducted my transactions.

"You go after what you want just like a man," he said.

"What's wrong with that?"

He shook his head. "Nothing. I guess."

"I've learned the hard way," I said. "And I don't like wasting time."

"Then I'll leave you to get on with it. You'll be all right?" He was having trouble giving up his self-appointed rôle as protector.

I gave him a hug. "I'll be fine. And thank you for being there when I needed you."

The first thing I did was to clean up the place, starting with the kitchen that had been run by a man who had no interest in cleanliness, and ending in the dining room where I made sure the waitresses had fresh aprons and clean hands. Mining town or not, no one was going to serve tables in my restaurant with dirty fingernails!

One of the girls looked at me with surprise and what I thought was a hint of fear.

"You," I said. "What's your name?"

"Magda."

That caught my attention. "From where?"

"Hungary, missus." She was doing her best to be polite, at the same time sniffing back tears.

"Well, then, Magda," I said in rusty but grammatical Magyar, "would you want to disgrace your country by having people say we're all peasants?"

Her mouth opened. "You?" she said at last.

"Yes. And if you know anything about cooking, and if you do what I tell you, I'll take you into the kitchen as cook's helper. I just fired that dirty old man in there."

Already I was remembering the meals I'd made in past years—food with the flavors of my long-ago home.

She clasped her hands. "Missus . . . anything you tell me, I will do. My father died in an explosion in the mine, and there is my mama and four little ones."

She reminded me of myself, with her long yellow braid and that flash of determination. Here was one who wouldn't end up walking the street, selling herself, not if I could help it.

"Just close your eyes and think about something else." That was Bessie Earp's advice when she hired me in Wichita.

Except it wasn't as easy as that. My first customer was a kid in from a cattle drive, a kid hardly old enough to leave home. We went to my room, and he stood there, his Adam's apple moving up and down, his eyes looking everywhere but at me. Obviously, he'd been to the bath house and the barber. I could smell soap and shaving lotion, and it was all I could do to keep from smoothing the cowlick on his freshly cut hair.

"Come sit beside me," I said, patting the bed.

He did, gingerly. I asked him his name and where he was from and what it was like on the Texas trail, and after a couple minutes he relaxed and I kissed him like he was my child instead of a paying customer.

"Is this your first time?" I asked.

"Yes, ma'am." He was polite, well-raised, and blushing like a girl.

Some woman had done a good job with him, and now it was my turn to teach him a few more things. If my son had lived, I'd have prayed that he learned the right ways with a woman, and that he found one capable of showing him.

"Take off those spurs and boots," I told him. "Then help me out of this dress. There's no hurry about anything."

The men who came to Bessie's weren't all like him, and think-

ing about something else wasn't always easy. As a result, I learned more than a woman needs to know about the peculiarities of humanity, men in particular.

I made up my mind that Magda wouldn't ever have to go through what I'd gone through, that she'd have what was denied me—the freedom to choose.

"Wash your hands and face," I said. "Then come back to the kitchen."

It turned out to be one of the smartest moves I ever made. Magda had learned cooking at her mother's knee, and she had an uncle who refused to work in the mines. "I won't be buried before I die," was how he put it.

Karoly was a hunter. He kept me supplied with venison and elk and anything else that walked or flew, usually for the price of a few meals and some rounds of ammunition. After a few months, he proposed, but by that time George Cummings had come back into my life, a disaster had I only known it.

IX

"There's a gentleman looking for you, missus." Magda was obviously impressed, either by the fact that I had a caller, or by the man himself.

"Who is it?"

"He say his name is Yurp. Something like that." Magda was still having trouble with English.

"And he's the last person I want to see."

She frowned. "He's very handsome."

"He's trouble." I took off my apron. "Never mind. I'll go

find out what he wants."

By keeping busy, I'd managed to dull the edges of grief. Sometimes a day would go by without my thinking about Doc. Now here was Wyatt, bringing back what I'd tried so hard to forget.

He was sitting at a table, his back to the wall, sipping a cup of coffee, but, seeing me, he stood up. "Well Kate," he said, smiling a little.

"I'm not Kate any more. Kate's dead and gone. My family always called me Mary."

He pulled out a chair and held it for me. "Mary, then. I was in town and heard you were here."

"Where's Josie?" I asked, hoping he hadn't abandoned her the way he'd done Mattie.

"Out shopping. I had enough of it. Thought I'd just drop by and see how you were. If you needed anything."

"I'm fine."

My short answers made him uncomfortable, and I was glad of it. Once I thought I knew him well, but I'd never really understood him. Maybe no one did, not even Josie Marcus. Not even Doc.

As if he'd read my mind, he said: "He was a good man. None better."

And you killed him, I thought. *You dragged him along and never thought what it did to him. Or to me.*

It was uncanny how he seemed to know my feelings. He said: "I couldn't stop him, Mary. He lived on his own terms, the way he wanted. And I miss him. I never had a better friend."

"You never will, either." I felt tears beginning, and anger. Damn him! He'd brought it all back, the whole tangled mess. Once I thought I loved him, that he was the prince in the fairy tale who'd rescue me from the life I hated, that he'd ride up to

Bessie's whore house and take me away. And then in walked Mattie, the wife he'd left back on the farm, and all my dreams vanished the way dreams usually do. And then I found Doc.

I pushed back my chair. "I have to get to work. Give my best to Josie."

He reached out and took my hand. "I'm glad you were with him, Mary. Glad he didn't have to go alone."

"He shouldn't have had to go at all. Not so soon. And whose fault is it?" I yanked my hand away and stood there trembling with pent-up rage.

Wyatt stood, too. "Not mine. Not yours, either. He made his choice. And for what it's worth, he told me he wanted to finish up and go back to you. Only it didn't work out that way, and I'm sorry."

It was like being shot, hearing him say that. Like having a slug tear through me, ripping apart all the walls I'd put up to keep the pain away.

"Please." I choked on tears. "Go away. You only make it worse."

He put on his hat and looked at me, and I saw a hint of my own sorrow in those ice-blue eyes. "Stay well," he said softly, and left, stopping at the counter to pay for his coffee before opening the glass door and going out onto the street.

I stood a minute, trying to compose myself. Damn him! Always so sure of himself, always in control. It was what made him so dangerous—both in a gunfight and with women. Whoever he was after never stood a chance.

I was wishing I'd never left home, never met a one of the men I'd loved and lost, when from behind me came a voice.

"Mary! Mary Holliday! What are you doing back here?"

X

George Cummings wasn't the kind of man I'd have picked for myself twenty years before, but I'd lived in the West long enough to learn that what was necessary for success wasn't always what was acceptable in drawing rooms.

He was a rough diamond, and he had a merry eye that promised a woman a good time. In spite of misgivings, I was drawn to him, or maybe it was that I'd simply had enough of feeling sorry for myself.

Working was fine and profitable, but I've never been one to sit at home alone doing nothing when the work was done. And there was plenty of fun to be had in Aspen—ball games, horse races, touring theatrical troops, dances, none of which I felt comfortable about attending alone.

A decent woman needed a male escort, and George was the answer to my unspoken prayer. With his beard trimmed and in clean clothes, I thought he would solve my problem quite nicely, so I smiled and said: "Why, George Cummings! Have you struck it rich and come to town to spend it all?"

He had those wicked hazel eyes, and they shot sparks at me. "I've come to take you to the Independence Day celebration," he said. "And I won't take no for an answer."

"I'd be delighted." The words slipped out. I was thirty eight years old, but I wasn't dead. Not by a long shot. It was past time for some fun.

The face in the mirror was the one I'd been looking at all my life—long, with high cheekbones under eyes that slanted just a bit.

"Cat's eyes," Doc had called them. Gambler's eyes, giving nothing away.

And there was the thin Horony nose that I'd thought was elegant until the day that whore in Wichita gave me the name I couldn't get rid of. Big Nose Kate. It made me sound like a clown. An elephant. A creature in a freak show instead of a woman with an interesting face.

Fortunately, no one in my new life had ever heard the hated nickname, and I had no intention of revealing it. I was Mary Holliday, recent widow, respectable restaurateur. A woman who, as Shakespeare wrote, had played many parts. And played them well!

I smiled at myself and searched for gray hairs. Not finding any, I smiled harder. I was ready to live again. Fortunately Doc had always insisted on my being well-dressed, and paid generously for it. There were enough clothes in my trunk to see me into the next century with a little careful needlework. And very few of the dresses had bustles.

"Bear traps," Doc had called them with a wicked grin. "How can I pinch your bottom, if it's protected by that contraption?"

It seemed he was in the room with me, lying on the bed and watching me dress as he often had, and teasing me in that slow, Southern drawl I loved. Only this time, I refused to give in to sorrow.

"Quit haunting me," I told him. "You're dead, but I'm not, and it's not fair, you coming back all the time, making me feel bad. And guilty. I'm not guilty, and you know it."

I was talking to myself. The face in the mirror mocked me. "Damn' fool," it said. "You're the one lugging the baggage around. Put it to rest once and for all."

I snapped back into reality and pulled out a yellow linen suit with hand embroidery on the jacket and skirt—several years old but still flattering, and best of all there was a parasol to match. Only the ladies of the Aspen social set would have anything like it, and I could be proud, and George Cummings would be pleased to have me on his arm.

"So there!" I said to the empty room, and stepped out into the brilliant July sunlight where George stood waiting.

The whole town was on holiday. Buildings were draped with bunting; flags flew everywhere; and Main Street was lined with people waiting for the parade that was led by the fife and drum corps playing spritely marches. They were followed by the wagons of the local fire departments; each one decorated with crepe paper and painted signs, the firemen, shouting and spraying water at the screaming crowd.

Around us rose the mountains—Aspen, Smuggler, the tip of Snowmass, ice-covered even in the middle of summer. It was a far cry from Tombstone that always managed a certain drab, sinister appearance, or even Globe, buttoned into its jagged hills.

So I was happy. Happier still to see Alex and Eva and the children coming toward us.

"We decided to take a holiday," Eva said. And then in my ear whispered: "And here we find you already with a man."

"It's nothing," I protested, but she flashed a conspirator's smile.

"You could do worse."

"Or better." I was thinking of Baby Doe and Tabor and the millions of dollars he was taking out of his mines, the mansion he had built for his new family in Denver. Not that I envied her. It just seemed, somehow, that there had to be a middle ground between absolute wealth and utter poverty, that too much or too little money, either one, corrupted.

To my dismay, I saw Wyatt, with Josie clinging to his arm, walking toward us.

I made the introductions, praying neither of them would refer to my past, Josie in particular. Although I liked her and admired her beauty, she did have a way of going on about things.

"Kate." She reached out a slender hand. "How good to see you again. And looking so well. I was sorry about Doc. We both were. I guess Wyatt's told you."

"I'm Mary now," I said, cutting in on her. "It's what my family called me."

"Oh good!" She was all sparkle and the best of intentions. "Big Nose Kate was really an awful name when you think of it. Not flattering at all."

Under cover of our skirts, I stepped on her foot. Too late.

"What's this? What's this?" George had ears like a fox. "Who dared call this lovely lady such a horrible name?"

I took his hand. "It was a joke. Now let's go over and watch the horse races." How did I know he'd use it against me one day in the far future? How did I know that a slip of the tongue would contribute to my undoing?

Josie looked at me, stricken. "Shouldn't I . . . . ?"

"Hush!" I said. "Just never mind!"

Wyatt saved me. "Let's all go. There's a gray somebody brought up from Denver in the second race that looks promising." And he led Josie away, though she looked back at me bewildered, and, I thought, in some pain. I hadn't been exactly gentle, but it served her right.

George and I followed them, laughing. "Some joke," he said. "Who'd insult you like that?"

I shrugged. "It was a long time ago. I forget. So should you."

The gray Wyatt picked came in first by six lengths, and since we'd all placed small bets, we were in fine spirits as we made our way to the picnic grounds.

Josie tugged at my sleeve. "Did I say something wrong?"

"I'm not her any more," I hissed. "She's gone . . . Doc's gone . . . they're all gone. Even Mattie. Understand?"

She nodded. "I do. We never talk about any of it. But it's hard. How do we live it down? How do we forget it all . . . and what we did?"

A good question, one I'd been asking myself. "We don't," I said. "We just hope to God nobody brings it up."

Her dark eyes flickered. "Somebody always does. Wyatt can't hide and neither can I. I'm sorry, if I embarrassed you. I should have known better. It wasn't meant."

"I know."

"Friends?" She cocked her head under a bonnet covered with plumes, reminding me of Baby again—another adventurous woman who had no qualms about what she wanted or how to get it.

"Sure," I said. "Just call me Mary from now on."

"If you'll call me Missus Wyatt Earp," she said, and winked.

XI

Every week-end for the rest of the summer George made the trip over the mountain and into town. He was determined and persistent, and he never left without proposing at least once.

For my part, I wasn't anxious to give up a thriving business and move to what was little more than a prospector's shack in the woods. My life was under control, and I was enjoying the freedom.

Every Friday afternoon I walked over to the Wheeler Bank and made a deposit. I'd also visited the Aspen stock exchange and bought shares in some of the local mines. In addition, having learned from experience, I was hoarding a stack of gold coins in the bottom of my trunk. Mary Katherine Horony wasn't ever going to be broke and down on her luck again!

I listened to the men talking over at the exchange. Although the mines were producing millions of tons of ore, there was a limited market for silver. Even I could see that, and sometimes wondered how the boom would end. The country was run on the gold standard, leaving silver to find its own place—a risky one in my view and in the view of some big-time investors who were a lot shrewder than I.

The fate of Aspen—and every silver mining town—depended on the price of silver, and, for that matter, so did my restaurant and all the businesses that had grown up due to the mines.

George sometimes laughed at me—portioning out my profits, collecting my small interest on my stocks—but, when the end came, we were both glad I'd had the foresight to keep my eggs in different baskets.

One of the reasons I said yes, when George proposed for maybe the hundredth time, was his willingness to give up prospecting and take a job blacksmithing for the Smuggler Mine.

He announced his plan with a kind of glee, as if he'd outwitted me by removing the last obstacle between us. It was January, 1890, and we'd gone to the skating rink for the afternoon—one of those glorious Rocky Mountain afternoons, when the sun shines, the snow catches fire, and every tree and rock is etched in glass.

"I'll do it!" he exclaimed, his hat in his hand. "I'll do it and move into town, if you'll just say yes and stop putting me off. You drive a man crazy, Mary, and I'm tired of it."

His eyes were solemn, almost pleading, and I felt a surge of pity for him, so earnest, so determined. Pity isn't enough to build a good marriage, but I didn't know that, then. I thought I knew everything, but I didn't. Somewhere inside I was still that little motherless girl running away from her past, grabbing at any life line that was offered.

And what, after all, was my objection? He wasn't Doc. But neither was any one of the other men who'd come courting—miners who enjoyed my cooking; the clerk at the bank who was eyeing my savings account; the doctor I'd visited when I'd burned my hand on the stove whose false teeth came loose when he examined me; and Magda's Uncle Karoly who'd finally given up and married his brother's widow.

A woman without a husband was at a disadvantage in those times, whether or not she was a success in business, and George was a hard worker, often fun, and he was giving up a large part of his freedom for me. How could I object to that?

I took a deep breath and balanced carefully on my skates. "Yes," I said, and watched as his face broke into a grin.

"You will?"

"I will."

He pulled me into his arms, and we both staggered, clutching each other and laughing, and it seemed like the mountains caught the sound and threw it back—peals of laughter and the applause of the other skaters who joined in the excitement.

We were married in the St. Charles Hotel, in March in the middle of a blizzard. George, not wanting anything to go wrong, asked both Judge Wiley and Judge England to do the honors.

No sooner had Judge Wiley pronounced us man and wife, than Judge England appeared ready to do it again.

Amidst much laughter, George, dressed in a new suit and starched white shirt, raised his glass in a toast—and an explanation.

"For two years I've been courting Mary, and she finally said yes. But I wasn't about to take any chances, so I decided to marry her twice!"

"It's good you're settled." Eva was beaming. "You'll be happy now with a husband to look out for you."

Poor, innocent Eva! She believed that a woman was nothing without a man at her side—an attitude that suited my brother completely. Neither of them held with women's suffrage, or with the ability of a woman to think and live independently.

And none of us, on that blustery March afternoon, could foresee the future and my descent into poverty and humiliation, regardless that I had, indeed, married a man who had promised to take care of me, forsaking all others.

XII

I should have known that George and I were headed for trouble even before the wedding, when Horace and Baby Tabor sent us a silver tea service as a wedding present. George had stared at the ornate teapot, the creamer and sugar bowl, and the silver tray where they sat like it was a nest of snakes.

"What're we supposed to do with this?" His voice had been icy. "And what's that woman doing sending us presents?"

"She's an old friend." I was enjoying the weight, the dull sheen of the silver. It had seemed a century had passed since I'd seen anything as lovely as this.

"We don't hobnob with mine owners and their fancy women," he had said.

I had laughed. "Don't be silly! I've known Baby for years, and she and Horace really love each other. Besides, I owe both of them. A lot."

"Is that what you want? To be a society lady? Then you're marrying the wrong man."

I had wondered what he'd say if I had told him that my parents had hobnobbed with emperors; that we'd had not only a silver tea set but a service for twenty four and the Limoges china to go with it. I had pictured my mother sweeping down the stairs in a velvet gown, diamonds in her ears and around her neck, and my father in uniform, every bit as splendid. But that life was gone, and I was here, and, having accepted George's proposal, I had no intention of telling him about my past, the good or the bad.

"I knew Baby when she was poor," I had said. "I can't help it if she married the richest man in Colorado, or what people think about her. And no . . . ," I had held up a hand to stop his protest, "I don't want to be a society lady. It's too damn' much trouble."

He had grinned at that and came around the table to take my face in his big, rough hands. "We're ordinary people, aren't we?" he had asked, his eyes searching mine for confirmation.

I wasn't sure what made anybody ordinary. As far as I knew, we were all different, but to please him I had nodded. "I guess."

He had kissed me then, hard and with a hint of possessiveness, like he had wanted to leave a mark that told the world I was his. For a day or two I had been troubled—by the kiss and the conversation—and then I had forgotten as I got busy getting ready for my wedding.

★ ★ ★ ★ ★

Baby Doe Tabor met us at the train station in Denver.

"You'd never find a hack in this weather, so I came to get you." She was bundled in fur, only her face visible as she smiled up at George who was stunned into silence, whether from anger or amazement I couldn't tell.

Baby didn't seem to notice, babbling on and leading the way to her carriage, an ostentatious affair done in blue enamel, driven by a liveried coachman, and pulled by a matched pair of bays.

George grabbed my elbow. "Did you know about this?"

"No. She's just being nice. It's the way she is."

"Look at her. Look at the damn' carriage. She makes me feel like a dirt farmer."

I lost my temper. "Well, for God's sake, you don't have to act like one!"

"Is that what you think?"

"Listen to yourself," I said. "Having a hissy because a friend was worried and nice enough to come to meet us. It's a little silly, if you ask me."

He pulled away. "I'm going back to Aspen." With those words he walked away toward the ticket office.

This was my honeymoon. This was my husband whom I'd married only the day before, and he was walking away, hands thrust in his pockets, while Baby watched, as shocked as I.

"Go after him." Her breath came out in a cloud. "Hurry!"

I knew about male pride. I'd seen enough of it, God knew. And I thought I knew George, but obviously didn't. We'd struck a fear or an anger in him, and I didn't understand its source or how to take anything back.

I planted myself in front of him and said the first thing that came into my head. "Don't go."

"Why not? You and your fancy friend can have all the fun

you want without me along."

"You're my husband. This is our honeymoon!"

One corner of his mouth jerked up. "And you're my wife. You coming with me or not?"

"Let's find a hack and go to the hotel," I said, though at that moment I wasn't sure I wanted to go anywhere with him. "Please. Don't be like this. Just let me tell Baby to go on home."

His eyes bored into me. "Tell her, then. She's just a whore dressed up in fancy clothes. I don't want you to have anything to do with a woman like that."

A whore. I wanted to laugh. To cry. Instead, I put my head in my hands so he wouldn't see my face. A whore. So that was it. And what would he do if he learned the truth about his wife? Quickly I walked back to the carriage.

"It's me, isn't it?" Baby's cheeks were flushed from cold and mortification. "He's like all the rest. All those good people who cross the street when they see me." She laughed, a single, harsh note. "Well, the hell with them. I've got my life. What about you?"

"Please don't blame me," I got out, conscious of George, waiting and watching. "I don't understand, so I can't explain, but you're my friend. One of my only friends, and I'm ashamed. I brought presents for the girls, too. I wanted to see them. And Horace. And you. If I can get away, I'll come for a visit. Just don't be mad, and don't blame me. He's my husband, you see."

She stood there, looking like a little queen in her furs with the snow falling on her face. Then she reached out and hugged me. "We do what we have to, even at the cost of friendship. But it's all right, Mary. You go on and have fun. Just don't forget me." Then she slipped inside without looking back.

I watched the carriage drive away, watched until it disappeared in a flurry of snow. George had come up beside me.

"Happy now?" I asked, unable to keep the bitterness out of my voice.

He tugged at the brim of his hat. "Let's get out of here," he said, and pulled me into the storm.

Close your eyes and think about something else.

George got drunk that night, and what should have been joyous became an act I had to live through. The man I'd known for more than two years became a rutting bull, as clumsy and unfeeling as any buffalo hunter or cowboy off the trail.

I wanted Doc back, never mind his waspish tongue, his way of igniting anger. The proof of what we had was in our bed where all anger vanished, and what was between us was honest and true. I wanted Doc, but I had married a stranger.

XIII

In the morning George whistled as he shaved, admiring himself in the mirror. "Ah, Mary, Mary, what a pair we make!" he said, catching me watching him.

I managed a smile that set him off whistling again. It was as if the day and the night before had never happened, and we were the same happy couple who had set out so merrily from Aspen.

Who are you? I wanted to ask. *Who were you yesterday?* But I kept quiet, not wanting a repeat of his earlier performance. With Doc I could shout and vent my grievances, and they bounced off him like stones. With George I resolved to be wary. And quiet. And to stay out of his way as much as I could.

He made it easy for me that day, asking me what I wanted to do. We were at breakfast, and, in spite of myself, I was enjoying being served good food in fine surroundings.

"I need to do some shopping, if that's all right with you."

He pushed back his chair. "Just as long as I don't have to go along."

"What will you do?"

He flashed his merry grin. "Try out the billiard table. It's been a long time since I had a good game."

We were staying at the Windsor that boasted a saloon, billiard tables, and three thousand silver dollars laid in the floor in front of the bar—a decoration which at first had shocked him, but which now he decided was clever.

"There's how you can save your money, Mary. Glue it to the floor and attract more customers."

In spite of myself, I laughed. "My customers wouldn't appreciate me throwing money away. Most of them would be on their hands and knees, trying to pry it loose."

"You sure you don't mind shopping alone?"

On the contrary, I was delighted. The first thing I intended to do was call on Baby. I stood up. "It's fine this way. I won't feel like I'm boring you."

I'd never felt that with Doc. He'd gone with me much of the time, picking dresses and hats with the eye of a connoisseur, seeing to it that I was always dressed as well as he, and never quibbling over the cost.

"I'll just run upstairs and get my coat," I said, and then—so as not to appear too eager—"Have a good time. I'll be back for lunch."

"And I got us tickets for the show at the Opera House tonight. Some Eastern troupe doing Shakespeare. I figured you'd like that."

He looked so proud of himself, standing there on the morning after his wedding night—the typical bridegroom without the slightest notion or concern about what pleased the bride. From thinking of him as a monster, I suddenly saw him as a little boy, perhaps five years old. Not my own child, but belonging to some other woman who'd done a bad job. *Were all men like this?* I asked myself, then shook my head. I'd been fortunate enough to know men who were men, in bed and out. Just my luck I'd not married one.

"I knew you'd come!" Baby came toward me down the long, marble-floored front hall. "How'd you get away? Did he make a fuss? Here, take off your coat and come in and let's have a good talk. I'll ring for some coffee." She summoned a servant who took my coat and gloves and disappeared as silently as he'd come.

"Is it all right? With George?" she wanted to know when we were seated in a parlor the size of my restaurant, the walls hung with paintings, the floor covered by an immense Aubusson carpet.

"He doesn't know I'm here."

She leaned toward me, her silk skirts rustling. "Do you really love him? Tell the truth, Mary."

I met her eyes with a kind of shock at what I was going to say. "No."

"Then why?"

"I don't know. I thought I did, but I'm not sure any more. I guess he just wore me down."

Another servant appeared, carrying a silver tray and a steaming coffee pot. Baby gestured at the inlaid table in front of us. "Put it here, please," she said. "I'll do the rest." Then she began pouring the coffee into fragile china cups.

"What'll you do now?" she asked, handing me a napkin.

I shrugged. "Live with it. I've lived with worse mistakes. You don't know all of them, and you don't want to, either."

"Living down the past isn't easy." She sipped her coffee and looked at me over the gold rim of the cup. "Heaven knows, I haven't been able to. But you're tough. You made something of yourself, by yourself. And I have Horace. And the girls."

"I want to see them. I brought presents."

"You shouldn't have. We've tried not to spoil them, but it's hard." She rang for a maid, and, when the girl came, asked that Elizabeth and Rose Mary be brought down to us.

Didn't she see her own children? I wondered. And if not, what did she do with herself alone in this house that was more like a palace and as filled with servants?

"Are you happy?" I asked on impulse. "With all this . . . this . . . ?" I couldn't find the word for the opulence surrounding us and waved my hand. I'd seen Miramar and the Emperor's palaces in Mexico, but even in memory they weren't as grand as Baby's mansion.

"Horace and the girls are my life," she said with a hint of irritation. "This . . . as you call it . . . just makes everything easier."

"It's like a fairy tale." A chill ran down my back as I spoke, remembering that a lot of those old tales had bad endings.

"And if I had three wishes, I'd wish the same for you," she said.

"Too late for me."

She shook her head, and her blonde curls bounced. "It's never too late. You just have to believe." And then: "Here they are, the darlings!"

A nursemaid stood at the door, little Rose Mary Echo Silver Dollar in her arms, and Elizabeth Lillie by her side, dressed like a small angel in white taffeta.

"Mama!" She ran to Baby, who lifted her onto her lap.

"This is my best friend, Missus Holliday. No . . . ," she caught herself, "Missus Cummings. Can you say how do you do?"

Elizabeth looked at me from under her lashes, then smiled widely, Baby's smile in a tiny face. Hopping off her mother's lap, she came to me and curtsied, then asked: "Did you bring me a present?"

Baby and the nurse gasped in unison, but I held out my arms to the little minx, and she came willingly. "Of course, I did. But first you must ask nicely."

It was good to hold a child again, especially one as sweet and as sweet-smelling as this one, her hair still damp from a bath, her skin as fresh as a peach—child of privilege but innocent of her heritage and secure in herself.

How I wished for one of my own! A daughter, a son like little Michael with his blue eyes and utter trust in me, dead now for more than twenty years. Time had passed in a heartbeat. Soon I'd be too old even to think of child bearing. I put my package in her hands and blinked back tears.

She looked around at her mother. "May I, Mama?"

"First say, thank you. Then go over to the window seat with nurse. And don't forget your manners again." She turned back to me. Seeing my face, she said: "There's always something to keep life from being perfect, isn't there?"

"You seem to have everything," I said. "Children, the man you love, security."

"But for how long? I worry about Horace. I worry about kidnappers taking the girls. And you know what the silver market's been like. Sometimes I wonder if this isn't all a dream, and I'll wake up some morning back in Central City poor as a church mouse and still married to Harvey Doe."

"You know that won't happen," I said.

"I don't know. Sometimes I'm scared." Her blue eyes were wide. "Why me? It came so easily. It can get taken away just as fast."

That was true, as I knew very well. "Keep a stash," I told her. "Don't trust anybody, especially all those Easterners who come out and take advantage of your hospitality, then try to sell you something."

I'd read of the parties she and Horace gave—the private railroad cars, the oysters, caviar, champagne, hunting trips, foolishness. "Put some money aside, just in case," I said. Advice that had been given to me and that I'd never forgotten.

She sat back and laughed. I'll never forget how she laughed, peal after peal like church bells ringing. Then she said: "Oh, Mary, Mary, it's not that bad. It'll never get that bad, believe me."

Except it did. In July, 1893, President Cleveland repealed the Sherman Silver Act, and all the silver mines in the West shut down, putting thousands out of work and bankrupting many of Colorado's millionaires, including Horace Tabor and Jerome B. Wheeler, whose Wheeler Bank was where most of my money had been deposited.

XIV

In simple terms, the Sherman Silver Act was a subsidy, with the government buying several million dollars' worth of silver each month in an effort to provide a market. President Cleveland's repeal doomed the mines, the towns that had grown up around them, and the miners and their families whose lives depended on the production of silver.

In a matter of days, Aspen changed from a lively, prosperous community into a place of hunger and despair. The men gathered at the street corners and in the saloons, talking useless solutions, while their women stretched out what food was left and tried not to think of the day when there would be nothing to eat and no money to buy more. Their children collected coal from the railroad tracks, trudging along with buckets swinging from filthy hands.

My business slowed to a trickle, then stopped altogether. No one had cash to spend on a meal, and I hadn't enough to replace supplies that wouldn't be used. Along with the rest, George had lost his job, and he spent his days with his friends in the saloon.

It was the silence that bothered me most. No more trains coming in and leaving loaded with ore, no mine whistles announcing the changing of shifts, no rumbling of machinery, or even the tramp of feet as the men made their way up the mountains to work.

It seemed as if Aspen had changed into Sodom; that death had come swiftly, overnight, and all that was left was what had been there before—sky, mountains, the rush of the Roaring Fork, the laughter of magpies like a mockery of us all.

On the First of September I closed the restaurant with apologies to those who'd worked so hard and whom I couldn't afford to pay any longer.

"I hate this as much as you," I told them. "But I can't figure a way to keep going."

Magda patted my arm. "We know, missus. And we thank you for trying. For being so good to us."

I saw them out, shut the door, and sat down at an empty table, tired to my bones. Everything that I'd worked so hard for was gone. My savings had vanished; my stocks in the mines were worthless. All I had were the gold coins in my trunk that I'd never told anyone about, not even George. Especially not George who'd have drunk it up.

What to do? I hadn't a clue and couldn't think. I looked up as the door opened and Alex came in and sat down across from me. He hadn't been to town for more than two months, and in those months he'd grown older, more like our father, with deep lines running from his nose to the corners of his mouth.

"I figured you'd be here," he said.

"Where else? There's no place to go, except out of Aspen." I spoke what I'd been trying to avoid—an uprooting, a move to still another place, another beginning.

To my surprise, he nodded. "That's what I've been thinking. The mines are dead. At least for a while. But I can't make a go of farming without a market, and I sure can't find a buyer for my claims. Eva and I have about decided to pull out and go to California."

"When?" I whispered.

"Soon as we can. We just wanted you to know, and to say you and George are welcome to throw in with us."

Once I'd wanted to go to California—with Doc—but no more. My heart was buried in the Rockies and in the desert of Arizona. My heart and the best years of my life.

"I'll miss you," I said. "But I think we'll stay on. Maybe not here. I don't know. It all happened so fast it's hard to believe."

He was drawing rings on the table top with a callused finger. "I guess we all hoped, but that wasn't enough. Seems like we're two countries, East and West, and neither understands the other or gives a damn."

What he said was true. I'd seen enough of folks from the East—investors, tourists, wide-eyed spectators—come to town to see the inhabitants, the scenery, as if we were foreign species in a zoo. How then could the President, or even Congress, recognize our problems, speak our language enough to understand? And as far as I was concerned, California was as bad—only on the other coast—a place where I didn't belong.

"George and I haven't talked about leaving," I said. In fact, we'd hardly talked at all since that morning in July when the news came over the wire, and he went out, cramming his hat on his head as if he were in pain. "He's been drinking." It was a difficult admission, but Alex was my brother.

He sighed. "So has everybody. What else is there?"

"You saw them. The men on the street. Just standing and waiting."

He slapped his palm on the table. "And they'll be there until the snow flies, but I won't, and neither will you. Let me go find George and see if I can't snap him out of it."

"Go ahead. But I'm not going to California, so don't even suggest it."

"Stubborn," he said.

"A family trait."

"God help us all." He got up, then reached out and pulled me close. "I hate splitting up again."

For a minute I leaned against him, comforted by familiarity. "Me, too. But I can't keep hanging on your coat tails. At least this time I'll know where you are."

When he was gone, I put on the coffee pot and cut thin slices off a loaf of bread I'd made using the last of the flour. Then I went out and down the street to the house we'd been renting.

The locked trunk sat in a corner of the bedroom, its top serving as a bureau where I kept my hairbrush and comb, a silver-backed mirror Doc had bought me, a tray of hairpins, and a bottle of cologne. Removing those, I knelt and unlocked it, burrowed down to the bottom where my hoard was hidden, the very weight of it inside a stocking a comfort.

Two hundred dollars—a fortune to a great many, a ticket out of Aspen, and a new start. Without hesitation, I counted out fifty dollars, then replaced everything and turned the key, happy that I could at least give some security to Alex and Eva and the children, repay them for their kindness to me and to Doc that year that seemed so long ago, that summer when we had all tried to reverse the tide of his illness and failed.

He was so wasted I could almost lift him myself. On sunny days he sat outside the house, a quilt wrapped around him, sleeping fitfully, then waking to watch the children play. Sometimes he walked with me, a short way only, and we talked about the good times, avoiding argument because there was no longer a reason to argue, and because the passion that had fueled our fighting had gone, replaced by the painful acceptance that our luck had run out.

Sometimes he played the old card game, Skinning, with the children, the way Sophie Walton had played with him as a child, his fingers still quick enough to catch them unawares and leave them giggling.

"You cheated, Uncle Doc!"

"And how do you know?"

"I just know."

"Did you see me?"

A shake of the head.

"Then mind your tongue. Don't ever accuse a man of cheating, if you can't prove it."

"That's no fair!"

"Nothing's fair, Hattie. Nothing at all. Next time watch closer. Your deal."

Later, little Mary, my namesake, watched as he stacked the pile of pennies.

"Did you win them all, Uncle Doc?"

"Yep."

"Are you going to buy something nice?"

The ghost of a smile flew across his face. "No. But you are. You're going to buy candy for you and Hattie."

He leaned back and closed his eyes. I think he was already dead, that he had chosen to die, perhaps because of what happened in Tombstone where he, indeed, became a killer.

I like to blame everything on that town and on Wyatt. I like to believe that, if he hadn't had to run to Colorado with a warrant hanging over him, he'd have gone home again, with or without me, and lived the life he'd been born for.

The desert air had cured him, yet he stayed on with the Earps until, in fact, he had become what everybody said he was. A murderer.

And then it was too late—for him and for us all.

"I couldn't find him." Alex stood in the doorway, his hands spread, his expression one of confusion.

"It's all right." God knew, of late I'd not been able to find George, either. The man I'd married had disappeared, and in his place was a stranger whose mind wandered, who stumbled over words, who drank and looked at me as if what had happened were my fault. Of course, he wasn't any different from the rest of the men whose jobs had dried up, who wandered like ghosts and stared at the mountains, the mine shafts, the skeletons of empty buildings as if they could bring Aspen to life again simply by wishing.

I poured coffee and put my bread on the table. "Eat," I urged Alex. "Eat. And take this for your trip."

He looked at the coins I held out in astonishment, then

shook his head. "I can't take your savings."

"There's more. There's enough."

"Mary . . . ."

I pressed the money into his hand and closed his fingers over it. "Take it," I said. "I owe you, and you have a family to think about. George and I . . . we'll be fine."

"Big Sister," he said. "Always looking out for the rest of us."

"That's what sisters . . . and brothers . . . are for." I was close to tears, and so was he. "I'll be out to say good bye before you leave, and we'll keep in touch. Maybe even visit once in a while, who knows?"

"We started out so hopeful," he said, sounding the way Doc had sounded years before. "It's hard to understand why things happen like they do."

I stood and put my hands on his shoulders, not about to let him feel sorry for himself. "Think about our parents. And what they went through, coming here with nothing but a dream and a promise."

"And then they died."

"Stop it!" I shook him gently. "They came, and so did thousands like them. They didn't all die, and neither will we. We'll keep starting over."

He gave a grim smile. "You will, anyhow."

"It's the way I am. I can't just quit. That's the easy way. You're a Horony, same as me, and we're fighters, all of us, even when the dream turns nightmare. So what, if the mines closed? There's other ways of making a living. So what, if you have to move on? You're young, and I'm not so old I can't do a good day's work and get paid for it. As a matter of fact, I've been thinking of going back to Arizona."

The words slipped out, startling me. What had been a vague notion had become suddenly real.

"Why there?" He looked up at me, curious.

"Because of the mines. Copper. Gold. Silver. They can always use a cook and a blacksmith, and we sure won't freeze in the winter like here."

"Does George know?"

I laughed. "I didn't know myself till I said it. But now it sounds right, and besides . . . ." I hesitated, searching for the words to speak a vision. "Besides, I miss it. The desert. The mountains. They're part of me, and I can't explain, so don't ask."

They danced in my head as I stood there, those red rock mountains so different from Colorado's. And the purple shadows moving across as if they were being painted by a giant brush. And the green of the cottonwoods in the river bottoms, how they changed to gold in late fall, dancing, setting sail into the bright air.

Doc was there, too, at least in spirit; a man full of health and determination, a man who had loved me once, of that I was sure. Arizona was where I belonged. It was past and future. It was home.

XV

After all, it wasn't hard to convince George to leave Aspen. He listened to my argument and nodded.

"Might as well," he said. "There's nothing here for us, even if I went back to prospecting. The market's shot to hell, and I don't see anybody stepping in to save it." He fumbled for his pipe and tobacco, and I noticed that his hands were shaking.

Too much booze, I thought, and sighed. Well, we'd make a

new start, he and I, and maybe we'd get back what we'd lost in our marriage and financially.

"When?" I asked, thrusting the rest of the decision onto him.

He lit a match, puffed a minute, then sat back in the chair. "As soon as you can get ready."

So it was all up to me—the packing, the figuring, even the purchase of our tickets to Denver, then to Albuquerque, Deming, and Bisbee, where, with luck, the copper mines would stay productive until we had some money put by.

Pack up and move. Pack up and move. The words played in my head like a Negro spiritual, with all the anguish of those who know only too well what despair is made of.

I said: "Give me a week."

"Don't take too long. We don't want to be the last rats leaving the ship."

"A nice way to put it."

He laughed, a hollow sound unlike his old boisterousness. "There's thousands out of work and starving, and no good way to say it, except damn the government, damn the President, damn us all for a bunch of fools."

Not wanting to hear a repetition of that constant refrain, I went into the bedroom and started sorting through our clothes, but his words wouldn't let me alone. *A bunch of fools.* That's what came when you looked to someone else for salvation; when you expected the government to bail you out, feed you, clothe you; when you abdicated responsibility for self and drifted. That's what could happen to me . . . if I relied on George.

I said my good byes to Alex, Eva, and the children whom I might never see again, to Magda, Karoly, all my friends in Aspen and in Denver, and, risking George's anger, I said good bye to Baby Doe.

The Tabor mansion on Sherman Street had been the first thing to go—that palace with its Turkish carpets, plush velvet draperies, the conservatory filled with palms, ferns, orchids, the garden and its marble statues brought from villas in Rome, Florence, who knew where?

"Did you save anything?" I asked her as we sat in the tiny parlor of her rented house. She still dressed in silk, shivering in the cold, and I was in my old woolen traveling costume.

"I have the Queen of Spain's pearls," she said with what I thought was foolish pride. Getting up, she left the room and came back with an ornate box. Inside lay the pearls, her wedding gift from Horace Tabor.

As I held them, I thought that he'd been duped, that he'd handed over a small fortune for pearls that had probably been strung by some clever jeweler in New York City or Philadelphia, and that he'd believed simply because he wanted to believe, just as his wife was doing. But I held my tongue. Enough dreams had been shattered.

"Lovely," I said instead, and they were lovely, regardless of their lack of age or provenance.

Baby gazed at them, her blue eyes filled with tears. "I'll sell all the rest, but not these. I'll even go to work, if I have to."

She did sell the rest—the diamonds, the sapphires, the rubies and emeralds—and, in the end, the Queen of Spain's pearls. Now, she's up at the Matchless Mine with the girls, wearing rags and miner's boots and waiting for the price of silver to rise, for the mother lode to be discovered, for the return of the days of glory. The Matchless, H. A. W. Tabor's greatest purchase, root of his fortune, seed of his destruction and hers.

We've seen the heights and the bottom of the pit, she and

I, and what has it gotten us? Are we wiser? More sophisticated? Better, for our hard-earned knowledge? This is a question I can't answer, except to say that life must be lived—and dealt with—to the best of our ability. Beyond that, who ever knows?

George was happy in Bisbee, having found a job immediately, and happier still to have a new bunch of cronies to drink with. We rented a tiny house perched precariously on the side of a mountain overlooking town, and I spent a week scrubbing, washing, arranging the few things we'd brought with us. That done, I went out to call on my neighbors.

Anna Pasquale was twenty two, a little woman with her hair in a bun and a catch in her throat as she talked in a mix of languages about leaving home and making the long voyage to America.

How different the trip had been for me! No cramped quarters in steerage, no noise or disease, no waiting in line at Ellis Island, the taste of fear in my mouth. Although at the time I had longed for Hungary, I was still child enough to be enthralled by what I saw—ocean, clouds, sky, the occasional leap of fish, the sound of wind in the huge sails that drove the ship westward like the wings of a white bird.

And then there was Mexico, all color and light, scents and sounds. Was it then that I fell in love with mountains and deserts, I wonder, or was it later?—Doc and me in New Mexico, our backs to the Sangre de Cristos, our eyes on the roll of the high plains, and around us the music of the language of Spain like the notes of a guitar on a summer night, like the falling of rain?

"I'm going to beat this, Kate."
"If we don't freeze first."

It was Christmas Eve, and Las Vegas was deep in snow with the temperature at zero. In spite of the cold, the townspeople were reënacting the Posada, *the search of Mary and Joseph to find shelter for the birth of their son. Long shadows fell on the snow and on the walls of the houses that lined the narrow streets as the candle-lit procession moved from house to house, and the sound of ancient hymns resonated in the pure, dry air.*

Doc stood with me, watching, as the singing died away, and his hands closed on my shoulders.

"I will beat it. I'm not ready to consign my soul to hell."

"And I'm not ready to let you." I leaned against him, still under the spell of the procession. "Maybe what we just saw was a kind of sign. Like we've been blessed."

"I'd like to believe you."

"Other people have gotten cured here," I said, and shivered as an icy wind blew around the window frame.

He leaned down and kissed my ear. "It's Christmas Eve. Let's forget about the cure for tonight. I have a present for you, and from the look of things, you need it."

"What is it?"

"Greedy as a child," he said. "I think that's why I love you."

My heart jumped. "Do you?"

"Most of the time." He grinned, wicked as a cat, and handed me a package wrapped in tissue and tied with silver ribbon.

It was so beautiful I hated to open it. "I have something for you, too," I said, "but you'll have to wait."

"My pleasure." He sat on the bed and crossed his legs.

I untied the ribbon carefully, then curiosity got the better of me. "Oh, hell!" I exclaimed, and ripped open the paper to the sound of his laughter.

Inside the box lay a shawl, a lovely thing of blue and black embroidery, with twining silver threads and silken fringe. I wrapped it around myself and found it warm in spite of what appeared to be its fragility, and I danced, there in that small room, whirling and stamping my feet, as wild and as happy as any Gypsy, while Doc watched and clapped his hands and, for a few moments, forgot that death hung over us both like a pall.

"Brava," he said, when I collapsed, breathless. "Sometimes I think you're somebody I've never seen before and can't catch. Like swamp fire. Who are you really? Do you know?"

I'd been so many selves, acted so many parts. "I'm me," I said finally, then got up and rummaged in my trunk for his gift that I'd managed to hide.

"Your turn."

I'd gotten him a vest, a fancy one embroidered with flowers and vines and our linked initials hidden in the design.

"Clever of you," he said, spotting our names right away. "Is it marriage you're after?"

I answered softly. Though I wanted marriage to him above all else, the time wasn't right to ask. "Just luck for us both. I thought it might do that."

"Ah, Kate, Kate." He held out his arms, and I went into them gladly. "I'm not sure I deserve anything. I've made such a mess of it. But we'll have better days. I promise."

And then I wept as if my heart had broken. Wept like a woman with nothing more to lose—not her man, not her self, not anything meaningful. It was as if I saw it all, that Christmas Eve in little Las Vegas, New Mexico—the future that held nothing but violence and the pain of loss.

XVI

"Please. Take." Anna offered a chipped plate that held a braided cake. It brought back memories that shoved against each other like children playing. Wedding cakes and merriment. Cakes rolled over logs and baked in huge ovens. Cakes in the shape of rings, decorating the arms of the newborn.

"*Kolacs!*" I exclaimed.

Her eyebrows rose at the unfamiliar word. "Is old recipe. From *Italia*. My mama, she make, and now me. Is good."

And it was. Light, yeasty, faintly flavored with fruit I couldn't identify, a treat from a woman who might have been a master baker had she been born in another place, a different time. I ate two pieces, then left her with the promise of a recipe of my own, and all that night and the next day I thought and planned.

Keeping house was simple. And George, who never minded what he ate as long as there was lots of it, made no demands on my time, often working double shifts or staying late to drink with his new friends.

We hadn't much of a marriage. It seemed as if once he got me he forgot about me except at meals or on those nights when he grabbed me and relieved himself without a thought as to how I felt.

So I was bored. And unhappy. Alone in a town of strangers except for Anna and the Ortega family who lived in the house below. Bisbee wasn't Aspen. It lacked the shops, the cosmopolitan atmosphere, running water, and anything beyond the basic supplies needed for a meal was hard to come by. Certainly it hadn't a decent bakery. Oh, there were places to buy *tortillas* and plain loaves, but where were the pies, the cakes, the strudels for fancy occasions, desserts fit for the tables of the bosses and mine owners in their big houses?

I put on my hat, took my purse, and carefully descended the steep steps that led to the cañon below. From the bottom it was a short walk to Brewery Gulch with its saloons and gambling houses, its raucous mining town life complete with whores, dandies, Mexicans leading burros that moved slowly under burdens of firewood and canvas water bags, and around it all the mountains rose, cutting off the horizon, piercing the sky.

I found what I was looking for, then retraced my steps a little breathless. Anna came to the door when I knocked, a welcoming smile on her face. When we were seated at the round oak table in her kitchen, I told her my plan.

"We're going to start a bakery, you and me. I've already rented a store. It'll be extra money, and God knows we can use it."

To my surprise, her face turned solemn. "My Tony . . . he won't like," she muttered.

There it was—that old-country way of thinking. Annoyed, I wriggled in my chair. "Look," I said, "I'm sure he won't mind the extra money, and, anyhow, I'll do the selling. You stay home and bake. I'll buy you the supplies and get a boy who'll make deliveries, if we need to. Let me handle the business part . . . I've done it before. What do you say?"

She looked at her hands that already showed signs of hard work, then up at me. "*Si*. I will. Is good idea, and I have so many recipes and nobody to eat them."

Within a year we had more business than we could handle. I hired two more women, miner's wives with a flair for pie crust and *empanadas,* and two little Mexican boys who made our deliveries with a great sense of pride.

Word got around. For a taste of paradise, people came to Mary's Bakery. There are still times when I wish they hadn't.

XVII

"I'll take six of those . . . and six of these." The young man pointed, then raised his eyes to mine. "Don't I know you from somewhere?"

"No!" I was firm. The last thing I wanted was to be recognized.

"But . . . ?" He seemed perplexed.

For my part, I couldn't place him, and said: "I'm new here. My husband works at the mine."

"Funny. You look familiar." He took the cookies and fished in his pocket. "I don't forget faces."

In the years I'd been away I'd changed, put on weight, and there was gray in my hair that I now wore differently. I smiled. "Everybody has a twin, or so they say."

He looked at me again, and I decided that I didn't like him, but smiled harder. "Enjoy the cookies."

"I will. And I'll remember. It'll come to me."

I hoped not. "Perhaps," I said. "Perhaps."

It came to him all right, just like it came to everybody he met, including George who came home drunk and shouting.

"Bitch! Whore! A joke! You said it was a joke, but it wasn't. You're a whore like that gal in Denver, putting on airs." He picked up a kitchen chair and smashed it against the wall. The whole house shook.

"Stop it!" I might as well have had no voice for all the attention he paid.

"You made me a laughingstock. My wife. Big Nose Kate."

"It's not what you think."

"Don't tell me what to think. Don't tell me anything. It'll be lies." He reached out and slapped me. Hard.

I fell against the stove and whimpered as the corner of it slammed my hip. No man had ever hit me except that snake Behan, when he got me drunk and forced me to sign the paper, saying Doc had held up the stage. But George was my husband, and, though he'd changed, I still couldn't believe what he'd done.

"You're drunk," I accused him. "When you're sober, I'll talk to you. Not before."

He staggered and leaned on the table. "I've got a right to get drunk. My dear wife, the Tombstone whore."

Anger was replacing pain. Inside me pure rage was building—at him, at life, at the young man who'd leaked my past to the town. I wrapped my fingers around the handle of an iron skillet. "Don't you hit me again, George. You hear?" Then I watched as my warning played through the haze of liquor.

"Big Nose Kate," he sneered, but backed off. "Why'd you lie to me?"

I took the offensive. "Get out and don't come back till you can walk straight. Until you can listen to reason and keep your hands to yourself. You hear me?" I hefted the skillet.

He went, still snarling. I hoped he'd fall down the steps and break his neck, but he made it to the bottom and turned toward Brewery Gulch and consolation in a bottle.

I cleaned up the pieces of the chair and threw them in the woodbin, anger bubbling like boiling oil. This was what I'd come to—the wife of a drunk who hit me. At that moment, I'd have rather still been a whore.

George didn't come home for three days, and I can't say I missed him. Marriage wasn't all it was supposed to be. The way it seemed, the woman got the worst of it and put up with beatings along with everything else. I wasn't the only wife in town sporting a black eye, though it shamed me to be seen with one, as if I was to blame for whatever had happened. Well, in a way I was, but the facts of my past couldn't be helped.

As mad as Doc got sometimes, he never laid a hand on me, just lashed out with that tongue of his and let me have it in words. But then, Doc was a gentleman. George, obviously, was not.

When I heard him fumbling at the door that evening, I took the offensive again and was waiting when he walked in. "Well?" I said, giving him a hard look.

"I figured you'd be gone." He wasn't drunk, but he'd had a few.

"Gone where?"

"Wherever whores go."

"I don't know what you've heard, or from whom, but I want you to listen to me, and listen good." I pointed to the chair. "Sit on it. Don't smash it like you did the other one. Just sit there and shut up."

His mouth dropped open in surprise, but he did as he was told.

I stayed standing, the better to avoid him if he lost his temper and came after me. Why it was so important for me to justify my life to him, I didn't understand. Still don't. Thinking about it, maybe I was explaining me to myself, and about time.

"You think you know it all, but you don't," I began, my eyes on his. "In the first place, you're a man. It's easy for you. You can always find work, a place to sleep, get along, somehow. But for a woman? A girl?" I laughed bitterly, remembering myself at sixteen, frightened, wanting, needing my mother's arms and kindness, except that she was buried in a

Davenport, Iowa cemetery and I was alone, without advice or instruction.

Taking a deep breath to banish emotion, I went on. "When I was sixteen, I ran away. On account of a man, George. A man who tried to rape me. Did I ask for it? No, I didn't. I was scared witless. Does that make me a whore? Does it?"

He stared at me like he was hypnotized, and responded with a reluctant shake of his head.

Satisfied, I said: "I was all right for a while. I even married and had a son, but, when he died, everything stopped. You wouldn't know about how that is. You're not a mother. And you wouldn't know how it feels to be in a strange town alone, no money, no job, starvation staring you in the face, and no way out except . . . . No!" I stopped him from interrupting. "No, you stay still and learn how it is for a woman with nothing that's worth anything, except her body. Men pay for that. They *pay*, George! You know they do. The world's filled with prostitutes and the men who use them. The world's full of scared girls selling themselves to be able to eat. And maybe dream about the day they can be decent again, take their bodies back. And their souls, if there's anything left of them."

"Stop!" The word came out guttural.

"I won't. You think I'm filthy and degraded, but who made me that way? You and your kind, thinking women are nothing but animals. I was lucky to meet Doc Holliday, let me tell you. He wasn't happy about what I'd done, either, but he was a gentleman. He never raised a hand to me, George, unlike you. He never left me to explain a black eye to the neighbors. I should've known better than to let myself be talked into marrying you just because we were friends and both of us lonely. We don't suit, you and me. You think I'm a whore, and I think you're a damned disgusting drunk and a lousy lover. That's something I do know about, only I'm stuck with you, God help me."

He was on his feet in an instant, and I realized my mistake. I'd brought him down to what he saw was my level, and he had pride. Misplaced, maybe, but pride it was.

Before I could reach the skillet, he was on me, shaking me so hard I saw stars just before he cracked my cheek open with one of those big blacksmith's hands. Then he tossed me away, limp as a doll. I hit the edge of the stove again, and heard another crack when my arm snapped.

I think I screamed, in anger and pain, before I passed out.

When I came to, Anna was there holding a cloth to my face and sobbing.

I said—"My arm."—and nearly fainted again, when the split in my cheek widened.

"Doctor." She forced herself to stop crying. "I get. You stay."

For sure I wasn't going anywhere. I closed my eyes and lay on the hard floor. "Go," I whispered, trying not to move the muscles in my face.

I heard her quick feet taking the stairs, and the mine whistle shrieking like a crazy person, for the change of shifts. Where was George? I wondered, turning my head slightly. Gone. He'd done his worst and gone, and good riddance.

I wasn't dying, though I wished I was—wished I could drift away past the pain, above the cañons, the red hills, the topsy-turvy shacks of miners and prospectors. Lying there I felt old, worn out, as lost as I'd been at sixteen, and no place to go. Forty five years had come and gone, and I had nothing to show for my life—not happiness or security or children to care for me. A wasted life is what it was, and the best part of it gone where I couldn't bring it back.

DOC HOLLIDAY'S GONE

★ ★ ★ ★ ★

Anna, in spite of my protests, moved me into her house, helped by the doctor who set my arm and stitched my cheek together. I didn't know which were worse, the wounds or the fixing of them there on the kitchen table.

"You shouldn't be alone, Missus Cummings." The doctor, a man with spectacles and a ratty beard, patted my shoulder.

"I'll be fine," I said through the darting pain in my face.

He peered at me out of eyes like bright pebbles. "You will. You're healthy enough, not like some I see. But you won't be able to do much for a while or defend yourself, if you have to."

I tried to laugh and failed. "He won't be back."

"You can't be sure. The world's a sorry place. No explaining what people will do."

While I didn't think George would attack me again, I agreed with him on principle. "The bastard," I said.

He wasn't shocked. "Exactly my point, Missus Cummings. Now let's get you on your feet and into bed."

I slept on a pallet in Anna's kitchen for two days, and, when I woke up, I'd come to a decision.

"I'm getting a divorce."

Anna turned to me, shocked. No one, especially Catholics, even thought of such a thing. You married for better or worse and stuck to it.

"Talk to the priest," she said. "He will help."

"To hell with the priest. He's not the one who's married."

She crossed herself, probably to keep from getting tarred by my heresy. "Is not good," she insisted.

I raised up slowly. "Getting beat all the time isn't so good, either. Don't worry. God won't condemn you, just me. He gave up on me a long time ago."

Her eyes widened in horror, and she crossed herself again. Then, taking no chances, she made the old sign of the horns with her fingers before she dropped to her knees beside me.

"Please, Mary. Is ask for trouble. Think. I am friend, and I tell you, don't do this thing."

But I did, and it was easier than getting married. Living in Bisbee afterwards was not.

XVIII

Business fell off slowly but surely, and it was a while before I realized why. Divorce was a stigma, and a divorced, one-time lady of the night carried a double curse. Anna, for all her superstition, had been right. Women, who'd come in to buy and gossip, stayed away, pretended not to see me if we met on the street, as if my reputation, like some dreadful disease, was somehow communicable. And all because of that pudding-faced young man and his memory. Wouldn't I give him a piece of my mind when I saw him?

It was summer, and the rains were late. I was tired, discouraged, irritable on the day I went to have the splints taken off my arm.

"How is it?" Dr. Feldman sat me in a chair and checked out the scar on my face.

"It'll be good to have two hands again."

He nodded, then cut the tape and removed the heavy splints. "Good as new," he said after a minute. "Just don't use it too hard at first."

I sighed, thinking of my loss of business.

He was perceptive. "Is something wrong?"

"You might say so."

"The divorce?" Behind his spectacles, his eyes were bright and compassionate.

"Partly."

"We live in peculiar times, Missus Cummings," he said. "There are many who believe a woman should allow herself to be mutilated or even murdered instead of trying to save her own life. I'm not one of them, however."

I leaned back in the chair, comforted by his understanding. "Thank you," I murmured.

He nodded, as if to say thanks weren't needed, then poured water out of a pitcher and washed his hands while I watched, appreciating his attention to cleanliness.

Doc had been like that, always freshly shaved, always insisting on a bath and clean clothes for us both. I sighed again, and Feldman heard.

"Can you cook as well as you bake?" he asked.

I laughed and decided to boast. "I ran one of the best restaurants in Aspen, and I'd still be there, if the mines hadn't closed. And before that I had a hotel in Globe. I'm a cook and a darn' good one."

He came to stand beside me, and ran a finger over the scab on my face. "You heal fast. I doubt you'll have much of a scar in a few months." Then, as if he'd made a decision: "Would you be interested in moving out of town?"

For one minute I had the notion he was making me a proposition, and my heart sank. But when I opened my mouth to protest, he cut me off with a blush of apology.

"I'm sorry. It's not what it sounded like. I have a friend who's mining near Pearce. Has quite a few men working for him. He's looking for a cook. It sounds like a kind of rough operation, not like what you've been used to, but you'd not be bothered by anybody, and from what I understand the pay is good."

I was forty five years old, a little plump, with a mark on my cheek, and gray woven through my hair, but youth dies hard if it ever does. I chuckled to myself. Who would want me now? And worse, why had I misunderstood an act of kindness?

"Can I tell him you're interested?" He was watching me as if he could read my thoughts.

I didn't hesitate. "I am."

Within a week it was arranged. I'd met with Percy Clark, the mine owner, accepted the job, and given him a list of the supplies I needed. I'd turned the bakery over to Anna, Lupe Ortega, and Lena Sestric, and taken my share of the profits, storing the money, as always, in a stocking in the bottom of one of my trunks.

To hell with Bisbee, George, and the so-called ladies who'd ostracized me! And to that young man who said he'd been a child in Tombstone at the time of the troubles. I gave him a piece of my mind one afternoon in the middle of the street, called him every bad name I could think of, and marched away before he had a chance to answer. Naturally the ladies jabbered—at my language, at how I'd "forgotten myself," as, of course, was to be expected from someone like me. What did they know, those twittering creatures who gave themselves airs? And what did a kid know about how I'd lived, where I'd been, what I'd had to do?

Once more I was on the move, waving good bye to my true friends from the seat of a wagon loaded with supplies and the trunks that held all that was left of the me that I'd been.

Once upon a time . . . . That's how all the old tales began. Once upon a time there was a princess. Me. Only the happy ending hadn't happened, and I doubted that it would. I was an aging female drifting across the endless sea of America, across the high desert that's like a sea in itself—sand, mountains, blue sky and never an end to it, on and on with the horizon always moving away, until you feel like you're swimming in the air like the shadows that fall and sail on in whatever direction they please, and the vastness takes you like a current, and you go with it, not caring, swept away.

XIX

The Sulphur Springs Valley fans out like the delta of a yellow river as it runs into Mexico. To the east, the Chiricahua Mountains thrust up like the frozen waves of an ancient sea. The copper-colored Mules and the Dragoons form the western boundary of the great valley, hemming it in, keeping it in place.

The Apache leader, Cochise, is buried somewhere in the Dragoons. Over the years, several search parties have climbed over those rocks and passes, hoping to find him—or what's left—but I've always wished them bad luck. Let the dead lie. Let him be, that Apache who, like the rest of his people, loved the land where they were born, and fought for it. And lost.

I can understand him because this is my country. By adoption, it's true, but I love it in an almost sensual way, feel it in my bones, respond to it with something like passion—as if I want to take it inside me, all of it, grass, mountains, spirals of rock, cañons that twist into secret places that might or might not speak out like oracles to one who knows how to listen.

I was mostly silent on that trip to Pearce—silent and looking, and I saw some of the changes that had happened because of the white man and his cattle and greed. The range had been overstocked and overgrazed. In many places the grass was gone, and tumbleweed and catclaw had taken root. Other stretches were bare, and dust devils coiled up from the surface like transparent serpents.

In the fifteen years I'd been away, the face of these valleys had been wiped clean and repainted, not for the better. So I was silent, and stunned, but happy, nonetheless, for I was home again.

Dr. Feldman had been right about one thing. Pearce, compared to Bisbee, was downright primitive. Percy Clark came out to meet me and take me to the shack that would be my headquarters. It contained a stove, a large table, and rough shelves on which were stacked rusty pans and Dutch ovens and a mess of tin plates and cups. A cubbyhole off to one side had a cot and a rickety table with a pitcher filled with sulphurous water. A layer of grit and grease covered everything, and cobwebs hung from the rafters. Both rooms were stifling and would only get worse when I fired up the stove.

I glanced out the back door and saw a ramada. "I want the stove moved out there. And the table, too," I said to Percy. "There's no way I can cook in here and stay on my feet. Who had the job before me?"

Percy looked embarrassed. "Nobody. We've been kind of making do on our own . . . but my men don't like it much."

"I'll bet." I took off my hat and hung it on a hook beside the cot, then looked around for a broom and bucket, smothering a grin at the look on Percy's face.

"Don't worry. I'll have this place clean before it's time to start supper," I said, hoping to calm him. "It's a wonder you haven't poisoned yourselves in this mess."

He opened his mouth, then closed it, and turned away. In any operation—ranching, mining, running a hotel—the cook's word counts for something. Men live for their stomachs, and so do women for that matter. I had the upper hand

and intended to use it, both for myself and the hungry miners.

All in all, once I'd established some order and a routine, it wasn't a bad place to be. The men were respectful and friendly, and appreciated the meals I put out. And then there was the country, the freedom of it, the beauty that was like life, both violent and peaceful, and accepting of me as no human ever was.

On my Sundays off I explored, either on foot or on horseback, borrowing one of Percy's old saddle mares and heading out, returning with my saddlebags full of rocks, weeds, desert flowers that fascinated me with their toughness. I couldn't name them, only marvel over shapes and colors—orange, yellow, the purple of storm clouds, the shell pink of sunrise.

"Miss Mary's back. Better get her a bucket of water," someone would call when I rode into camp with my treasures, and they'd help me arrange the grasses and flowers, though they probably figured I was crazy.

For me, it was like having a family again—a family of rough but well-meaning brothers who flattered, teased, begged for their favorite meals, and did their best to keep me happy. A hard life, but I didn't complain.

I stayed a year, and then on one of my Sunday rides I passed by the little Cochise Hotel and met Mrs. Rath, the owner. She was a fussy woman with a fringe of false curls and an air of helplessness that was equally false, as I found out.

Seeing me pass, she invited me in, and was horrified to hear that I was cooking for the miners.

"My dear Missus Cummings," she said in a whisper, "you can't. It's not decent . . . you and all those men."

Hypocrite! I thought but said nothing.

"People will talk, you know," she went on. "Why not come and work for me? I've been needing someone with experience to help out, and that's hard to find here."

I sipped the coffee she'd brought, then said: "It's really all right. The men are my friends. I've not had any problem."

Her eyebrows lifted to the false fringe. "Not yet. But you know how men are."

"I'm a little old to worry about such things, don't you think?" I asked, trying for humor.

She shook her head, dropped her voice to an even lower whisper. "Some of them lust after anything, especially in a place like this. Even women of our age. Think about it. If you work for me, you'll have your own room, your meals, a decent place to bathe, and forty dollars a month." She paused to let her generosity sink in. "And Sunday's off, of course. What do you say?"

"It sounds interesting." And it did. The idea of sleeping on a decent bed in a room where the wind didn't cut through the cracks in the walls was appealing. But the woman herself made me cautious—all that piety and doom-saying.

She changed her tactics, when I didn't answer. "Please," she said, folding her hands on the table. "I really need the help. I wouldn't offer, if I didn't. And we women have to stick together. Safety in numbers, don't you know."

"I'll think about it," I said, and got up to leave.

"Fifty dollars a month!" Her eyes were like steel darts. "You won't be sorry!"

Well, I was and I wasn't. The widow Rath had a tendency to fuss over small things and overlook necessities, and her daughters were lazy creatures who gave themselves airs and looked down on me—the hired help. If I'd told them I'd once known the Emperor of Mexico, they wouldn't have believed it. "Mary's making up stories again," they'd say, snickering. "Mary thinks she's better than us."

No doubt about that! The poor girls didn't even know how to set a table, where to put the knives and forks. Not that the travelers coming through knew better or even cared. Still, I showed them, much to their irritation and their mother's.

"Snooty," they called me behind my back, then relished the fact that I was the one who changed beds and did the laundry, who oversaw the kitchen while they were off flirting with guests or with some of the neighboring cattlemen.

That was just as well. Their absence allowed me to do things my way, to enjoy the hanging of clothes on the line, while the hawks soared overhead and the thrashers whistled at me from the brush; to pretend that the kitchen was my own, that I was back once again cooking as I chose for appreciative diners. At least the people who ate at the hotel were appreciative—travelers who'd had their fill of beef and beans, jerky and cornbread. They talked to me, and I to them, exchanging news and stories. And it was one of those exchanges that led to my downfall.

He was a book salesman, taking orders for editions of Shakespeare, Dickens, the Old and New Testaments, and he was frustrated to find so few on his route who could read or who even wanted to.

I pounced on his sample of the Shakespeare, leather-bound and illustrated with engravings. It had been a long time since I'd held a book like that one in my hands, or read anything besides the week-old newspapers that came in on the train.

"Can I borrow it?" I asked him. "Just overnight. I'll be careful with it, I promise."

His face crinkled like wet taffeta. "Of course, Missus Cummings. Enjoy it, and tell your friends. Perhaps you might even start a reading room here in the hotel."

I snickered at the thought of the girls indulging in anything that would improve their minds. "Doubtful," I told him. "But it's been an age since I've read a real book."

"You've been out here quite a while then?" He was interested, not so much in me as to what I could tell him that would improve his business.

"Since the early 'Eighties," I said.

"Wild times then, or so I hear. Robbings, killings, bandits behind every bush and tree. Am I right?"

I thought back to those days, to Tombstone when it was alive, throbbing with dissension, rude but vital. We'd been young, all of us—Doc, Wyatt, Josie, myself—young and as devil-may-care as the town.

"It was different," I said. "But it's gone now, and all the actors with it."

Something in my tone struck him. He said: "I've heard stories. About outlaws, the Earps, Doc Holliday. Are they true?"

"Depends on what you heard and who did the telling."

He nodded. "Yes. I can see that. People will twist things just to make a good tale. Even Shakespeare, there, did it." He cleared his throat. "In Bisbee last week someone told me about a woman named Big Nose Kate. Did you ever run across her?"

Now it was coming! Now I'd hear it all again—distorted, a fantasy told by someone who hadn't known me, didn't give a damn.

I said: "I knew her."

"Then you've heard she was murdered. By that Holliday fellow. Buried out here somewhere, so they say. Pity to do that to a woman. But dramatic, you have to agree."

Laughter got the best of me. When I was in control again, I said: "She's not dead. And Doc wouldn't have done that. He was a gentleman, and they loved each other. I know that much."

His face fell, then brightened. "You knew them both?"

"Oh yes. And the Earps and all the rest."

"Interesting."

"Maybe."

Out of the corner of my eye I saw the widow, her eyes fastened on me with something like horror. *Trouble*, I thought, and cursed myself for talking too much.

"You never mentioned that you were involved with those people."

It was the next morning, and the widow was grilling me like my life was on the line, which in a way it was.

"You never asked."

"Well, I'm asking now. How is it you know so much?"

"I was there for a while," I said, and went on chopping peppers for the stew pot.

"In what capacity?"

I wanted to shake her until her fake hair fell off, until her teeth rattled and fell out, but I controlled the urge.

"I was visiting. Other than that, my life isn't your business."

She grabbed the knife out of my hand and waved it like a saber. "It certainly is! I have my girls to think of! And my hotel. We're reputable people, and I can't have someone whose life's indecent working here."

I'd have bet her life wasn't lily-white, either, but that hardly mattered. What did matter was that she was painting me black without knowledge or charity. I picked up the vegetables and tossed them on the floor at her feet.

"Fine," I said. "I quit."

And that was that. By the end of that week I had answered an ad in the paper and been hired as a housekeeper by one John Howard whom I'd never met. That didn't matter, either. All I wanted was out—away from hypocrites, prudes, and spoiled children.

When he arrived to pick me up, neither the widow Rath nor her daughters were there to say good bye, a fact that Howard noticed as he noticed most things.

"Where's the widow?" he asked, hefting my trunks into the wagon bed.

"Probably counting the spoons."

He made a noise that I thought was laughter. "Did you take them?"

"No."

"Too bad. She's an old biddy, if ever there was one."

With that, he helped me onto the seat, climbed up himself, and took the reins. "You'll be better off with me," he commented. "As long as you're not too particular."

About what? I wondered, and then forgot as we moved off at a trot through heat waves that shimmered above the valley floor.

Part Two

XX

Camp Supply, 1876

I'm holding the horse's big head between my hands. His breath is warm, his eyes have a glimmer of a twinkle in them. I'm saying good bye to Gidran who carried me safely out of Fort Griffin and across Indian Territory, and to the little mouse-colored mustang that was Doc's.

"Take care of him." It's a plea and an order to the buyer.

He seems to understand. "I will, that. He's a good horse."

"The best."

With the money from the sale I go back to Doc, trying not to cry.

He says: "Out here horses are a commodity. You know that. We're on our way to Dodge and Denver and need money not horses."

I wipe my nose on my ragged sleeve. "It's like I lost something. Some piece of me. Understand?"

"Sure. But vagabonds like us can't afford to be sentimental."

"I wasn't born to be like this!"

"Neither was I, sweetheart. Neither was I. It's the luck of the draw."

Jack Howard and I drove across the valley toward the mountain peak known as Dos Cabezas—Two Heads. The afternoon was brilliant, the sky a deep and cloudless blue. I was feeling young again, and adventurous. It was that kind of day. A little touch of autumn in the air, a hint of excitement that was infectious.

The team of sorrels trotted out boldly, and I admired the way Jack handled the reins. He wasn't anything to look at—sharp-featured and angular—but there was determination in him and a gleam in his eye, as if he made his own rules and stuck to them come hell or high water. I had the eerie sense of having known him before, and only hoped it hadn't been at Bessie's house which would have been hard to explain, especially if he should turn out to be like George.

"A nice team," I said over the sound of hoofs and wheels.

"They get me where I want to go." He glanced at me out of the corner of his eye. "Can you handle a gun, Missus Cummings?"

A strange question to ask one's housekeeper. "Yes," I said. "Will I have to?"

"You might. I've got claims, and I don't want anybody jumping them. Or me."

"Maybe you should have advertised for a bodyguard, instead," I said.

He chuckled, and it came out rusty, as if he'd forgotten how. "You'll do. You've got an honest face, and you aren't some flighty young 'un pining for city lights and compliments."

"Not any more."

"That's good, then." He clucked to the team, and we turned off onto a track that led into the mountains. "My daughter took off for the city. 'Not enough excitement,' she said. That's why I advertised. A man isn't made right for things that need doing in a house."

"And your wife?" I hesitated to ask, but, since I was working for him, I figured I should know something about him.

"Dead," he said shortly. "Died and left me with Jessie to raise, and I wasn't cut out for it."

"Not too many men are," I said to ease what was obviously a sore spot. "But don't worry. She'll probably make out fine."

"Huh!" He spat over the side of the wagon. " 'Twon't be my fault, if she gets herself in trouble!"

"No, indeed!" I agreed, deciding he was a man of character in spite of his cranky way of putting things. "Why do I have the feeling I met you before?" I asked then, because I couldn't escape the tug of memory.

He shrugged. "People get around. Like me. Born in England, made my way here, worked at jobs across the country. But here I'll stay. Mark me."

It came, then, in a flood. Me, holding Gidran's big head, fighting tears. Me saying: "Promise you'll treat him right." And the buyer stroking the horse's neck, not looking beyond my boy's clothes. "For sure, lad. I can see what he is, don't doubt it."

"You bought a big paint horse years ago at Camp Supply," I said to him. "Do you remember?"

He gave me an astonished look as if I were a Gypsy, reading palms. "How do you know that?"

"He was mine. I was that boy."

"I'll be damned. The best horse I ever owned. Had him till he died, like I promised." He spat again. "That was you? That lad?"

"It was."

"You fooled me. What the devil were you doing out there dressed like that?"

"A long story."

"And you'll tell me sometime."

"Why not?" Nights are long on the high desert, and a housekeeper earns her living in more ways that cleaning and cooking. I laughed. Maybe, just maybe, I'd lucked out at last.

★ ★ ★ ★ ★

Dos Cabezas never had the glitter and flash of the big mining camps, and the people who lived there liked it that way. There was a store, a livery, a church, a school, a post office, and the houses of the people who ran the businesses.

Jack pointed out everything as we drove through, and added a caution. "You can get what you need at the store, or wait till I go into Willcox, but I'm not made of money, so don't go running up a bill."

"Aren't your claims paying anything?" I asked, worried that I'd agreed to a life of poverty.

"I get by . . . but I'm no millionaire. Even if I was, I'd be out here where I'm free to do what I please when it pleases me. If you don't like it, say so, and I'll take you back."

But I did like it. All of it. The little town nestled in the hills, the quiet broken only by the thud of hoofs, the jingle of trace chains, and every now and again the squawking of startled jays in the oak trees.

"So far it suits me fine," I said.

Two dogs snarled at us, when we drove into the yard—the biggest dogs I'd ever seen. I stayed where I was, holding tight to my skirts and looking to Jack to tell me what to do.

He jumped down and ignored me. "Hey, boys," he said to the pair. "Did you think I'd gone off and left you?"

They quieted and stood, wagging their tails.

"Is it safe?" I called.

"Just come slow. They'll get used to you."

I certainly hoped so. Although I'd always wanted a dog, these hardly seemed like lap dogs. Their huge tongues hung out between curving, white teeth, and their eyes were unreadable as they stood, watching me.

"It's all right, Bear," Jack said as I put out a hand to the bigger of the two.

"That's his name? Bear?"

"He's damn' near as big as one."

The creature sniffed me, then investigated my skirt before wagging his tail. The other, slightly smaller, followed suit, and I got down on my knees and patted them both.

"I always wanted a dog," I told them, "but you're a bit more than I figured on."

"Don't mollycoddle them," Jack ordered. "They're guard dogs, not pets."

His tone, his manner, irritated me. "You're trouble is you've lived alone too long." I scrambled to my feet, and he jumped like I'd shot him.

"Don't think you're going to come here and boss me, woman! You can go at any time."

"And don't think I'll stand quiet and let you shoot off your mouth at my expense," I said. "It's obvious you need looking after."

His jaw dropped, and then, surprisingly, he laughed. "You've got a sharp tongue on you," he said. "But so have I. We'll have some disagreements, we will."

"I've lived through worse."

"And you've promised to tell me."

"Only if you behave yourself, and give me a free hand in the house." I wasn't about to take chances with his changeable nature. The rules were going to be laid out from the start.

"Why do I get the feeling I just sealed my fate?" he asked.

I grinned. "Because you have. Now let's see the house."

It was a house like any other in that part of the country. Put up fast with board and batten, quick shelter, added on to as needed. There was a front room, kitchen, and sitting room combined, complete with iron stove, plank table, a rocking chair, and two straight chairs. Behind that, two small bedrooms with narrow beds, primitive chests, and hooks on the walls for clothes.

Hardly a palace, I thought, remembering Baby Doe's mansion, the elegance of some of the hotels I'd stayed in—and some of the other places as well—the stone house in Fort Griffin, the adobe in New Mexico—places I'd turned into a home with my own hands and determination.

"Say it! It's not what you're used to!" Jack was beside me, belligerent as one of the dogs.

"You don't know what I'm used to," I snapped back. "Stop apologizing."

He took off his hat, and I saw that he was as bald as an egg with only a few grizzled hairs around his ears.

"Best keep your hat on when you're out in the sun." I spoke automatically, so used to taking care of someone.

"Looking out for me, are you?"

I guess I was. I nodded.

"That's nice." He put the hat back on and walked to the door. "I'll get you settled, then I've got things to do. You want to hear how I lost my hair?"

"How?"

"I was in one of my prospects. Took off my hat and laid it down. When I put it back on, damn' if a vinegaroon wasn't in it. Scared me so bad my hair fell out!" He stood there grinning, waiting for me to catch on.

"Liar!" I said with a chuckle.

"Damn' right. Now, tell me where to put these trunks of yours. Heavy as lead they are. What's in 'em?"

"None of your business, Mister Howard," I said, and preceded him out the door.

XXI

"I need wash tubs, lye soap, a washboard, clothespins, and some calico for curtains. And a coffee pot, a good frying pan, moth balls, and flour that doesn't have bugs in it."

We were facing each other across the table like duelists. I wasn't spending any more nights under dirty quilts, or fighting a losing battle with infested flour. And Jack wasn't happy. In fact, he was roaring.

"You'll break me! We'll both be paupers! You with your wash pots! The spring up the cañon's good enough, always has been. You'll use your legs and your wits, woman, or I'll let you go!" He slammed his cup on the table.

By now I had him figured. A lot of bluster, a lot of noise, and then he saw sense. I only had to stand up to him and stay calm, which wasn't always easy given my own temper.

"You want bugs in your bread? Fine. You want fleas in your blankets from those beasts of yours? That's fine, too. Just don't complain about your stomach or your itches. There! I've told you. Now make up your mind."

I got up and went outside where the view always pacified me. Rolling hills dotted with oaks and mesquite, yellow chamiza flowers, and the peaks of the mountains like sculpted faces turned to the sky. Closer to home was the garden plot I'd started to dig, and the sapling trees—apples, peaches, apricots. In a few years—if I lasted that long—we'd have fruit and vegetables of our own, good, fresh produce to supplement Jack's beans, beef, and occasional venison.

Oh, he was tight-fisted, but I knew he was taking gold out of those prospects he was so proud of, and I'd found where he kept his money in a sack under a loose floor board. There was more than enough for the simple way he lived, and which I intended to stick to.

"Missus Cummings . . . ." He was at my elbow, coffee cup in hand.

I said: "It's time you just called me Mary."

He blinked, distracted as I'd intended. "I . . . it's not right," he said after the minute it took to follow me. "People might get the wrong idea."

"There's nobody here but us," I reminded him. "We can do and say what we want. And anyhow, I'm divorced. Missus Cummings is long gone."

"What happened? With you and him?"

I told him, leaving nothing out.

When I finished, he was quiet, frowning. "It's not right, raising your hand to a woman. A man who does that isn't a man, and you such a little thing."

I gave him a pleading look, not having forgotten how it was to flirt and get my way. "And now here I am, trying to earn a living and having to fight for every little thing I need to make you comfortable."

He sighed. "All right. All right. This time you can have your way, but don't think I can't recognize when a woman's trying to get 'round me. I'm soft in the head this morning is all."

I smiled sweetly. "Thank you, Jack."

He stalked across the yard to the horse pen. "Save your thanks," he called back. "I deserve whatever happens. God help me."

He rode off without another word, and I spent the morning sweeping and laughing to myself. Jack Howard was ornery, penny-pinching, argumentative, and, in spite of it all, charming. He was himself, and there's a lot to be said for that.

DOC HOLLIDAY'S GONE

★ ★ ★ ★ ★

It's a funny thing, but I've never been lonely all these years, even though so much of my early life was spent in towns surrounded by people. Maybe a person gets so she has enough of noise, excitement, the tug and pull of other people's demands. I don't know. I haven't thought much about it until now. I've been too busy doing things—making this house comfortable, doing the garden and putting up the produce, writing letters and getting answers, making sure Jack didn't work too hard and come in bent over so I had to heat water and get him in a wash tub, then rub liniment on him and keep him inside while he groused about how, if he couldn't work, we'd end up in the poor house, both of us.

"Shoot me through the head, Mary," he'd say. "If it comes to that, shoot me and toss me in a hole."

"And leave me to look out for myself."

"My money's on you. You're the only woman I ever met who never complained. Can't stand whining females. Never could. You're all right, no matter what anybody says."

We came to understand each other, Jack and I, in spite of our shouting matches. All my years with Doc and that wicked tongue of his made it easy for me. I was used to a man who used words, instead of blows, to get his points across. In fact, I liked it. We kept our wits sharpened, our humor intact, and that was, I see now, our way of showing affection, as strange as that sounds.

Jack brought back the wash tubs and everything else on my list, and then watched as I stitched and hung the curtains.

"Damn' place looks like a brothel," he said, when I admired the bright calico.

"Is that where you were in town?"

He made a rude noise. "Waste of money."

"Why not?" I was baiting him.

101

"What kind of woman are you, talking like that?" His roar rattled the windows.

"Curious," I said.

"You're not supposed to be. You're not supposed to know about things like that."

I smothered a laugh. "Who said?"

He stalked across the room, and stood facing me. "Shut your mouth, woman. It's not decent."

"You're a prude, Jack Howard!"

"I'm not!"

"Seems like it. I mean, after all, we're here in the same house, we ought to be able to talk. And we both know what the world's like."

"There's better things to talk about!"

"Like what?"

"Like what's for supper?"

I burst out laughing, and after a minute so did he. "You made a fool of me, Mary Cummings," he said. "You and your wicked tongue."

"I wanted to see if I could make you laugh," I said. "You're always so ready to go up in smoke. Like one of those dynamite sticks you keep in the outhouse. And that's another thing. I want a door put on it. It's not right, me having to be out there for everybody to see."

He always took his shotgun with him and sat there in full view, which didn't bother him, but which I thought was awful.

His laughter ended as quickly as it had begun. "Nobody's sneaking up on me. Especially not out there. They want my claims, Mary. A man has to protect what he's worked for."

"I know that. But a woman needs some privacy."

He gave me a piercing look. "Just like a man's life is his own."

We were, it seemed, back to the beginning. "All right," I said. "I won't ask where you've been, if you'll put a door on the outhouse for me. Agreed?"

With another spurt of laughter, he sat down and plunked his arms on the table. "You drive a hard bargain, but I'll do it. And I'll see what I can do about piping that spring down here to the house for the wash and our water. I been meaning to do it, but there's never enough time. And just so you know, I've got no use for fancy women. Never have. Anyhow, now I've got you."

"But you don't," I said softly. "Have me, I mean."

"There's always hope." His eyes glinted up at me.

It was as if I was young again, slender, still pretty, believing in dreams. It seemed I was being given another chance at what I'd come to believe would always be denied me. So I weighed my answer carefully.

Finally, I went to him and kissed the top of his bald head. "I'm not pretty any more," I said.

He kept his elbows planted on each side of his plate and wouldn't look at me when he spoke. "A man wants more than a pretty face, Mary. And I'm a bit long in the tooth, myself."

I put my hands on his shoulders. They were rigid, as if he'd scared himself. "You suit me just fine," I said.

XXII

"I suppose now you'll be wanting to get married."

We were having breakfast—eggs, beef, fried potatoes—a huge meal that Jack said he needed to get through the day.

He caught me by surprise, and I looked down into my cup as if I could find an answer there. Finally, I shook my head.

"I've been married. It never brought me anything but trouble."

He took a forkful of eggs. "That's fine then."

But like a sinner, I had the sudden urge to confess and be forgiven, to have the slate of my conscience wiped clean. "There's a lot about me you don't know," I said.

"Let the past rest. I know enough."

"But . . . ." I was insistent.

"Mary, whatever you did is done. Same with me. I'm no saint, and probably neither are you, but we don't have to start blabbing just because of last night."

Regardless of consequences, I blurted out what bothered me most. "They called me Big Nose Kate! You understand me? You want to kick me out, now's your chance."

His eyebrows shot up to where his hair should have been. "That was you? Back in Tombstone with that Holliday fella?"

"That's only part of it."

"Then spit out the rest, if it'll make you feel better."

Why was he being so calm about it all? By now he should be shouting about women and deception, and how he never trusted a one of them. Taking a deep breath, I went on and didn't stop till I reached the end.

"That's it. All of it. Now you know and can send me packing."

He cut another piece of meat. "You should see yourself," he said. "Nervous as a whore in church. No offense," he added with what looked like a smile.

"But . . . ?"

"Stop with your buts, and listen to me. It seems like you did what you had to do like everybody else. Like I did. Staying alive beats dying all to hell, at least in my book. And you stuck with him, didn't you?"

"I was there when he died."

"Well, then. As for the rest, everybody knew the Earps and Holliday were the law. You were on the right side." Then he went on eating as if my revelation was of no interest at all.

I leaned across the table. "You don't mind?"

"Like I said. What's done's done. I killed a man in Tombstone back then. He tried to jump my claim."

"Why doesn't that surprise me?" I said.

"It shouldn't." His eyes crinkled with silent humor. "We're quite a pair, you and me."

"Why aren't you in jail?" I wanted to know. "Why aren't you in Yuma?"

"Self-defense. The fella needed killing like a lot of them in that town. A bad place, Tombstone. It's better here."

I looked past him through the open door. The desert broom was covered with silver plumes, and the mountains seemed farther away, their fall appearance, as if they'd drawn into themselves for protection against the coming winter.

"This is the best place I've ever been," I said softly. "I hope you don't ever decide you don't want me any more."

"Just don't start thinking for me," he said. "I can't stand a woman does that."

I figured with his quick temper somebody had to think for him at times, calm him down before he got apoplexy. But a clever woman knows how to make her influence felt without being caught at it. I sipped my coffee and didn't say another word until Jack, who was looking out the window, jumped up, scattering the dishes.

"Now what?"

"That damned Hurtado fellow's gathering cattle. Probably gathering mine along with his. They all try it. Every damn' year."

He grabbed his shotgun. I grabbed him. "You can't go shooting the neighbors," I said firmly. "Let me go."

He glared. "And what'll you do about it?"

"Bring our cows back."

He gave that cackle of his that passed for a laugh. "What do you know about it? Those cows are wild."

He could be infuriating, never believing I was capable of doing more than keep a house, set a table. I stamped my foot hard. It hurt, but I paid no attention. "I know as much as you. Now, go saddle me a horse and put that damn' gun away, because I won't need it."

He stopped short, belligerent as one of the dogs. "I won't have you riding out there with your skirt up to your waist."

"Oh, stop!" I said. "My skirt will be only above my ankles, and nobody's interested in an old woman's legs anyhow."

"I am!"

"And we're both long in the tooth, like you said." I sounded harsh, but inside my heart was pattering like a girl's, and I put out a hand and laid it on his arm. "Thank you for that. It was . . . it was nice."

"Huh!" he said. "You listen to flattery but not to common sense. Like every other woman," he added, refusing to look at me out of what was, I thought, embarrassment.

"And where would you men be without women? Out shooting at each other. Let me go, Jack. It scares me . . . you ready to kill somebody, and maybe get killed yourself. And then what?" What I said was the truth. I didn't want Jack dead, and I'd seen enough killing to last me.

"You mean it, don't you?" He raised his eyes to mine.

"Yes."

He cleared his throat. "All right. Just this once. You hear me? Either that, or you get yourself something decent to ride in."

"I will," I promised, with every intention of doing so as

quickly as I could. I'd missed my rides—the freedom I felt on horseback, and the land rolling past, each scene different from the last, each curve of the trail beckoning.

I scrambled up on the old horse without any help and rode off down the cañon. "See you soon!" I called back, and Jack waved, a stiff motion of hand and arm as if he wasn't used to waving to anybody, had never done it before. Probably he hadn't, I decided, as I headed for the dust cloud that was the main body of the herd. Probably he hadn't had much love in his life or any close friendships at all. He'd grown up distrustful of everybody and never had reason to change.

Well, I thought, *I'm going to change that. You just wait and see, Jack Howard.* Then I put the horse into a fast trot, laughing at how good it felt to be on the move again.

Regardless of Jack's state of mind, Florencio Hurtado was a gentlemen, and so were the other ranchers, Charley Busenbark and Harvey Newell, who'd joined him in the roundup. Seeing me, they all pulled up their horses and tipped their hats.

"We thought you were Jack. That's his horse isn't it?" Busenbark said with a grimace of what seemed like relief.

"I came, instead," I said, and introduced myself.

Hurtado was riding a rangy bay that was dancing under him, and I admired the way he controlled it, with a light hand on the bit. *"Señora,"* he said, "we'll find your cattle. You, please, stay here. Have coffee and rest until we come back."

Then he was gone and the others with him, leaving me to marvel at the courtesy that seemed born into every Mexican I'd ever known—so different from most of those who'd made their way West and had no knowledge or understanding of manners.

Jack had only four cows that ran loose on the range and

were bred by whatever bull wandered by. All, this year, had calves at their sides, good, big youngsters as wild as their mothers.

"If you wish, *señora*, I can take them to market for you and get a good price." Hurtado stood beside me, hat in his hand.

Jack wouldn't like it, but it was one less chore to do, so I smiled and nodded. *Gracias, señor*. I would be grateful."

"And *Señor* Howard?" His eyes were alight with humor.

"I'll manage."

"*Bueno.*" He turned to his horse. "My men will drive your cows back for you. They won't want to leave their calves, and I don't think you could manage four at once." He hesitated, then gave a small bow. "Even if you are brave enough to face Jack Howard by yourself."

Looking at them—bony mamas with wicked horns—I didn't think I could manage them, either. Facing Jack looked like a much easier proposition.

"His bark is worse than his bite," I said.

"A barking dog and a shotgun are always dangerous," came the response.

And Jack had admitted to killing a man. I wondered how many of his neighbors knew about that, and thus stayed as far away from the home place as they could.

"Perhaps you better leave the money for the calves at the post office," I said.

He bowed again. "As you wish."

That's how I got to know some of the neighbors—by interceding for Jack. And they are good neighbors, all of them, just wary of Jack's temper. There's the schoolteacher, who lends me books to read; the local ranchers who to this day have kept an eye out for our few cows; the Whites, our closest neighbors and best friends, who in these last years have made sure we never wanted anything, made trips to town for us, and never paid the slightest bit of attention to Jack's frequent bad humor.

It was Mrs. White who found me standing in the road that day in 1929, when Josie Earp's letter reached me. Wyatt was dead. The man I'd loved and hated, the man who'd cleaned up Cochise County then left with a warrant hanging over his head—left, taking Doc Holliday to ruin—was dead.

Almost fifty years had passed since those nightmarish days at Tombstone. I was old. Everyone who'd been there was old and dying. Where had the years gone? Where was our youth, and what had we done with all that energy, all those hopes?

Tears blinded me, and I stopped walking and stood there feeling lost, crying—not for Wyatt, but for the passage of time, the foolishness of passion.

The men were gone—all of them. The women, Allie, Josie, myself, and the lovely Baby Doe, remained—links with the violence of history, the reasons underlying that violence.

What would have happened if Josie had never come to Tombstone, intending to marry Johnny Behan but falling in love with Wyatt, instead? What would my life have been if Doc had loved me enough to leave the Earps and settle down somewhere? It seemed we'd all been the instruments of our own destruction, our lives braided together in a long rope that held firm even all these years later.

We were all widows. As for me, I'd been widowed or abandoned so many times I'd lost count. Even George Cummings was dead—a suicide. They said he'd had a brain tumor, and maybe that was so. Maybe that accounted for the way he'd acted, but who could tell?

"Are you all right?" Mrs. White was standing beside me, looking worried.

I nodded. "Just some bad news."

"I'm sorry. I'll get somebody to drive you home."

Company was the last thing I wanted, so I managed a smile. "I'll be fine. It's just a kind of shock when somebody you know dies."

"Come in the house and rest a minute, then," she said. "I'm just through baking, and the coffee's still hot."

She was a good woman, and kind. And young. I wanted to tell her to hold on to life, to savor every minute, to treasure her two sons, active boys as nice as their parents, because too soon everything would change, and she'd be like me—an old woman with a life that had passed in the blink of an eye, and nothing to show for it but a trunkful of clothes, old photographs, and memories.

I said: "I'll just go on home. Jack isn't feeling too well. Thanks just the same."

And then I went on up the dusty road in the brilliant late-winter afternoon, the sky so blue, the mountains so clear, it seemed they'd just been made. They'd been here all along, though. They'd seen it all, silent witnesses. They'll be here when we're gone, all of us. And there was a comfort in that, like there's a comfort in believing in heaven.

It's first light now—that ghostly pale gray that forecasts morning—and the wind has died down. I'll get my shawl and walk down to the Whites'. And then?

Then, who knows? It's hard to think about the future when the present is so sad. But everything changes. In eighty years my life has changed more times than I can count, and the world around me with it. I've gone from horses and stagecoaches to trains and automobiles; from waiting months for news of my family to being able to hear their voices over the telephone. There has been a war in Europe, a prolonged, fierce thing, and the Hungary I knew, the land of my birth, is a different place from the land that lives in my heart.

But all the time these things were happening, I was here, in these mountains that belong to me because I've looked at them, loved them, more perhaps than I've ever loved a person, and with good reason. People get old and sick. They die, and nothing's left of them. But the land's different. It's always been here and always will, and there's a mercy in that, a strength I once took for granted.

The road to town has never been so long. Three miles seems like a hundred. My feet drag in the dust, and my breath comes hard. The sun is lifting, a great jug pouring light down the cañons, turning the leaves of the mesquites to jade.

A new day—and empty. So empty without Jack to make me laugh, fire my temper, touch my hand. I'll go on alone as I've done so many times before, my tears like salt in my mouth. So many tears—for all of those I've loved and buried, for all the miles traveled, running away, moving toward something.

Where am I going? Who am I now?

Epilogue

Dos Cabezas, Arizona
April 6, 1931

Secretary of Board of Directors
of State Institutions
Phoenix, Arizona

Dear Mr. Zander,
    No doubt you have received documents in regard to my application for admittance to the pioneer home from

Mr. C. O. Anderson, my Attorney.

When may I leave Dos Cabezas for that home? I have money to pay my fare to Prescott, but when I arrive in the city I won't know where to go or what to do with myself. I would like to leave here as soon as you have accommodation for me. I am very anxious to leave here as I have no income to pay my expenses here.

If you write me when I may come, please give me a few days to dispose of some furniture and a few other things. If I stay here much longer, I won't have money enough left to pay my fare or anything else.

Please let me hear from you at your earliest convenience.

I remain most respectfully,
Mrs. Mary K. Cummings

MRS. SLAUGHTER

I

Governor Lew Wallace was frustrated. In place of a diplomatic post in Italy, he'd been offered the governorship of New Mexico Territory, and he'd accepted only because he needed the money and because he'd hoped that, in the far reaches of the West, he'd have the peace and solitude necessary to finish the novel that had occupied his time for so many years. Instead, he'd inherited a war, and it was difficult, if not impossible, to ascertain just who was in the right, who were the killers, and who the preyed upon.

It was enough to keep him awake at night, pacing the cold floors of what was called the Governor's Mansion, a sprawling adobe compound in a city that had seen Spanish conquest, Indian uprisings, and now the machinations of white men bound and determined to become rich in a land far enough from Washington to escape justice.

In September, 1878, he had been sent to replace Governor Samuel Axtel. From then on his troubles had mounted. It was impossible to gain a hold on the warring factions—Dolan, Murphy, McSween, Tunstall, Chisum, the Kid known as Billy Bonney and a few other aliases, the drunken Colonel Dudley at Fort Stanton, and the crew down at Seven Rivers that had earlier been known by the ignominious name of Dog Town.

In his whole life—that encompassed the Mexican and Civil Wars—he'd never seen such a labyrinthine mess. And all the time the manuscript, BEN HUR, lay untouched and unfinished in his desk drawer.

"All right," he snapped at the young lieutenant who stood at the door. "Come in and let's go over that list again."

At least, he could attempt a beginning, weed out the bad from the good, the outlaws from the citizens simply trying to make a living and survive in this magnificent country—a country of mountains, desert, sky—populated by descendants of the early Spaniards, homesteaders, and the dregs of Texas who'd been chased out of their stamping grounds into what was now his domain.

Adjusting his spectacles, he peered down at the paper where unfamiliar names were written along with those only too familiar, then he glanced up at Lieutenant Dawson.

He pointed to the first. "John Slaughter. Who's he?"

"A Texan, sir. He came in a few years ago with some cattle he sold to the fort, and Chisum claimed he rustled some of his. It turned out that time he was only cutting out his own, and since then he's come and gone. Now they say he's stolen Tunstall's cattle, or what was left of them. And he was under suspicion of murder a few years back."

Murder. Everyone was murdering someone, or so it seemed, and it had to be stopped. If it wasn't, New Mexico was lost, and he'd go the same way Axtel had—in disgrace, replaced by another poor fool without the faintest notion of the hell that awaited him.

"Who was the victim, and why wasn't this Slaughter tried?"

The lieutenant shrugged. "Bitter Creek Gallagher. A drifter. Slaughter claimed self-defense, and there weren't any witnesses. At least not any who wanted to testify. Slaughter's a hard man, and his riders are as bad or worse than he is."

"Where is he now?"

"Probably down near Seven Rivers with the rest of them. Some that's on the list."

"Who?"

"Joe Hill, for one. Jesse Evans. John Selman. Probably

some other hardcases he brought in from Texas. Hill works for him, when he's not off working for himself."

Wallace sighed. New Mexico was big enough for every hoodlum running out of Texas to hide in. "All right. Bring him in as soon as you can, and any of his cronies you can find."

"Yes, sir." Lieutenant Dawson turned sharply on his heel.

"Dawson!"

"Yes, sir?"

"Be careful. I want him alive and able to talk. Understand?"

Dawson nodded. "Slaughter's a cut above the usual saddle tramp, sir. I doubt he'll give me any trouble."

Wallace leaned back in his chair. "Even the best of families has a rogue or two, and there's no accounting for it. Shut the door on your way out."

Alone again, the governor opened a drawer and pulled out his manuscript. He'd been working on it so long the pages were wrinkled and torn, battered, the way he felt. There were times, and this was one, when, like Diogenes, he doubted the possibility of finding even ten honest men in the entire territory.

II

"Soldiers! There's soldiers coming!" No matter that the war had been over for almost fifteen years, the sight of blue-coated men still frightened Mary Anne Howell. That was one reason she'd been glad to leave Missouri with her husband, Amazon. The other was that the damn' Yankees hadn't left them with anything except feelings of fear and hatred. A way of life was gone and, with it, her confidence.

"Go see what they want, Vi, honey."

Eighteen-year-old Viola Howell wasn't afraid of much except maybe Indians and snakes. She put a calming hand on her mother's arm. "Sit down, Mama. I'll take care of them."

She stepped through the door and stood blinking in the brilliant, late-winter sunlight. "May I help you?' she inquired of Lieutenant Byron Dawson who had dismounted at first sight of her.

A pretty little thing, he thought, removing his broad brimmed hat. Pretty, and defiant, her brown eyes meeting his directly.

"Sorry to bother you, miss, but we're looking for a man named Slaughter. Somebody said we might find him here."

With an effort she controlled herself and forced a smile. "Is it important?"

"Yes, ma'am."

"Oh." She lifted a hand and covered the quick pulse at her throat. Never would she betray John to a bunch of damn' Yankees! Let them go search! "I'm afraid I can't help you," she said. "He's waiting for a herd to come in and might be anywhere."

Anywhere in that broad plain west of the Pecos covered a lot of country, Dawson thought. The girl was lying through her teeth like everybody else he'd questioned, but he couldn't blame her. The situation was such that a man couldn't trust his own neighbors, let alone the law.

"I'm sorry to have bothered you, miss."

She didn't answer, just nodded, and stood watching as he mounted his horse and trotted out of the yard, his men in formation behind him. When they had disappeared behind a rise, she turned and went inside.

"They're looking for John," she said to her mother, her

face white. "I'd better go find him."

"You'll do no such thing. It's not our business, whatever it is. Let the men handle it. I think I'll lie down for a minute. I have a headache coming on."

"You do it, and I'll bring you a cloth for your head." Viola was thinking fast. With her mother out of the way, she could take her mare, cut across country to the post office where John had been headed. It was pitiful the way he waited for news of his children whom he'd left with friends after his wife died of smallpox. He was a good man. She knew it. And she loved him. She knew that, too, although she'd have died rather than admit it to anyone, especially her mother.

A half hour later, she slipped a bridle onto the mare and rode off slowly, hoping the dust muffled the sound of hoofs. Her mother, brought up in comfort, disapproved of the way she sometimes rode—bareback and astride—disapproved, in fact, of almost everything she did or wanted to do, regardless of the fact that the rules on the frontier were not the same as those that had governed her youth.

Viola frowned, thinking about how inept she was at things that mattered in a wife. She couldn't even cook, hadn't the vaguest notion about how to fry an egg, or what went into a stew. That was a cook's job, her mother maintained. A lady didn't go into the kitchen except to check that things were in order and see that she wasn't being stolen blind by her help.

Viola sighed. Being a lady was fine except when you butted up against reality and discovered that lady equated with useless. What man out here wanted a woman who couldn't do anything except play the piano and sing and look pretty while doing it?

John Slaughter didn't strike her as the type to admire a helpless female. He was a man who knew what he wanted and aimed to get it. One glance at his face had told her that much, and for her it had been love at first sight although she'd done her best to hide it. Ladies never showed what they felt. That was as bad as showing their legs.

She grinned, looking down at her own slim legs that gripped the mare's sides. Somehow she believed that John Slaughter wouldn't mind the sight. *If* she found him before the lieutenant did.

At that she pushed the mare into a lope, forgetting appearances. There was a time and a place for everything, and she, Cora Viola Howell, wasn't about to let the man she loved be taken away, perhaps put in jail, just because she was admiring her own legs.

Seven Rivers had grown from a few adobe huts into a town boasting stores, saloons, and its own post office where Slaughter's big black stood hitched. She slipped off the mare's sweated back and ran inside, found him standing beside the stove, a letter in his hand.

"Mister Slaughter!" She was formal still, in spite of her feelings.

He looked up quickly, a man cautious of sudden approaches. Then he smiled. "Why, Miss Viola. What's the matter?"

"The soldiers. They're looking for you. I thought . . . I thought you ought to know."

The change in his expression was swift, quick as a threatened snake's. "What?" he said. "What, what?" in that way he had of stuttering when taken by surprise.

Her eyes blazed, fierce in the dim room. "They asked where you were. A lieutenant and some men with him. I said I didn't know."

"So. So. They've come, have they?" He put a careless arm across her shoulders, noted how firm she stood, how full of fight, noted the loyalty in her eyes as if she'd take on the world. Except she was a girl, over her head in the turmoil of the place, the times. She didn't understand, had no knowledge of what he'd done, only that ferocity which he understood deep in his bones.

"I'll take care of it." He gave her a smile that didn't reach his eyes.

"You mustn't let them take you."

"They won't. Not for long, anyhow." Wasn't he doing only what the rest were, even her father, if she'd known it? Making money with cattle that strayed among his own? And if his riders brought in others, it paid to look the other way because money was where you found it. New Mexico was a hot bed of thieves, and no one was free of sin, least of all John Chisum.

He tightened his arm around Viola's shoulders. "Go on back home, honey. It'll be all right, and that's a promise. And tell your daddy to get ready to move."

She reared back at that, her eyes frightened. "Move?" she said. "Move where? Not again."

He had a plan, he and Amazon. In Arizona nobody questioned your papers or your bill of sale. You sold your cattle in town, to the forts, the reservations, and got paid. Then you repeated the operation, only, if you were smart, you ran Mexican cattle across the line and sold them as your own. Nobody cared as long as they got beef to eat. Nobody gave a damn, and John Slaughter gave less than that.

He pulled her close. "Do you trust me?"

She felt bonded to him, her blood running hot, screaming like the hawks screamed over the mesas. "Yes," she said. "Yes, I do."

And with that, her destiny was sealed.

III

Back at the house she found chaos—her mother hysterical, her father attempting to comfort.

"You!" Mary Anne turned on her daughter. "Where have you been? The minute my back's turned you go sneaking off and leave me to face trouble."

"What trouble, Mama? What's happened?" Viola put her arms around her mother and felt her trembling.

"They came back. The soldiers. For your father."

"Papa?" She looked across the room at Amazon. "Is this true?"

" 'Fraid so, honey." Amazon Howell was a big man with a weathered face and a thatch of graying hair.

"Why?"

He shrugged. "They say I don't have a proper bill of sale for the cattle I brought in from Nevada. It's true. I don't. And there's a bunch of unbranded calves they say I stole."

"They can't believe that."

"They do. And John's cows are in with mine . . . some they claim he rustled from what's left of Tunstall's herd. Looks like we both have to go up to Lincoln and try to talk sense into the governor."

"Another Yankee!" Mary Anne snapped, her tears gone. "It's not bad enough they took everything once, they have to try again."

"No sense going over that." He put a hand on her shoulder. "We're not the only ones, nor the only folks with unbranded cattle, either."

"But. . . ." Viola was puzzled. "But isn't that kind of like

122

taking what's not yours?" She had to ask to keep things straight in her own mind, but she wasn't sure she wanted to hear the answer.

Her father smiled. "It's the way it is. There's Chisum up at South Spring, helping himself to our stock . . . there's Dolan and Murphy who rustle anything that moves . . . and there's us down here, the little folk, trying to even it up. Only big cowmen have the governor's ear. They can say we stole their cows, and now we've got to stand up and say we didn't. And hope we're believed."

She listened, and the knowledge sank in. If you were big enough, you could do as you wished. If you were John Chisum, you called the shots, while she and her family and men like John Slaughter got sent to prison. Rustling, it seemed, was only a crime if you got caught and couldn't defend yourself.

"Still, it doesn't sound right," she said.

"Everybody does it."

Mary Anne's mouth was a grim line in her once beautiful face as she turned to her daughter. "Leave it be. I told you before, this is men's business. And dinner's ready."

In a daze, Viola sat and pretended to eat, but she was turning over what she'd heard in her mind. The Commandment plainly stated—"Thou shalt not steal."—and she'd been brought up to believe that.

Now everything was changed, like a backward reflection in a mirror. Both her father, whom she worshipped, and the man she'd come to love, were thieves by their own admission. And how, she wondered, was she supposed to reconcile that?

IV

She was born just before the Civil War began, but she remembered very little of those years. For her life had begun on the trail, in a wagon train headed to Montana, the first time Amazon took her up on the saddle with him.

She had spent her babyhood surrounded by women —frightened ones—because Amazon had been off fighting, but her five-year-old mind recognized the warmth and security of his big arms, the pride in his voice as he praised her fearlessness, and how that voice rumbled in his chest as she leaned against him. It was a new experience, and she reveled in it, made excuses to leave her mother in the wagon and ride with the father she had missed without knowing she did so.

With them was her brother, Stonewall Jackson, still an infant, and Sally, her mother's black servant who had refused to be left behind. It was Sally who drove the wagon, cooked their meals, and soothed Mary Anne during fits of weeping for her lost home. Although she was delighted to have her husband back safe, she looked on the journey as the end, rather than the beginning of her life. Behind them lay the known and familiar. Ahead, who knew? They might be murdered by Indians or die of cholera. The trail was marked by the rough graves of those who hadn't made it. They shaped her nightmares, those rough crosses, those rude stones with their pitiful names and dates, solitary reminders of lost hopes.

What Viola remembered were her mother's tears, and how they put a pall on her own new-found happiness. Was it then, she wondered later, that her own survival instincts were honed? In the attempt to be something more than a lost and weeping woman? To be admired instead of pitied for female weakness?

Whatever the case, by the time the family reached Montana, her babyhood was ended and her character formed. For the rest of her life she would be independent, determined, and as unlike her mother as possible.

It was she who, along with Sally, supervised their constant moves as Amazon failed in one job after another from gold panning to restaurant owning, and as Mary Anne grew more timid and bitter-tongued.

But when her father announced they were moving to a farm in Nevada, even the indomitable Sally gave up.

"I think I'll be stayin' here," she said. "My seat bones are tired of that wagon." And she was tired to death of trying to keep Mary Anne's spirits high.

At her announcement, Mary Anne burst into tears, but Sally was adamant. "Miss Vi's old enough to help. As for me, I'm gettin' married and stayin' put."

So it was ten-year-old Viola who drove the wagon to Nevada, who set up the house, and then turned her efforts toward helping her father with his sheep and cattle, but who paid no attention to the rate at which the herds increased or how often they were bought and sold.

Perhaps she should have, she thought now, elbows on the table. Looking back, she realized that the herd they'd brought into New Mexico was larger than the original, but her mind had been elsewhere—seeing to Mary Anne and the new baby, James, and on the excitement of the journey—the desert spread out around them like a painted quilt framed by mountains, a country that went on and on, harsh, lonely, fascinating in its moods, in the odd shapes of the plants that grew, surviving year after year through sheer determination, nothing more.

Well, she hadn't come this far to quit, either. Somehow the governor had decided that Amazon and John threatened his vision of law and order, and so her own life and future hung in the balance.

She straightened her shoulders and looked across the table at Amazon. "I'm coming with you to Lincoln," she said, and her tone brooked no opposition.

Amazon nodded. Mary Anne wailed. "You can't!"

"Yes, Mother. I can. And I will." And if necessary she was going to break the two men she loved out of jail. Then she'd be on the governor's list, too. Lady outlaw. She didn't care, not as long as the men were safe.

The door opened, and John came in, weariness carved on his face. "Reckon we've got to go see the governor, Cap," he said, calling Amazon by the name he'd preferred since the early days when he'd been a riverboat captain.

"Looks like it. What do they have against you aside from cattle?"

"Murder. That saddle tramp Gallagher. And then there's the cows of Tunstall's." He smiled briefly at Viola who was staring at him.

"Tunstall is dead," she said.

"Yes. And some of his cattle are in with mine. Better me than Murphy and Dolan. They took the rest."

Everybody knew how, after the murder of the Englishman, Tunstall, Murphy and Dolan's riders had looted his place, cleared off his range. No matter whose side you were on—and sometimes it was hard to tell—their greed hadn't gone unnoticed by the smaller cattlemen.

"How do they know you have his cows?" she asked after a minute.

He shrugged. "Somebody must've been watching me pretty close. But those cattle have Missus Casey's brand on 'em, and I aim to tell Wallace I bought them from her. It'll be hard to prove, seeing as she's gone back to Texas." He walked over to the hearth and stood warming his hands before he spoke again.

"While Wallace is trying to prove I'm guilty, I'm heading for Arizona, and I'd advise you to do the same, Cap." He turned to Amazon, and the two looked at each other in silence.

"I won't go!" Mary Anne's face crumpled.

"Now, Mother, don't get upset before time." Amazon reached across the table and patted her hand.

She shook it off. "Don't treat me like a baby. I'm just sick and tired of always being on the move, never settling, never having anything. I want a home. A place that's ours for once and for all."

Each of them heard the misery in her voice and understood it, Amazon most of all. For nearly fifteen years he'd dragged her across the West, always hoping to better their circumstances, to give her what she desired. And now here he was, threatened with jail, simply for doing what everybody did. Suddenly he felt old—too old to keep on moving.

"I'll think on it," was all he said.

Viola studied their faces in the lamplight—her mother's, tearful and defeated, her father's, perplexed. And at the last, Slaughter's, whose eyes blazed at the thought of confrontation. He was a fighter, she thought, just as she was, and never mind that he was twenty years older and under suspicion of murder.

She had pieced together the facts from listening to others. How Gallagher had been rustling John's cattle and come at him with a shotgun. Self-defense is what it had been, and no one had ever said otherwise until now.

She stood up. "I don't know much about Arizona," she

said, "but any place seems better than here."

If she wasn't so damn' young, John thought. She was a woman in a thousand, standing there ready to take on whatever enemy threatened. He wanted her—so badly it was all he could do to stay where he was, hands held out to the warmth of the fire. He was a thirty-eight-year-old widower with two children, a weak set of lungs, and no prospects except jail. Hardly an ideal candidate as a husband.

She turned then and met his eyes, and he was stunned to read the stirring of passion in her, a need that seemed as great as his own.

V

To the east and south the high plains rolled and tumbled as if they were alive, as if there was a giant heart beating under the buffalo-grass-covered hide of the beast that was earth. From the back of her mare, Viola could see a hundred miles or more. Distance here wasn't measured by human invention but by the sweep of wind, the motion of clouds, the lure of El Capitán, snow-covered, rearing at the edge of sight.

Here the Río Hondo spilled out of its narrow valley, and the valley itself beckoned, offering shelter to those who had come across the plains and grown weary of unbounded space.

"It's grand!" she exclaimed. "Isn't it?"

John, riding beside her, agreed. "And free for the taking."

"Is it like this in Arizona?"

"It's different."

"My mother's against it. She wants to go on to Texas." And for herself, she'd go where Slaughter went, if it was ten thousand miles.

"We aren't likely to change Wallace's mind," he said. "You know that. Staying here could get dangerous."

"You're saying my father's a thief. And yourself, too."

He heard pain in her voice, and a tinge of anger. She was young. And innocent. A jewel in a den of opportunists, and he'd fallen for her. He sighed. "An unbranded cow has no owner," he said at last. "It belongs to whoever finds it. And a man who doesn't mark his cattle is plain foolish."

What he said made sense, but would the governor understand? Somehow, she doubted it, and when Byron Dawson rode up, she was glad of the distraction.

"We'll be stopping here a while, Miss Howell. I thought you might want to know." He pointed toward the narrow river, a silver thread under the noon sun.

"Race you there, Lieutenant!" For a moment her face shone with mischief, and then she was gone, feather-light on her mare, laughter spilling out in her wake.

Watching them, John felt too old to make a fool out of himself over a slip of a girl, no matter how much he wanted her. He sighed again.

Amazon, who had come up beside him, read the longing on his face. "Best not wait too long, man," he said with a grin.

"You don't mind?"

"I'd like to see her settled. Mind you, she's a handful, but her heart's pure gold."

For a moment he was happy. Then the knowledge of what lay ahead of him blotted it out. "I can't ask her to marry a jailbird, Cap."

Amazon spat. "There's not enough evidence to convict either of us. Nor enough jails to hold every man who ever took a few unbranded cows. Wallace knows that. This whole thing's just to put a scare into people, but it won't work."

"Maybe not. But I'm planning to leave as soon as I can. *If* I can. Then we'll see."

Up ahead, Lieutenant Dawson was helping Viola off her mare. She was still laughing. The sound was sweet as music, as painful as a shard of glass.

"By God, he'll not have you," John said under his breath. "And that's a promise."

VI

Lincoln was smaller than Viola had expected, simply a main street framed by a few wood and adobe buildings, with Bonita Creek murmuring between its banks, and behind it, a mountain covered with oak and juniper.

"Is this all?" she asked her father as they rode past the Ellis House and the Torreón, a tower of yellow stone that had been built to protect the town from raiding Apaches.

"Reckon so, honey. But don't go by size. There's places that attract trouble, and this is one."

She felt it then, the violence, the ghosts that seemed to linger in the burned ruins of the McSween house. "How long do we have to stay?" she asked.

"Long as it takes Wallace to make up his mind."

In that moment she made up her mind a second time. They were leaving Lincoln and New Mexico, and be damned to anyone who tried to stop them! She wasn't about to spend her life waiting for her father's and John's release from jail and catering to her mother's whims. She might as well be imprisoned, too, sentenced to spend her youth reaching through the bars of a cell toward a dream that was leaving her behind.

The Wortley Hotel sat at the western end of the street, an adobe building much like all the others. In the late afternoon, lamps were already lit, and fragrant piñon smoke wreathed its chimneys, welcoming travelers.

Obviously, she thought, the governor was also staying in the little hotel, and, therefore, she could arrange to meet him before her father and John went to testify. She, after all, was a woman, and he, well, he was merely another man, and a Yankee at that. If not for him and his blue-coated kind, they'd be back in the big house in Missouri, instead of here in a wilderness accused of everything from murder on down.

She waited until her father and John were shown to a room before questioning the clerk at the desk.

"The governor is staying here, isn't he?"

"*Sí, señorita*. And it is an honor to have such a man in our town." The young New Mexican, hardly older than she, smiled widely, impressed by her beauty as much as by the visit of the territorial leader.

Viola smiled back. "Is he here alone?"

"Oh, no. He brings with him many men . . . a *mayordomo*, a *segretario*, even soldiers."

"And does he eat with the rest?"

"He eats in his room, when he is finished his work. It is said that he sits all night writing, but I don't know this for certain."

When he turned to reach for the key to her room, she quickly scanned the register, noting the location of the room she wanted. It wouldn't be seemly to knock on his door, but she could be waiting outside and would be, even if she had to get up in the dark.

A rooster crowed outside, and others joined in, announcing sunrise although the town in the valley lay in darkness. It was cold—the water in the pitcher only a few degrees warmer than the room—and Viola shivered as she washed, brushed out her hair, and recoiled it at the back of her head.

Day came slowly, a subtle change from black to gray, and, when she looked out, she saw that the town and the red hills surrounding it were deep in snow. The scene was one of brooding desolation, and she wrapped her arms around herself in an attempt to stifle the chill that came from within as much as from without. For the first time she doubted the success of her plan, the future she'd imagined with such surety. Here, in this valley of cold shadows, optimism had no place. Here were only greed and the wickedness of men.

Voices and the rattle of china in the hall brought her out of her dark mood. Obviously, in spite of the weather and his night-time occupation, the governor was an early riser. And she intended to be waiting when he opened his door.

The glow of a lamp brightened the passage. Against it, he stood in silhouette—a tall man, and slender, even in the greatcoat and hat he'd put on for his walk to the courthouse.

"Your Excellency." Viola hadn't the faintest notion how to address him, but chose the most respectful way she could think of and cursed that her voice wavered like a child's and not the woman she wanted to appear.

At her words, Wallace turned toward her, and she saw his face—*a scholar's face,* she thought, noting the spectacles, the high forehead, dark hair, graying in places.

He took off his hat, bowed slightly. *Who on earth was this girl, and what did she want, hovering like an apparition in the shadows?* "What is it, child?" He bit off his words as she came close. *No child certainly, but a young woman, and beautiful with her large eyes and carefully arranged dark hair.* "Speak up. Don't be afraid."

"I'm not."

If she was, she hid it well, he thought, noting the tilt of her chin. "Good. Who are you and what is it you want?"

She took a breath. *Where to start?* "My name is Cora Viola Howell. My father is Amazon Howell who you've accused of being a cattle thief."

Ah. Now it was clear. He nodded and held out his arm. "Walk with me, Miss Howell. Did your father send you to plead his case?"

How dare he say such a thing? On top of it all, he now accused her father of cowardice! She drew away, eyes flashing. "He did not! It's my idea. My father has always been an honorable man, sir. A riverboat captain, an officer in the Confederate Army. He has always tried his best for his family. If it hadn't been for the war . . . ." She stopped, not wanting to hurl accusations at this Yankee.

The war. Always one came back to that—a war that had accomplished its purpose but that had left so many—black and white—homeless and destitute. And here was another war with equally dark results. Worse, he had no way of ascertaining who was innocent, except, perhaps, for this woman who stood filled with the courage to fight for those she loved.

"What do you want me to do?" he asked quietly. "Your father is in possession of cattle without a bill of sale."

"It doesn't mean he stole them! Or that John Slaughter stole his! You have to believe me. And them."

"Slaughter's is a different case. As I recall, he's also a murderer."

"It was self-defense!"

Behind the spectacles Wallace's eyes were keen. "You know this for a fact, Miss Howell?"

"I know John. He's not a Regulator or involved with any of the others. He's a businessman. A cattleman."

Wallace stroked his beard. "And what is Slaughter to you?"

Everything! But that was a secret that belonged only to her. "He's a friend. A family friend. And a good man. Oh . . . ." Her hand tightened on his arm. "I'm not asking for much. Only that you understand that without my father, my mother and I won't have anyone. And my mother isn't . . . ." She searched for the word. "Isn't strong, sir. She depends on him, and so do my brothers."

"No other family?"

"No, sir. Just us." She looked at the stern but kindly face lit now by the lamps in the small lobby. "I beg you . . . don't send him to jail. Or Mister Slaughter. All I'm asking is that you give them a chance."

The tears in her eyes were real, and the desperation, he had no doubt. And she was several cuts above most of the women he'd seen—those who lived with the wanted men on his list. She was educated, too, judging by her speech. He couldn't afford to ignore her, even if he wanted to. Educated citizens were a valuable asset—more so than the riffraff that poured into the territory, the law on their heels.

He patted her hand. "Miss Howell, don't cry. I'll give your father and John Slaughter a fair hearing and the chance to prove themselves. And . . . ." A smile flickered across his face. "I won't mention our meeting. Agreed?"

The smile she gave in return was worth any promise, and he doubted she had any idea of its effect. He wished he had a child like her, willing to face the enemy with nothing but her beliefs.

"Yes, sir. Thank you, sir." She choked over the words. "I owe you my life!"

"You owe me nothing. Only your honesty."

And who was honest in this land? The weight of her errand

lay on her like a stone. "God bless you," was all she said.

"And you, Miss Howell." He bowed again—she deserved the courtesy—and, replacing his hat, set out for the courthouse to listen to the excuses of her father and those of John Slaughter, family friend.

From the door to the room he shared with Amazon, John Slaughter heard the entire interview. He'd gotten up early and was on his way out when Viola had stepped into the hall and intercepted Wallace.

So that was why she'd insisted on coming along! Why she'd faced down Mary Anne's objections with a cold determination he hadn't understood! He'd thought she only wanted an outing, or perhaps a flirtation with the handsome lieutenant. But he'd thought wrong. Viola Howell was a most unusual woman, one any man would be proud to have at his side.

Well, if she would have him, he'd keep her beside him as long as he lived. And God willing, that would be many years.

"He let me off, but John's been sent to jail at Fort Stanton." Amazon stood in the door to his daughter's room, distress creasing his broad face.

Viola felt her legs give way. She'd been so certain. So sure of herself. "Why?" she asked. "What reason could he have?"

"Those Tunstall cattle, pure and simple. We both told Wallace how it was, but he wasn't listening. Seems like he's deaf where the real trouble lies."

"But. . . ." She was clutching the bed post that, at least, seemed solid. "What can we do?"

Amazon shook his head. "Nothing. We'd just best head home before your mother worries herself sick."

And leave John? She let go of the bed and took a step toward him. "We can't just go off and leave him in jail. He's our friend. And he's got nothing to do with this . . . this *war* that's going on. All he wants is to go to Arizona. We have to help, Papa."

He was watching her closely and hid a smile. So he hadn't been wrong, after all. The girl was smitten with the Texan who had a dream of a cattle empire. No matter that the man was hardly bigger than a banty rooster. As far as Amazon was concerned, Slaughter still stood head and shoulders above the scum that was causing all the trouble.

He stepped into the room and closed the door behind him. "How do you figure we can help?" he asked his daughter quietly. "We're only a little bit better off than he is."

"We'll go back to the governor."

Her chin was set firmly. She reminded him of himself in the days when he'd been young. Cock-sure and determined.

"I've been," he said.

"Then I'll go myself." She came closer and put a hand on his arm. "Let me try. And we won't tell John or Mother."

At the thought of Mary Anne, he snorted. "Honey, we can't tell her the half of it."

She took it as approval, although that hardly mattered to her. "I'll talk to him in the morning before he leaves."

Her certainty alerted him. "What've you been up to?"

"Nothing," she said. "Yet." But she didn't meet his eyes.

She had the spirit of a man, and all the charm of a Southern woman. Her mother's charm that had swept him off his feet years before and that, in spite of her disappointments and sharp tongue, still captivated him. In his experience there was nothing like a woman who'd made up her mind about what she wanted. He almost pitied Wallace—and Slaughter, too.

"Mind you remember who you are and act like a lady,"

was all he said, and he was rewarded by a smile of pure mischief.

"A lady is as a lady does." She linked her arm through his. "Is it dinner time? I'm hungry."

She was waiting for the governor in the morning, hands clasped together to stop their trembling.

"Miss Howell," he said. "Are you always up so early?"

"Yes, sir. When I have to be."

"And what is it today?" he asked, although he thought he knew.

"John Slaughter. I . . . I hoped you'd let him go."

"And you want to question my reasons, is that it?"

For a moment he thought she was going to cry, that female trick that had undone so many men, himself included. He hoped she wouldn't. It would spoil everything, including his opinion of her.

Instead she squared her shoulders and drew herself up. "Yes, sir. And to tell you my own reasons."

"Heaven help me," he said with a chuckle, and was rewarded by a sharp glance.

Was he making fun of her? She struggled with sudden anger. He hadn't the right to laugh simply because she was a girl who had come to plead for the man she loved.

"Perhaps I made a mistake." Her voice was cold. "I thought you, more than all the rest, were a fair and honest person."

"I thought so, too, my dear. But fairness isn't always simple. Not when I'm surrounded by deceit and must discover the truth by myself. Perhaps you can help me. I'd be glad of it."

That earned a swift smile. "I don't know how much help I can be," she said. "But I do know that Mister Slaughter doesn't deserve jail. He isn't a part of what's happened here except as someone passing through who got caught up in the troubles. If I may say so . . . there are others who need punishment more than he does."

"Who?" His eyebrows rose above his spectacles.

She shook her head. "I only know what I've heard. That hardly gives me the right to say. But there have been murders right here in this town, and the killers are still free. And out there"—she waved her hand—"are little people who're afraid to sleep at night for fear they'll be murdered in their beds or all their stock rustled. Murder is a worse crime than owning unbranded cattle, I think."

If it were only that simple. But, of course, it was. "I ask you again, Miss Howell, what is Slaughter to you?"

This time she gave him a direct answer. "The man I hope to marry."

It was as he'd suspected. Well, there wasn't anything wrong in a woman fighting for the man she loved. "I see," he said. Stalling for time to think, he reached for his handkerchief and wiped his spectacles. "And neither your father nor Slaughter plan to settle here?"

"Mister Slaughter has only been waiting for the rest of his cattle. We've all been caught in something we had no knowledge or warning of. Please believe that."

Strangely enough, he did. There were always minor players in every great drama, always the small folk who got dragged along by the turbulence. Some survived, while others were crushed and lost, but he would hate to see this girl become one of the latter, hate to see her spirit crushed, the fire gone from her magnificent dark eyes.

He made up his mind quickly. "Give me your word, my dear, that you and your family and John Slaughter will leave New Mexico."

The responsibility overwhelmed her. How could she speak for the rest? If she gave her word, her family might never forgive her. Well, she'd gotten herself into it and now, somehow, had to get herself out. She put out her hand, and Wallace took it. "You have it, sir," she said.

Wallace walked the short distance to the courthouse, head bowed against the cold wind that funneled down the street.

Love strikes where it will, he thought, although it was odd that so young a girl should have fallen for a man old enough to be her father. Still, there was steel in Slaughter, a toughness that belied his size. By no means an ordinary man, in another time he might have sought him out, learned something of this land about which he knew so little. And in another time he'd have delighted in the girl, the determination behind her lovely face.

Perhaps he'd put her in his book. She belonged there. Well, if he ever had time to get back to writing, he'd think about it. He would, indeed.

At his desk, he picked up his pen, dipped it in the ink pot, and scrawled a brief message. Then he called his secretary.

"Have this taken to the fort," he ordered. "Tell them John Slaughter is to be released on his own parole, but that someone will be checking his cattle and his papers shortly. Then bring me all the information you have on this boy they call Billy the Kid. I keep wondering if he isn't being falsely accused."

Viola found the note slipped under her door. **John Slaughter released**, it said. **Pending his departure and that of your family for Arizona, and may God go with**

you. It was signed simply with the initials: **L.W.**

For the first time, she understood her own power. For the first time, she realized that a woman was not simply baggage carried along on a man's quest. And she had done it all with dignity, unlike her mother's nagging complaints. She had done it with her mind, her wit, and, she conceded, her smiles. It was a lesson that was never to be forgotten.

She permitted herself a dance around the little room, arms wide, feet skipping under her skirts. Nothing was impossible. Any obstacle could be overcome. She was nineteen years old, filled with hope and with the knowledge of her own indomitable will.

With the note tucked into her pocket, she went down the narrow hall to find her father.

VII

God the weather was miserable! Cold and wet, and it had been even colder in the jail cell at Fort Stanton. John came into the hotel, shaking water off his coat and stamping his feet. What he wanted most was a hot meal and a good wash, and with luck he'd find Amazon and Viola still here, waiting for decent weather before heading home. He wondered what she was thinking—her father released, himself sent off to prison in spite of her pleas. Damn Wallace! Damn them all! He was free and intended to stay that way!

Viola half rose from her chair at the sight of him, haggard, wet, but with eyes shining. "You're here!"

"It seems Wallace can't make up his mind," he said. "First I'm sent to jail, and the next thing I'm out and given three months to come up with a bill of sale."

"How?" Relief and concern were written on her lovely face.

"It doesn't matter. As soon as the cattle come, I'm out. I doubt he'll follow me."

"And we'll be with you," Amazon said.

She squirmed in her chair. With any luck she wouldn't have to tell them about her promise to Wallace. "What about Mother?"

Amazon sighed. "She'll come along or be left."

"She won't like it."

"Child, she's been unhappy for years. Nothing to do with you or me. She wants what isn't there any more, and there's nothing we can do about it. I'm hoping to settle in Arizona, once and for all. Maybe then she'll come alive again." Or maybe not. He wasn't sure of much these days, least of all his wife's frame of mind.

A surge of affection swept her for this man who had done his best for all of them. "It'll be all right, Papa. You'll see. And neither you nor John will ever have to worry about being tried as criminals."

She sounded almost smug. John, who had been watching her, wondered what she knew, what else she'd done. He wouldn't have put it past her to threaten old Wallace and keep it all to herself. Maybe on the long trek he'd find out.

He pushed back his chair. "If you'll excuse me, I'm going to wash the jail off me and get ready to start back. Is that all right with you, Cap?"

"The sooner the better."

The ride home was for the most part silent, each of them isolated by their own thoughts.

John left them on the second day to round up riders for the

drive to Arizona, and Viola and Amazon continued on alone. Mary Anne met them at the door, her face creased with worry.

"I worried every minute," she said by way of greeting. "Anything could have happened. To any of us."

Amazon gave the reins to Stonewall. "Put the horses up, Son, and rub 'em well. Thanks for looking after your mother for me."

"It wasn't anything." Stonewall couldn't wait to be old enough to ride with the men. He'd been humiliated when his sister had gone off and he'd been left behind like a child.

Amazon remembered what it felt like to be on the verge of manhood. "I left you in charge because I knew you'd handle it," he said. Then he put an arm around his wife's waist and led her into the house.

For the rest of her life Viola remembered the scene that took place—the bitter accusations, the anger, her mother's tears that, once started, never stopped until Amazon, tried to the limit of patience, laid down the law in a voice that, although stern, was filled with anguish.

"I've done my best for you, Mother. Done what I figured was right with what we had, and Lord knows we didn't have much. Now I'm asking you to go with me one last time. If you don't, I'll send you on to your San Antonio cousins. But I'm going to take one last chance, and the children are coming with me. You think on it. Don't answer now. Morning's soon enough." Then he crossed the room and went out, leaving a stricken Mary Anne and a stunned daughter alone.

"He means it," Viola said to break the silence that seemed to have dragged on forever.

When her mother answered, it was in a monotone, without hope or her earlier hysteria. "He's all I have."

What of her and her brothers? Obviously, they didn't

count. "Then you'd best keep him," she said bitterly. Then she, too, went out and left Mary Anne to her decision.

VIII

They pulled out at the end of March, 1879, the Howells, John Slaughter, and one thousand head of cattle driven by Slaughter's men—Joe Hill, Billy Grounds, Jesse Evans, and a surly Texan known only as Curly Bill. John's servant, Bat, drove the combination supply and chuck wagon, and young Stonewall Howell was on the seat of the wagon that held all of the Howell's possessions. Beside him, a sun-bonneted Mary Anne, who had decided that life with Amazon was preferable to that with her unmarried cousins, sat silently, although at times her lips moved as if she was praying.

Perhaps she was, Viola thought, and perhaps they needed praying for. They were a rag-tag bunch, thrown together out of necessity, even the cowboys, most of whom she knew were in trouble with the law and as eager to leave New Mexico as her father and John.

The way some of them looked at her made her feel vulnerable, aware of herself as female and defenseless, even though she was carrying the pistol Amazon had given her as they left.

"Keep it on you," he said, his face betraying nothing.

"Why?"

"In case you need it, why else? We're going through some hard country, and the Apaches aren't going to like it, either."

"In hard company," she said, slipping the pistol into her belt.

He looked at her sharply. "Anybody been bothering you? Speak up!"

She decided not to mention the men, their eyes hungry as wolves. "No. Nobody."

"That's good, then. Just don't go riding off out of sight. Anything happens to you, your mother'll have my scalp, and never mind about the Apaches."

She reached out and patted his hand. "She'll be all right when we're settled once and for all."

"It's been hard on her. All this. And you've been a good daughter." He cleared his throat and looked after the slow-moving herd. "Best catch up now, and remember what I said about keeping in sight."

She had no intention of disappearing. Her intention was to stay as close to John as she could manage. The thought of being on the trail with him excited her. Surely she would have chances to find him alone, away from Mary Anne's supervision. Surely she hadn't been mistaken about the longing in his eyes. Except, what she knew about courtship was nothing at all. She'd never had a beau, never spoken about such things with anyone, especially not with her mother. Oh, she and Josefina Beckwith had giggled about boys often enough, but she'd been a child then, unaware of the lightning strike of passion.

With a sigh, she lifted her reins and set the mare into a long trot, keeping well upwind of the herd and the dust it raised, a cloud that rose high in the air and announced their passage to anyone watching. Pray God there were no Apaches. Her fear of Indians stemmed from their trek to Montana, the threat of Indian attack and snatches of conversations she'd overhead but hadn't understood, not until they came upon the remains of a wagon train that hadn't made it through. Until the end of her days she would see the carnage—bodies sprawled like rag dolls, and overhead the buzzards attracted by the sight of death, the bloodied faces and scalps.

MRS. SLAUGHTER

They followed the Río Peñasco, then turned north through a country of grass and brush, cut by rocky washes and miniature cañons, swept by the wind that came out of the southwest, steady and cold. Overhead, the sky was a hard and perfect blue, ragged only at its edges where the mountains rose, Sierra Blanca the highest of all, a white beacon marking the way.

Although the Howells had come to New Mexico on this same route, everything seemed new to Viola, as if she was seeing it for the first time, and the beauty of the land pierced her, grabbed her throat, clutched at her heart.

Time after time she drew up and stared around, putting out a hand as if to touch the mountains, opening her mouth to capture the wind that tasted of snow and pine trees, sage and rock and trail dust, and to her it was sweet, as everything she sensed was sweet because John was nearby, sharing these moments with her.

It seemed to her that they came upon the mountains suddenly. One day they were driving over the plains, the next they were camped at the base of the trail that led over the pass. The pines were thick here, and patches of snow still lay in their shade. To the north, Sierra Blanca gleamed red in the sunset, as if the snow was burning with a cold fire.

They camped for the night between the hills, the sighing of the pines, the rush of water, a song in counterpoint to the sound of cattle bedding down. One of the night riders was playing a harmonica, and the tune drifted back to camp like a lullaby.

Viola walked away from the light of the fire and stood listening, looking up at the sky. Had she ever seen it before? she wondered. Had she ever bothered to notice the stars? It seemed she'd been so caught up in herself and her narrow world she hadn't seen much of anything, or even cared.

145

Now she tilted her head and let the pale light sweep across her, and she thought the sky seemed covered with ice crystals, billions of tiny flakes that glinted like snow that had fallen upward.

"Magnificent, isn't it?" John had been watching for the chance to find her alone.

"I don't think I ever saw so many stars." She turned to him slowly. "I don't think I ever saw anything at all. I've been asleep all my life like the princess in the story."

It was an old tale. Even he had heard it somewhere, sometime, but had paid no attention until now, standing next to her whose eyes reflected the immensity of the night.

"It took a kiss to wake her," he said. "If I remember the story right." Then he wondered if he'd misunderstood and made a fool of himself.

He meant it! Suddenly she was frightened. She'd never been kissed, had only lately tried to imagine such a thing. "I don't know how!" she blurted, and hated herself for her ignorance in front of this man far more worldly than she.

He chuckled, from relief and happiness. "It's the easiest thing in the world to learn," he said. "And a pleasure to teach."

From somewhere, she never knew how or why, came courage, and with it the mischief that, with her, was never far from the surface. "I'll be a good pupil, sir," she said.

He didn't wait. Life had taught him to take the advantage and that there were few second chances. In his arms she was light-boned, but with a hint of steel, and after the first kiss she laughed up at him with a recklessness he recognized.

"Well?" She was teasing, barely containing what he thought was joy.

"I say, Viola . . . I say . . . marry me." The words were out before he could stop them, even if he'd wanted to.

She leaned against him, almost as tall as he was, her lips next to his ear. "Yes," she whispered. "Yes, gladly."

Oh, more than gladly! They were bound, had been from the first, and blessed, she thought, when she could think at all. Life was a gamble, as was love, and she was ready to throw her heart out and follow where it led, regardless of what troubles lay ahead.

She pulled away slowly. "Let's not wait. I'm tired of waiting."

So was he, by God. "There'll be a judge in Tularosa. Or maybe a priest, if you want."

"I don't care." And she didn't. "Let's go tell my parents."

He took her hand. "Amazon knows."

She looked at him, amazed. "You mean . . . you mean you asked him?"

"No. But he told me to hurry up about it. I tried."

That was her father, all right. No nonsense there. Mary Anne was a different cup of tea. "My mother will have lots to say," she said, "but I won't listen, and neither should you."

"I won't." As a rule, he didn't listen to anybody, particularly not dissatisfied women.

They were both rebels, both risk-takers, she thought. Odd that until now she hadn't realized that about herself. But then, as she'd said, she'd been asleep, undisturbed by want or turmoil. This was what butterflies felt like emerging from their cocoons, spreading their wings, tasting freedom. And freedom, she decided, was precious, almost, but not quite, as precious as love.

IX

"I won't have it! He'll ruin your life! Gamble it away. And he's too old. He's got children, and you're just a child yourself. What'll you do with them? They'll walk all over you, and so will he. All he wants is a place to leave them so he can run around the country with a herd of cattle, getting into trouble."

Mary Anne had been carrying on for ten minutes, and all Viola wanted to do was scream. Worse, she was certain that her mother's objections carried well beyond the thin walls of their tent, and that not only John but the cowboys were listening to it all.

"Please!" she hissed at her mother. "Hush! You don't understand."

Mary Anne came so close that she could see the wrinkles on her face. "Don't hush me! I'm your mother, and I can see it all. He's been after you for months in that sly way of his."

"And I've been after him."

Her mother reeled back, one hand to her heart. "Are you in trouble? Speak up."

Bewildered, Viola shook her head. "No. Why should I be? And where's the disgrace in wanting to get married?"

"You'll rue this day . . . wait and see."

"Now, Missus Howell, calm down." Amazon had come through the tent flap. "I've already given John my permission."

"Men!" Her mouth tightened in scorn. "He's a rustler. A murderer. And you're handing your daughter over to him."

He put his arms around her. "There's plenty worse than John Slaughter around. I'll sleep easy, knowing Viola's with him, and so will you, once you think about it. He'll give her a good life."

"He's too old!"

"He's not!" Viola jumped into the fray, hands clenched. "And I think I have sense enough to pick out a decent husband."

"I brought you up for better things." Mary Anne's lip quivered. "I wanted something better for you than a life with a man who's not settled and not likely to be, that's all. Those are my feelings, but, since you're both set on it, I wash my hands of the whole thing."

As her mother had intended, Viola felt guilty and ungrateful, the wayward daughter she'd never, in truth, been. "Don't be angry, Mother," she said. "Please just try and be happy for me."

"I'm not angry. Just disappointed."

Because of her. Because she'd made a choice and stood up for herself. Because she loved. She looked at Amazon, her eyes filled with tears, and saw understanding on his face.

"Go on out and find him, honey," he said. "I've got a few things to talk over with your mother."

John was standing by the chuck wagon, lighting a cigar with a twig he'd pulled out of the fire. For a moment she stood studying his face—a pugnacious one but with kindness in the lines around his mouth and in the dark eyes that met hers across the flames.

"I guess you heard," she whispered, ashamed. "I'm so sorry."

"Not your fault. Not anybody's fault, and she'll come 'round. Don't worry. Day after tomorrow, you and I'll ride on down to Tularosa. We'll stay there till they catch up. It's a pretty place. You'll like it."

But for the next two nights she would have to put up with

her mother's aggrieved complaints and accusations. Well, it would be the last time. With her head against his shoulder, she nodded agreement.

"Nothin' like a young bitch to wake up an old dog." From where he hunkered by the campfire, Curly had been watching the two lovers.

"Wish it was me, instead of the boss," Jesse Evans muttered. "She's a fancy piece, all right."

"And neither of you's fit to wipe their shoes!" Bat, whose loyalty belonged only to John, stepped out of the shadows. "Best you both mind your own business and keep your mouths tight shut."

"Just wishful thinkin'," Curly said. "No harm meant."

Bat gave him a hard look. "Make sure you keep it that way."

They were trash, both of them. He couldn't figure why the boss had hired such men, but he sure could keep them in line, come to it. The camp cook held the reins in more ways than one.

Before their nasty tongues had started wagging, he'd been thinking of a special wedding dinner—a cake, maybe, if he had the right fixings. And he'd make damned sure those two hands and their pals got the crumbs. He would, indeed, or his name wasn't Bat Hennings.

The trail was steep, the pines thick, the sky a narrow opening framed by branches. Up and up—and over her shoulder Sierra Blanca, immovable, serene. At her side, her husband-to-be on his big, black gelding, telling her his life and his plans.

She hardly heard, didn't care what the future brought as long as he was in it, as long as she was with him. Mrs. John Slaughter. She repeated the words to herself and laughed low so he wouldn't hear and think she was crazy.

Missus Slaughter, she said to herself. *That's me.* Only it was someone else, a different Viola from the one she was now, a woman she didn't know, couldn't foresee.

"I don't want you to be worrying about my children," John was saying. "When we're settled, I'll bring them to stay for a week or two and then send them back to Texas."

So much for Mary Anne's prediction. Viola flashed him a smile. "I don't mind a ready-made family."

"Those are my plans. I'm not going to burden you with children." Sometimes it was hard to believe he'd ever been married, ever fathered Addie and Willie, his life had changed so drastically. And now it was about to change again, for the better.

By tomorrow evening this lovely woman would be his. Too old was he? Not with his blood running hot as a young stud's at the thought of her he wasn't.

X

They came down into a country of red earth and deep arroyos, yellow grass and juniper trees that clung to the gullies with thick, twisted roots. Against the foot of the mountain, apple trees were blooming, and the perfume rode the air as lightly as the bees that flashed and sipped and buzzed among the flowers. The town, it-self, was prosperous, built of adobe, shaded by cottonwoods, watered by the *acequia* with its source in the river that rushed down the cañon.

A perfect place for a honeymoon, Viola thought, then blushed.

John, who had been watching her, asked: "Second thoughts?"

She shook her head. "No. It's only . . . ." She stopped, confused. How could she tell him her fears, her eagerness? Such things weren't talked about, not in her family, not in anyone's. A woman kept her feelings to herself. "It's nothing," she said finally. "Do you think I'll be able to wash and change my dress before?"

"We'll stop at the hotel. While you're getting ready, I'll find the judge."

When, as a child, she had pictured her wedding, it had always been in a church, with attendants and her parents looking on. She would have a new dress, in the latest fashion. The dress, of course, had changed with the times, but always she would be carrying flowers and smiling, the way all brides smiled out of sheer bliss at having been chosen.

How different was her reality—alone, with her husband to be, in a town where she knew no one, had come as a stranger, her best dress strapped behind her saddle, and only her father's blessing to give her courage.

Not only had she been chosen, she, too, had made her choice, and that she saw was more important than waiting, breathlessly, for a man's declaration. By choosing she had defined herself as a person, as John's equal, and she intended to have an equal voice in their combined future.

For now, however, she wanted a bath, the luxury of warm water after having been in the saddle for days, and the scented soap carried in her saddlebags. When she went to John as a bride, it would be at her most desirable, in her pale blue silk dress with kid boots on her small feet, smelling of lavender water instead of horse sweat and trail dust.

What in God's name had he done? John paced the hall outside the room where Viola, now his bride, was getting ready for bed. He'd married a child! He'd allowed himself to be carried away by his own hungers and now had to prove himself equal to the task of educating her without shocking her sensibilities.

He tried to remember his first wedding night, but Viola kept intruding—her laughter and how she'd taken his arm and leaned against him, offering her lips as soon as they'd been pronounced man and wife.

"Mister Slaughter," she'd whispered, looking up at him with adoration and a hint of something more, as if she expected him to take her there and then. But damn, how could she know her affect on a man? She couldn't, and he'd go slowly. She was too precious to hurt.

With a curse he put out his cigar and knocked on the door.

"Come in."

She was already in bed, her dark hair spread out on the pillow, her eyes shining. With a smile, she held out her arms. "Why, Mister Slaughter," she said, "what took you so long?"

And with that, he forgot his fears and good intentions and went inside and locked the door.

So *that* was what marriage was about! Viola grinned and gave a healthy yawn. That was what the wives and old ladies whispered about when they got the chance; what her mother had never mentioned at all. Well, her body hadn't lied any more than her heart had mislead her.

Life was a wonderful adventure, and the world and John Slaughter were hers. She threw back the covers, got out of bed, and stretched, admiring herself and the body she'd given over so joyously. A glance in the tiny mirror showed her no different except for, perhaps, a glimmer of knowledge in her eyes, lips that seemed bruised from too many kisses. What fun it was! She dressed quickly. The morning air was cold; John was waiting to take her to breakfast, and, after the night's activities, she was starving.

"Well, are you happy now?" Mary Anne made her question sound like a curse.

"Yes," Viola said. "Yes, I am."

She and John had ridden out to the herd, racing each other and laughing, and even her mother's dour countenance couldn't darken her spirits. She was no longer the dutiful daughter. She was a faithful wife. Her allegiance was to John, and she gave it gladly.

Old Bat helped her dismount. "This is one happy day, Miz Slaughter," he said. "Mister Slaughter, he was needing a wife somethin' awful. Now he can have a family again. Seems he ain't himself without a family. A place where he can be his own self, 'stead of what folks make him out to be."

Did he mean children? she wondered. And what was expected of her that she didn't understand? "I'll do the best I can," she said with a smile. "And I hope you'll help me."

"Yes'm. I'll sure do that."

"I don't know how to cook, Bat."

"Nothin' to it. I can show you easy. But cookin' don't make a home."

His words went straight to her heart. She'd been worried about all the wrong things, when what was most important—love, kindness, respect—had been furthest from her mind.

"You're a wise man," she said.

He shook his head. "No'm. I just know what's needed."

"Like in a recipe."

He chuckled deep in his throat. "If you want to put it that way. I made us a honey cake for the wedding, and after, I can play my fiddle. Seems like we ought to celebrate, even way out here."

John had told her about Bat's music-making. "None like him," he'd said. "He can make the thing talk."

"I'd be proud to have you play for us," she said, realizing the worth of the black man's loyalty. "We'll have us a dance!"

She was something, this new wife. Pretty as a little bird, and with sweetness written all over her. Mr. John had outdone himself this time. Yes, he had!

Bat checked on the cake he'd hidden in one of the wagon's cupboards. Just as well to keep it out of the sight of those no-good trail hands. Then he pulled his fiddle out from under the seat where he kept it wrapped in a piece of quilt.

That night they danced to the enchantment of Bat's fiddle, even Amazon and Mary Anne who finally, breathless and laughing, sat down on a log beside the fire.

"Goodness! I haven't had so much fun in I can't remember when!" She patted her curls and looked at John and Viola who were waltzing in a circle.

Amazon sighed with relief. Maybe his daughter's marriage would mean happiness for them all. Over his wife's head, his eyes met Viola's. She was smiling, her cheeks flushed, the filigree earrings John had given her brilliant in the firelight. *Good or bad, life went on,* Amazon thought. He'd had enough of the bad, but the future looked promising.

"Are you ready for bed, Missus Howell?" He bent close to his wife's ear.

"Wedding fever! It's best left to the young," she said, but she put her hand in his and let him lead her to the tent.

XI

They headed out the next day, Viola on horseback and John at her side, down into the valley where the white sands edged the trail—a mysterious stretch of what appeared to be empty dunes—empty except for a few fragile trees that cast dark shadows on the whiteness out of which, somehow, they grew.

"I think this is the strangest place I ever saw," Viola said. "It's just here . . . for no reason. And lonely." She looked north across the pure white expanse of gypsum and shivered. What was the purpose of such a place? What could live there, and how?

"There's supposed to be mustangs running in there." John answered her unspoken question. "That means water and grass. But it's not my idea of cattle country."

"And where we're going is?" She was eager to be settled in her own home.

"It's fine country. You'll see soon enough."

"How soon?"

He glanced at her. "A few weeks. If you're tired. . . ." She worried him, small as she was, riding like a man day in and day out with enough energy left at the end of each day to welcome him with passion.

"I'm never tired. I'm just curious. Who can get tired, when there's so much to see? And do." She gave him a wicked, sideways look.

She was a flirt. A temptress. And he loved her the better for it. Still, he spoke what was on his mind. "I say, I say, Viola, I don't want you exhausting yourself. There'll be a lot to do when we get to Arizona, and we don't even have a place to live. We'll have to camp out like we're doing, and it won't be easy."

"I'm not afraid of hard work. Not when we're building a life together." She was serious, hoping to impress him with her sense of purpose.

Odd that he hadn't looked at it that way himself. Until this minute he'd simply been doing a job, trying to get ahead, gain an advantage, and stay there. But his life had taken a new path. He had a past, and now, with this bright-faced girl at his side, the future seemed a pleasant prospect.

He said: "I hope I don't disappoint you."

She gave an unlady-like snort. "You won't. And even if you did, it wouldn't last."

"You're sure of that?"

"Mister Slaughter," she said, turning to look squarely at him, "life is full of little problems, and we can't escape them. But I do love you with all my heart."

With that, she pressed a heel against the mare's side. "Now let's take a closer look at this sand just in case we're never back this way. I want to be able to remember it all. It *is* our honeymoon trip. Something to tell our children about."

They crossed the Río Grande at Las Cruces, then strung out across a wide and desolate plain bordered by mountains—the Hatchets, the Floridas, Cooke's Range, and on the floor of the valley the white cascades of blooming yucca rose in stalks as high as her head, like candles marking the way.

On and on, and every day the wind in their faces, strong gusts out of the southwest, stirring up sand devils, spiraling, dancing whirlwinds that made the cattle restless and the horses unmanageable. At night they shook the dust out of their clothes, splashed precious water on their faces, ignored the grit in old Bat's beans, and fastened their eyes on Arizona.

"You'll look sixty, time you're thirty at this rate," Mary Anne told her daughter whose face was tanned in spite of her wide-brimmed hat.

"I'll still be me," came the stubborn reply.

Mary Anne rummaged in the back of the wagon. "Here," she said, handing Viola a small bottle. "Use it every night, and try not to lose it. And just for once take my advice like it's meant."

From the unmarked bottle came a faint scent of roses, a scent Viola had associated with her mother since childhood. And her face was as smooth as a child's in spite of the hard life she'd led. Now the secret was being passed, mother to daughter. The realization, that her mother cared for her more than she'd ever shown, came swiftly. Love showed itself in so many ways, some so small as to go unrecognized.

Viola put out her arms and hugged her in a rare display of affection. "So that's how you stayed so pretty," she whispered.

"I've done the best I could. I'm telling you to do the same." Mary Anne submitted to the embrace for a brief moment, then stepped away. "Men are fools for a pretty face."

If she put her hand on paper and outlined it—fingers and the spaces in between—the result would look like a map of southeastern Arizona, Viola decided. Here were mountain ranges that separated broad valleys, each range different from the next, each valley more lush than the last. But the common denominator of them all was grass that grew as high as her mare's shoulders, that leaned in the wind and rippled as if it were fluid, an endless, inland sea. Grama, galleta, red clover, love grass, brome—the names sounded like a song, one of the liquid tunes Bat coaxed out of his fiddle. Cattle, grass, an end to striving.

She dreamed of a home, an island in the ocean of grass, an end to the trail and constant motion. She dreamed of feather-beds and meals on a table set with fine linen, a roof overhead instead of the endless sky, and children. Always there were children, laughing, playing, tugging at her skirt, at John's coat tails.

Someday, she vowed, *someday I will have these things.* For now they struggled, as all newcomers to a new country struggled, to have money in their pockets, to make a life regardless of hardship. For now, life was the trail with its dust and sounds of hoofs and horns, the sameness of days, wind, sun, and wind again, motion of grass, dancing of new leaves on mesquites and cottonwoods.

XII

When they reached the San Pedro River, Amazon and Mary Anne left them and headed south toward Tombstone. John had a beef contract with J. L. Hart, the agent at the San Carlos Reservation, and, although he and Mary Anne did their best to discourage Viola from going with him, their best wasn't good enough.

"You should come with us and get settled," Mary Anne said, "instead of trailing along with the men."

"A woman's place is with her husband," Viola insisted. "I belong with John." Besides, she had no intention of staying with her parents and becoming a daughter again.

"I didn't know you were a stubborn woman," John said.

"Now you do. How soon do we start?"

He knew when he was bested. "As soon as we put a little weight on these steers."

They were a sorry lot, she thought. Texas longhorns, gaunt from the long drive, their ribs like washboards, their heads almost too heavy for their bodies. "They hardly seem worth selling," she said, looking them over.

"Beggars aren't picky. Neither's the Indian Agency. The Indians are starving. They're not cut out to farm, and that's the truth. When they get hungry enough, they jump the reservation and go back on the war path. And Hart isn't the most honest fellow I ever met."

"Will we . . . will we see any? Apaches, I mean?" As usual, at the thought of Indians, she was terrified.

"I said you didn't have to come. You'll see more than you bargained for."

With a visible effort, she controlled her fear. "But I am coming. Indians or not. If the agent is dishonest, why are you selling to him?"

He gave her a blank stare. "Understand this. In this business everybody shades the law, no matter what you think. He's got the money. I've got the cattle. What he does after . . . that's not my problem."

"But. . . ."

"This is business, my dear," he said. "Best leave it to me."

What Indian Agent Hart did was a common practice. He paid for cattle, then turned half the herd back to the supplier, supposedly to be put on grass until they were needed, but which were actually resold elsewhere. The agreement benefited both parties who profited twice, splitting the money from the second sale. The only losers in the game were the Apaches who existed on weevily flour and handfuls of beans.

The Apaches that crowded around Bat's wagon were, therefore, far from the way Viola had imagined. Half-starved, with barely enough clothes for decency, they begged for tobacco, sugar, coffee without any appearance of shame.

Still, she held to Bat's arm for fear they would drag her off the seat. "Go faster," she urged him.

"They're just hungry," he said. "They ain't gonna hurt us. Tell the truth, they don't look like they got strength enough."

She knew she'd see them in her sleep—the broad, dark faces, the impenetrable eyes, the hands held out in supplication. And she knew she would feel an unexamined guilt in the face of such misery.

"In a war," John had told her, "there's winners and losers. The Indians are the losers, though they're putting up a good fight. But you're better off with them on the reservation than losing your scalp when you're asleep."

Oh, yes, better! But . . . there were women in the group, and scrawny infants, and she, who had never known real hunger, drew back in fear and revulsion and chided herself for being helpless.

Her confusion changed to indignation the next morning as she sat watching a young lieutenant cut out the cattle he wanted. He turned back what seemed like half the herd.

She squirmed in the saddle. "He doesn't know a cow from a donkey," she muttered to John. "At this rate, we'll go back with all our cattle. What on earth is he doing?"

"Throwing his weight around." John's eyes twinkled, as if he knew a joke that she didn't. "And don't worry. If we can't sell here, we'll sell in Tombstone. The town's booming."

"But there's nothing wrong with those steers," she protested. "Even I can see that."

"Keep watching." He was still smiling.

To her amazement, she saw their riders run the rejects back again, and this time the lieutenant made no objection. "He can't tell!"

"Greenhorn," John said with hidden satisfaction. The

young man, whether knowingly or not, was only adding to the general confusion. By the time John settled up with Hart, half the herd would be back in his possession, and he would, indeed, sell it in Tombstone.

He turned his attention to the horse the lieutenant was riding—a well-muscled gray that was too good for him or for the Army. He had in mind a good poker game after dinner—when his money was safely in his pocket. In his mind, letting a well-trained horse go to waste was more sinful than gambling.

John and Viola had been given a room in the officers' quarters, and she was delighted at the fact that they would be sleeping in a real bed for a night.

When John told her he was going out and not to wait up, she was disappointed enough to show it. "Where?" she asked. "Can't I come, too?"

"Business."

"And wives aren't allowed?"

He tugged at his beard. "I say, Viola, you aren't going to turn into a nag, are you?"

She was horrified. Become like her mother? "No, Mister Slaughter, I'm not," she said, her tone cold. "You just go on about your business."

He kissed her cheek. "Don't sulk, my dear. It doesn't suit you."

By midnight, the young lieutenant, Cowper, an Army scout, Clay Beauford, and Hart were well on their way to being drunk, and most of their money was on John's side of the table. As usual, he'd followed his rule of never mixing liquor and cards, and he was pleased with his night's work. Not for the first time, either. He'd gambled with old Chisum back in New Mexico for cows that had actually belonged to Chisum, and had won that time, too.

"Guess I'm out." Cowper threw down his cards.

"Me, too." Beauford tilted away from the table.

"One more hand." John shuffled with a gambler's ease.

"I'm broke till payday," Cowper said.

John smiled. "What about that horse you were riding?"

The lieutenant's chair crashed down on the dirt floor. "That horse has been with me three years."

"And can be replaced. My wife took a fancy to it."

"Replaced how?" He squinted across the table.

"Out of my remuda. Agreed?"

"I. . . ." Cowper hesitated, looked at his pay on the table beside John. "He's a good horse."

"And the Army uses up good horses faster than a good man can blink. Shall we play?"

"Count me out," Hart said. "I don't need a horse. Damn' redskins'd likely try to eat it when my back's turned."

John flicked him a quick glance. "Better watch how you renege on the beef rations, then."

"Better watch your mouth." Hart lit a cigar and stared at John through the smoke.

John nodded. "Of course. Like you'll watch yours." The threat was there just below the surface. "Gentlemen," he said, "are we ready?"

Viola eyed the big gray with suspicion. "That's the lieutenant's horse," she said.

"He's mine now." John refused to meet her eyes.

Realization came swiftly. "That's where you were last night! Gambling with our beef money!" God, what if he'd lost?

"Now, Viola . . . ," he began.

She threw up her head. "Don't now me, Mister Slaughter.

We could've been paupers, thanks to you."

"I don't lose."

Her mother had been right. The man was a risk-taker, a gambling fool, and she was married to him. "That's what they all say!"

He lifted his reins and moved off, and she followed, hurt, angry, suddenly unsure of everything. "Promise me. . . ."

He kept on riding. The big gray had a fast jog that was almost a dance, and her mare had to trot to keep up. Now she'd done it. Precipitated an argument, when all she had wanted was to be reassured. "I'm not nagging," she pleaded. "Honest I'm not."

"Making a big thing out of nothing, then," he said.

"It scares me. All that money at risk."

"I didn't stake it all, and I have a good market for the rest of the herd. I'm not the fool you think I am."

His stern response made her feel childish, as if she were the fool. "I'm sorry," she said. "Am I forgiven?"

He glanced at her then, saw her flushed face, her eyes filled with tears. Still, he had no intention of giving up his happy habit of winning at poker, not for her, not for anyone.

"You said you'd get over little disappointments," he reminded her gently. "And you may be disappointed, but last night I doubled our money and got me the horse I wanted. So . . . so what do you have to say to that?"

She swallowed hard. Admiration struggled with her mother's warnings and her old beliefs—and after a long moment won out.

Mimicking him, she said: "I say, I say, Mister Slaughter, what'll we do with the money?"

"We'll go to Tucson. Send the boys down the valley with the cattle, and you and I will have a decent honeymoon and pick up my children. Not for long, just long enough for me to make sure they don't want for anything. Do you mind?"

"Not at all." How could she mind? At this rate, they'd be rich in no time. And above all else, she wanted to be rich.

XIII

Willie Slaughter, almost three years old, had forgotten his father and had never really known his mother. He looked at John and Viola out of round eyes while he chewed on a moldy bacon rind.

Viola took in his filthy clothes, matted hair, dirty bare feet, and lost her temper. No matter that Amazon had provided a poor living, even as children, she and her brothers had been fed and kept clean. This child, John's child, looked like a rag-amuffin and was starving to boot.

She knelt down in the dusty yard and held out her arms. "Poor baby. Come here to Aunty Viola."

Willie did so eagerly. Although unaware of his own miserable state, the pretty lady seemed to promise what, unconsciously, he yearned for—warmth, sweetness, a soft breast for comfort. Once in her arms, he gave a delighted squeal and held fast.

She kept her voice level so as not to alarm him, but over his head her eyes blazed with fury. "What's been done to this child is unconscionable, Mister Slaughter. He needs a bath, clean clothes, and decent food. And possibly a doctor. Why, I can feel his poor bones, and I don't like the way he was coughing. Give me your handkerchief."

John had been stunned into silence by the sight of his son. He'd left money with Mabel and Harvey Ryan for his and Addie's care, but they'd turned the boy out and used the money for themselves. Sick at heart, he gave her the handkerchief and watched as she wiped the child's streaming nose.

"Poor little mite. We'll have you better in no time. Can you smile for Aunty? Can you?"

Willie regarded her solemnly, as if he'd forgotten—or had never learned—how to smile.

"This child has been neglected," she said after a minute. "But no more. And I'll hear no more about sending him and Addie back to Texas, either. Their place is with us, with their father, no matter what. And I'm going to give those awful people . . . that dreadful woman . . . a piece of my mind! It's shameful is what it is!"

She turned on her heel and started walking, indignation in every line of her body. Over her shoulder she said: "While Willie has his bath, you're going to buy him some decent clothes and a pair of shoes, no matter what they cost. And something for Addie, too. We can't forget her, the dear thing."

At that moment, John knew he would forgive Viola anything—her tantrums about his gambling, her tight-fisted ways. She had opened her heart to his motherless waifs and taken them in, and that was what counted. They were a family, and she was at the center, dispensing love and down-to-earth pragmatism. By some stroke of good fortune, she was his. No. He shook his head. He was hers. And heaven help them all, he thought, when he returned and heard his wife's voice raised in wrath.

"You'll get me a tub of hot water this minute or I'll have the law on you for mistreating a child and stealing my husband's money that he gave you in good faith! God knows what you've done to Addie, though she's clean enough. But I'll find out. You can bet on it!"

Frightened, Willie began to cry, a high, thin wail, and Viola's voice lowered. "There, little one. No one's hurting you.

We'll have you all clean in a trice, as soon as the water comes. *Won't we, Missus Ryan?*"

John couldn't hear the other woman's response, probably because she, too, was frightened out of her wits. His guess was proved correct when Mabel Ryan came scuttling toward him looking like a small, round spider.

"I didn't mean no harm, Mister Slaughter. Honest I didn't. I just couldn't take care of the both of them and run this hotel. Not with my Harvey laid up like he's been." She clasped her hands as if she were praying.

"Do what my wife w-wants," he stammered. "I'll settle with you later. And I *will* settle, Mabel."

She turned white and fled.

In the room he found Viola wielding scissors, locks of Willie's baby hair on the floor around both of them.

"Pray he doesn't have lice," she said in greeting.

"What's lice?" Addie, who was sitting on the bed enthralled, asked.

"Bugs," Viola answered.

Addie laughed. "Willie has bugs, Papa."

Viola turned, scissors in hand. "I haven't found any by some miracle. So be good and don't scare your brother. I'll be checking you next."

"No!" Addie ran to John and clasped his leg. "Don't let her find bugs, Papa!"

As if on cue, Willie shrieked and wriggled off the chair. "No-o-o bugs! No-o-o!"

Family life. John hadn't envisioned it as a mad house. He disengaged Addie's hands from his trouser leg and lifted her back onto the bed, then turned to Willie. "Be good and do what Aunty says." Then he beat a hasty retreat.

Viola seethed but tried not to show it. The little boy was skin stretched over bone, and he had bruises on his knees and shins. But for all that, he seemed a perfectly bright three year old, splashing in his bath and giggling when the water caught her in the face.

"Aunty's wet," he crowed in pleasure.

"Aunty Vi will take her bath later." She tried to sound stern but failed, and giggled instead.

Addie joined in, then asked: "Are you really our Aunty?"

"I guess I'm your step-mama. Your daddy and I are married."

"Are we going to stay with you? We don't like it here." Addie came to stand beside Viola, her eyes serious.

"Yes, indeed, because your daddy's been missing you, and because I always wanted a girl and boy of my own." And be damned to Mary Anne and her hateful predictions! These two needed her. And God knew how many other orphans there were in the world. If she had her way, she'd adopt them all.

"Bring me a towel," she said to Addie. "I'm putting you in charge as my helper."

"Because Willie's still a baby." Addie skipped over to the dresser where Mabel had left two skimpy towels. Handing one to Viola, she said: "Is Missus Ryan a bad lady?"

Viola sighed. How to explain? "Let's just say she should have kept you two together."

"I told her, but she wouldn't listen."

"Did you?" Viola pictured the scene and smothered a laugh.

"I told her my daddy would come back and be awful mad. That was before I knew he was bringing you. You yelled really loud."

At that, Viola's laughter bubbled over. "I guess I did."

Addie's eyes gleamed in admiration. "Yes," she said. "It was fine."

XIV

Home! They were headed home to a place near Charleston in the San Pedro Valley. Viola let her imagination run wild as she pictured a snug adobe house shaded by cottonwood trees. The children would have their own room, and a swing hung from one of the large tree branches. And she and John would have rest and privacy in a real bed behind a door that closed. Best of all, Bat would be around to supervise her cooking lessons. She was going to learn to cook so many things, to be a good wife to John and mother to the children, who were bouncing like excited puppies in the wagon.

She did her best to keep them occupied, teaching the names of the mountains, having them count the hawks and buzzards that spiraled overhead, riding the wind as easily as kites. But they were overjoyed at being with their father and new aunty, and their happiness spilled out, uncontrolled.

Viola could smell the river long before they reached it—the sweetness of water in dry, desert air, the darkness of old leaves rotting on the banks.

"Almost there!" she said to Addie and Willie. "Now how do you think I can tell?"

In unison they shook their heads. Viola sniffed the wind like a hound. "Use your noses. What do you smell?"

They imitated her so perfectly, John chuckled. "A real bunch of little Injuns."

"They need to learn about the country," Viola said. "It's their home now."

"So it is."

Addie interrupted. "Flowers. I smell flowers."

"What else?"

"Something soft."

Viola was delighted. "Very good! That's water. You can tell when it's close by, just like you can tell when it's raining, by using your nose."

Willie sneezed, and she took him on her lap. "You must cover your mouth when you do that," she instructed. "Will you remember next time?"

He sneezed again.

"His manners have been neglected along with everything else," she said.

John cleared his throat. "I have no doubt you'll take care of all that."

"Count on it!"

"Look there!" He pointed ahead, and she saw the river, its curving course marked by trees whose tops appeared to explode in the midday sun. On the far bank, cattle were grazing, taking advantage of the shade.

She squinted to read the brand, and was startled to see John's Z, a duplicate of Amazon's but on the right shoulder.

"Why," she said, "why those are ours! Where on earth did they come from?"

John smiled into his beard. Obviously the boys had been busy. There were enough unbranded cattle in Mexico to stock a hundred ranches, and everyone knew it and took advantage of the fact.

"Mexico." He pointed again, this time to the south. "There it is. Those mountains you see are almost at the border."

"So close. Yet so different from here."

"It is at that. A hot bed of renegade Apaches in addition to the rest." He slapped the reins once. "Now let's get across the river and see what they've done about a place for us to live."

She leaned forward, hands clasped. "Hurry!" she urged.

"Hurry. I've waited long enough!"

Ten minutes later she was doing her best not to cry.

Called by the Spanish word, *jacal*, the house she had imagined was built out of ocotillo stalks held together with mud and frayed lengths of rope. The floor was hard-packed earth, the roof assorted branches laced together and covered with sacaton. Some of the ocotillo had begun to put out leaves that did little to disguise dangerous thorns. The door was a cowhide hung from a rod jammed between roof and walls.

On the hearth of the clay fireplace, Viola saw one of Mary Anne's treasured Dutch ovens, a pot that she remembered from childhood. Though Mary Anne had left her fine mahogany chest of drawers, her dining table and chairs on the trail to Montana, Sally had insisted on keeping the cooking pots.

"We don't need no chests. We got nothin' to put in 'em. But we all got to eat."

Funny how clear Sally was in memory, standing there beside the wagon, one arm around a tearful Mary Anne, determined to see her people through their troubles.

What was needed, and what Sally had in plenty, was courage. The frontier wasn't the place for weeping women, timid men. Somehow, her mother had made it through those difficult years, although they had shaped her, marked her, embittered her.

And if Mary Anne could do it, swallow one disappointment after another, so could she—Cora Viola Howell Slaughter—who had cast her lot with the man she loved, and who, because of that love, would do whatever was required of her.

She put her carpetbag down on the table—three rough planks on crude sawhorses—and squared her shoulders.

"Looks like my work's cut out for me," she said. "I'd best get to it."

XV

The summer rains were heavy and constant that year. Every afternoon, thunderclouds rose over the mountains, changing shape, feeding on their own energy, until at last they covered sun and sky and burst open in crashes of thunder.

The river swelled to the top of its banks, and the roof of the *jacal* leaked steadily, rivulets of muddy water that soaked the beds and turned the dirt floor to pudding.

Viola gave up trying to keep the house clean, the sheets and clothes washed. Mud was everywhere, and in the mud were toads, released by the rain and surging like a wave out of earth and into the fields and through the rawhide door. She stationed Willie and Addie at the opening with brooms Bat had made out of sacaton, with orders to sweep the creatures away. They worked diligently, accompanied by much shrieking, and Viola didn't know what irritated her more—the constant noise or the sight of the creatures skulking in corners and hopping underfoot.

At least she hadn't had any snakes inside, she thought. Only toads, tarantulas, and vinegaroons that released their vile odor as soon as they were threatened.

She was trying to cook dinner, but it was impossible to concentrate. The air was sultry, made even hotter by the fire that, somehow, she'd managed to start with wet kindling. Her head ached; her hair had come out of its bun and hung in her eyes, glued to her skin by perspiration. Lord, she was dripping wet, and her hands were filthy. If, as Mary Anne was so fond of saying—"A man liked a pretty face."—then John would soon ride off and leave her with the screaming children, a pot of boiling potatoes, and an army of critters intent on storming the door.

She picked up a long-handled wooden fork and leaned over the kettle, so absorbed in her own misery that she never saw the toad sitting by the hearth. It picked that minute to jump against her leg and entangle itself in her petticoat. She screamed, tipped the potatoes and hot water onto the floor, just missing her feet. Everything ruined! Everything! Her dinner, her life, her sanity. Still screaming, she ran out the door toward the river, where John found her, trembling, her tears mixing with rain on a face smudged with mud and ashes.

"Ruined, ruined. Everything's spoiled!" She sobbed against his shoulder, unable to control herself, too weary to try. It seemed she'd been working like a field hand for months, learning to cook, keeping the dirt and dust at bay, lugging water for the family wash and hanging it up to dry, only to have to do it all over again a few days later. And what had she to show but potatoes on the floor?

"What's ruined?"

"Everything!"

"Come back to the house and get dry, my dear, then we'll see what's the matter."

She snorted through her tears. "House? It's not a house. It's a mud hole full of varmints."

"That bad?" He could feel her shaking, more from emotion than cold.

"Worse. Next thing, we'll have them in our bed."

He sighed. Sometimes he forgot how young she was. Perhaps he'd asked too much of her, first with the children, then with what even he had to admit were miserable quarters. He patted her shoulder, then took her hand. "Let's go see what I can do to help."

Reluctantly, she let him lead her back. Her headache was worse, and she'd had a nagging pain in her stomach all afternoon. All she wanted was to lie down on dry sheets and sleep—and let supper take care of itself.

He saw Addie and Willie at their stations and the overturned kettle, potatoes lying in the muck. "Wash them off," he directed. "Get some clean water out of the barrel. Aunty Viola's going to lie down a while."

She held tightly to his arm. "Yes, please," she said, and then felt a rush of blood between her legs—warm, the blood of her womb. Oh, God! She had been so busy, she'd overlooked the fact that she'd missed her monthlies. And now she was losing a child. John's child. Hers. At the realization, she wept harder.

How she'd wanted a child of her own. And now, for a reason she couldn't understand, it was leaving her body as if fleeing from a foreign place. She was not wanted. Her body was unsuitable. She lay down and tasted tears, bitterness, the emptiness of a leaking and useless vessel.

"I want my mother," she whispered, and was stunned that, truly, she longed for Mary Anne, the touch of one who had loved and lost several children.

Her blood was on his clothes. He knew enough to understand what was happening, but not why, and he called to Addie who was dutifully washing each potato and dropping it back into the pot.

"Call Tad," he said. "He's out in the south pasture. Tell him to go get Missus Howell and quick. Can you do that?"

Addie read his pain, denied it in herself. Aunty Vi was ailing, and the burden rested on her own narrow shoulders, the swiftness of her feet. "Yes," she said. "Yes, I can." Then she was gone, a tiny figure parting the tall grasses, a black speck in the hugeness of afternoon.

MRS. SLAUGHTER

★ ★ ★ ★ ★

Viola drifted in and out of consciousness. It seemed that she and Stonewall were back in Nevada, huddled together by the fire—for comfort more than for warmth.

"Stay here," Amazon had told them. "Don't bother your mother unless she calls for you."

From behind the closed door they could hear their mother's moans. Once she screamed, and the sound cracked through the stillness like breaking glass.

"Is Mama going to die?" Stonewall whispered, clutching his sister's shoulders.

If she said what she thought, she'd say yes, and then it would happen, and she and her brother would be alone here, keeping watch over the dead.

"I don't know, Stoney," she whispered back.

"What's the matter with her?"

"A baby's coming."

He shut his eyes. "Don't want a baby. I want Mama."

"So do I," she said. "So do I."

By the time Amazon returned with the doctor, the baby had been born and had died. It was buried quickly. They never saw its face.

"Don't cry any more. It won't help." Mary Anne wiped her daughter's forehead where the dark curls were matted with sweat. "You aren't the first to lose a child, though it hurts every time, God knows."

"John," Viola whispered.

"He's outside. Soon as you're cleaned up, I'll call him. Hush, now. You're messing your face."

She didn't give a fig about her face. It was her body that had betrayed her. The body she'd never thought about, worried about, had betrayed her—and John.

"She'll be all right." In spite of herself, Mary Anne took pity on her son-in-law. He was haggard, his expression anguished. "I . . . I didn't know," he said. "She never told me."

"I doubt she knew herself. It was too early. But there's time enough for a family, John."

"I lost one wife. I couldn't stand to lose Viola."

He meant it, bless him. Possibly he was a better man than she'd given him credit for. She reached out and patted his arm. "Go on in. But she needs to sleep."

"I guess I ruined everything." Viola's voice was weak.

John knelt beside the bed. "You're all right. That's all that counts."

She saw his worried eyes, and how his mouth drooped at the corners, read devotion in every gesture. "Next time. . . ."

"Next time I'll take care this doesn't happen. I'll take care of *you*."

"I'm so sorry," she said.

He leaned and kissed her cheek. "Be well, my dear."

"Ummm." She was almost asleep.

The rain had stopped. In its place, without warning, they heard the singing that rose from the riverbanks, a music that wound around them, the *jacal*, the darkness of night like a silver wire or the vibration of Bat's fiddle strings.

Viola opened her eyes. "Listen!" she said. "What on earth?"

"Toads. Calling each other."

She lay back on the pillow, exhausted but with a growing excitement. Out of the mouths of those repulsive creatures came magic—a chorus of exultation, a celebration of life—and it was joyful, insistent, too demanding to be ignored. Instinctively, she understood.

You sang to your mate, crooned in your throat, threw up

your head to the sky and embraced the world and the one you loved. And you put fear, pain, loss out of mind and went on making music, moving in rhythm with the ancient dance and giving thanks.

"Next time," she murmured, reaching for his hand. "Next time I promise." And fell asleep.

When he came into the front room, he found Mary Anne braiding Addie's hair. She looked up briefly. "Asleep?"

"Yes." He sat down on a bench and drummed his fingers on the table. "When . . . when she's up to it, I wonder if you'd take her to your place. I have to leave for Hermosillo to pick up some cattle, and I'd rather not leave her alone."

Mary Anne gave a dry chuckle and pushed Addie off her lap. "She won't like it."

"Can't be helped."

"You'll have to be firm. She'll say she's going, no matter what."

"Not this time."

"Who's going to tell her?"

John stood up. "I'll do it in the morning."

XVI

As they expected, Viola was furious. Sick or well, she would go with her husband, and that was that.

"I say, I say . . . I didn't think you were a fool, Viola. But you're beginning to convince me." John paced the floor beside the bed, startled at his wife's vehemence.

She pushed herself up, anger giving her strength. "How dare you, Mister Slaughter!"

"I dare, my dear, because I don't want to lose you. You

and the children are going to your parents. I've made up my mind, and that's that."

She punched the pillow with impotent wrath. "I hate it! Hate having my mind made up by somebody else! Even you. I hate being in bed. I've never been sick in my life, and I'm not now. I want to go."

He thought she might fly at him if he attempted to touch and comfort her, but Christ she was lovely in her anger. Hair tumbling down, dark eyes made larger, brighter by hot tears. He jammed his hands in his pockets.

"The answer is still no," he said and, turning, left the room. Behind him he heard the thud of her pillow as it hit the wall.

Of course, he was right. And so was her mother, much as she hated to admit it. She wasn't up to the long trip to Hermosillo. Even the buggy ride to her parents' milk ranch was tiring.

Amazon had, for once, been lucky. When he and Mary Anne arrived in the valley, he'd sold off his herd and bought the ranch and the dairy cows from a widow who wanted to return to Tennessee. The sale included a stone-floored adobe house and the Mexican couple who had worked on the place.

It was the house Viola had imagined for herself—shaded by cottonwoods, thick-walled, with a massive wooden door and shutters that could be closed and barred against any trouble, including marauding Apaches.

"By the time I'm home, you'll be well again," John said, kissing her good bye.

"Hurry back." She held to him for a minute, fighting down fear. If anything happened to him . . . .

He read her mind. "Nothing's going to happen. Don't worry."

Other women were brave. Left behind, they went about their lives, taking on duties and doing a man's work, and if they had fears, they kept them hidden lest the children, too, be frightened.

She clenched her teeth to keep her chin steady and stepped back. "Go with God," she said, and watched him mount the gray and ride off down the valley, watched until the distance swallowed him and he was one with grass and plain.

Amazon came up behind her. "Don't fret, child. The man has work to do, and you can't be around every minute."

"I just have a feeling," she said. "I can't explain it."

He chalked that up to her miscarriage. In his experience, women were prone to fancy at such times. "Put it out of your head. It can't help and might hurt. And your mother and Inez have supper nearly ready."

Obediently, Viola spent the next few weeks doing as she was told. She ate, she slept, she began teaching Addie her letters, but a part of her was cut off, shut away. A part of her brooded and mourned, not only for herself but for the lost child, for the emptiness she carried within, as if at any moment she or John could disappear, be taken by the wind and dispersed in the vastness of the valley. Life hung by a thread as illusory as a spider's web, and no one, least of all herself, knew the precise time when the thread would be broken.

She was at the corral watching Stonewall break a horse. He had a way with them and, in addition to helping Amazon, had begun to work on the rough strings belonging to several local ranchers.

"I call this one Traveler," he said over his shoulder. "He's one of those Nez Percé horses that found his way down here." The horse, white with leopard spots, stood in the middle of the corral, eyes showing white, muscles bunched.

"He looks like a handful," she said. "And how do you know where he came from?"

"We saw enough of them up north. Don't you remember?"

She didn't. Anything to do with Indians had been blotted out, and, besides, it was Stoney who went chasing after horses as if he wanted to own every one he saw.

"Are you going to ride him now?" She had a vision of her brother, bones shattered, face down in the dust.

"Not today. I've got a hunch about this one. He's smart, and he's thinking, but right now he doesn't much like or trust me. I could take the buck out of him, but he wouldn't be broke. Today I'm just getting him used to the sight and sound of me."

She relaxed. One less life to worry about. At least for the day.

The sound of a horse coming fast caused them both to turn and squint down the lane that led to the house. She recognized the horse before she identified the rider, and stood for a second, one hand to her throat as if to still the scream.

"It's Tad!" And then she was running, lifting her skirt high above her boots, her white stockings flashing in the sunlight.

"John!" The word hung in the air between them like a dust mote.

"Miz Slaughter . . . ma'am." Tad dismounted, came toward her, hands stretched out to catch her if she fell.

"It's John. Isn't it?"

He bobbed his head, couldn't meet her eyes, couldn't bear to see her expression. "Miz Slaughter . . . we were ambushed on our way back. Mexican bandits. I was . . . I was riding point . . . out ahead when they jumped the others. Mister

Slaughter, he yelled at me to keep going, to get to you. I wanted to fight but he . . . he cussed me out good. Last I saw, they were surrounded. It looked mighty bad."

No husband. No child. No solid ground anywhere. She'd been right to fear, wrong to stay behind. Better to have gone and died fighting alongside him, to let the buzzards pick their flesh, their bones sink into common ground.

She fought the pain, the blackness behind her eyes. Had he suffered? Gone quickly? No one knew, not Tad standing beside her, not herself. And his body lay in some unnamed, unmarked place in an alien country far from home. It wasn't right.

She wiped her eyes on her sleeve, then stood straight, disregarding Tad's hand on her shoulder. When she spoke, it was slowly, each word enunciated as if she had just learned the language. "I am going to bring him back."

"Ma'am! You can't!"

"You'll kill yourself, Sis." That was Stoney who'd followed her.

"Yes . . . I . . . can." Again the painful spacing between words. "And I will. With or without you."

"Ma'll have a hissy."

Color flooded back into her face. "Ma be damned! Hissy or no hissy, can't or won't, I'm going to bring my husband's body home for a decent burial. And there's an end to argument."

Without waiting to hear further, she spun on her heel and walked quickly toward the house, the men following her, looking at each other helplessly.

"Don't argue with her," Stoney advised. "It'll only make it worse. She don't know what she's in for, and, believe me, she don't care. We'll just have to go along and try to keep her out of trouble."

They left the next morning, Viola driving the wagon with Stoney and Tad as outriders, leaving an outraged Mary Anne and a stoic Amazon behind.

The children hadn't been told. Time enough when their father's body was put in the ground, when the mourners gathered, when the dream had come to its end.

"Aunty Vi's going to meet your daddy," she told them, holding back tears with an iron will. "You stay right here and be good, and I'll be back before you can blink. You hear?"

Addie put her arms around Viola's neck. "I want to come, too. I want my daddy."

She buried her face in the child's hair and prayed for strength, for the ability to be a mother to Addie and her brother, now orphans for real. "No, honey," she whispered after a minute. "It's a long, hard trip. Maybe some other time." Except there would be no other time. Never again. She stood up quickly, turned away, hiding the tears that couldn't be hidden, and without looking back climbed unassisted onto the seat of the wagon.

Two riders pulled up and watched the slow procession. "Who d'you think that is?"

"Nesters. Just what we don't need any of."

The bigger man squinted. "Looks to me like part of the Slaughter outfit. There's a woman in the wagon."

"What's a woman doing out here?"

"Let's go see!" He slapped his reins on his horse's rump and took off at a lope, pulling up alongside Viola and staring at her with barely disguised lust.

"It's Missus Slaughter, ain't it? Billy Clanton. This's my brother Ike. We're neighbors." He grinned, and the expression in his eyes reminded Viola of a wolf.

What on earth did he want from her? Whatever it was, she

wasn't about to give anything away, not to one such as he. "I'm Missus Slaughter," she said, her voice cold.

"I was looking for your husband. He at home?"

She bit her lip before answering. "No. He isn't. But . . . but I expect he will be shortly. Is there a message?"

He shook his head. "Naw. Just wondered if he was around anywheres."

"I'll be sure and tell him we met." She picked up the reins in dismissal, aware that his eyes lingered on her body for what seemed too long a time. Trash! That was it. Both these men were trash, neighbors or not. "Good afternoon, Mister Clanton."

She drove off without looking back, and after a minute said to Tad: "I lied. Don't say it. But I didn't like those men. And what's happened isn't their business."

She seemed so small, sitting there on the wagon seat, small but tough for all a good wind could have blown her away. "You did right, ma'am," he said. "The boss has run them off once or twice for takin' what's not theirs to take, if you get my meaning."

She clucked to the horse. "Sometimes I wonder if anybody out here is civilized," she said. "And sometimes it isn't worth thinking about." But in spite of herself she kept picturing the two brothers, their pale eyes and how they sat their horses, as if they were looking for trouble and knew just where to find it.

It seemed to her that they moved in slow motion down the valley, along the river, heat waves dancing, San José Peak and Cananea dancing in the distance, and the little slant-sided mesa that she kept watching, neither mountain nor hill, simply a small, distorted cone rising out of the hot and rippling ocean that was grass—and herself lost in it, lost in a continent of loneliness, a widow on a quest, a lone female on a wagon seat headed into Mexico to bring back the remains of what had been, what in her mind would always be, a great and enduring love.

XVII

Tad rode ahead, watching for any sign of Indians or Mexican bandits. You went into Mexico, you took your chances. John Slaughter had understood that, and look where it got him. He was dead, but Tad had no intentions of endangering the lady boss any more than she'd already done by insisting on this journey.

It was a sorry business, and her not well. She was a tough little thing, but he'd seen how she nearly fell over from exhaustion when they'd camped the night before—how white she was, and how her eyes seemed too big for her face.

With any luck, he'd find the bodies first. Or what was left of them. He was going to spare her that much, at least—the sight of death and what happened after. Out here, it didn't take long for a body to disappear, not with a thousand hungry critters in search of a meal, and the sun burning down like a brand.

At the thought, he spurred his horse into a lope and rode up a small rise. From the top he'd be able to see ahead and behind, spot danger, if it was possible to spot those damned Indians in their disguises, the *bandidos* who knew every hidey hole in the country.

The wagon was coming slowly along a bed of rock, Stoney riding beside, his young face set. A good kid, one who didn't panic easily. Any sign of Indian trouble, he knew what he had to do. If necessary, he'd shoot his sister. Better dead than a prisoner of the Apaches.

Damn it all! He'd left life on the farm to find adventure. Only what he'd found was harsh reality—not that much different from home, except that out here death lurked in a thousand places and didn't wait patiently to take you in old age.

He spat out dust, reached for his canteen. They'd made a dry camp the night before, and it was imperative that he find water for the horses before they camped again. Regretfully, he limited himself to one swallow.

In the distance something was moving. He squinted hard, saw dust and what looked like a team of horses pulling an unwieldy wagon. But the country played tricks. He'd seen mirages—on the plains, in the middle of the desert—seen the enormous reflections of men on horseback, lakes of water where nothing existed but sand.

Motionless, he sat watching, shaking his head at what he thought he saw. If that wasn't Bat and the chuck wagon, he'd eat his hat. Cautiously he rode down the rise toward what he hoped was more than a ghostly vision.

"No, suh! We ain't dead! Mister Slaughter, he's comin' behind with the herd." Bat's grin split his face into two parts.

"How?" Tad slumped in his saddle, too stunned to talk.

"They made it to the pile of rocks where I was and holed up. Then we shot it out. There's six dead men back there, but they ain't us."

"You're sure?"

Bat's grin disappeared. "Now why would I make a joke over that?"

"You wouldn't. But just the same, I've got the lady boss comin' behind with a wagon to get the body."

"Then you better go tell her there ain't no body. Leastways, no dead one. And don't go scarin' her. You break it to her easy. That's a fine lady."

"He's alive! John's alive?" All the determination that had held her body upright vanished, and she huddled on the seat, her face in her hands, tears coming unchecked. So many tears! How could one person produce such a flowing, and where did they come from? She wept and didn't stop until Bat pulled up and came to her side.

"You goin' to mess your pretty face," he said in a parody of her mother. "And Mister John, he sets a store by that face. Now you come on down here and set in the shade and let Bat get you something to eat. I bet you ain't ate right in a week."

It seemed longer. It seemed a year since food had any appeal, since life itself was anything but forced labor. She had lost a child and a husband, except that John was alive. She couldn't quite take that in, couldn't quite believe what they were telling her. Hope was such a precarious emotion, prey to dangers she couldn't name, couldn't begin to imagine. Fear hovered, held her by the throat, refused her permission to believe what the men were saying.

And then he came riding on his big gray—out of the haze of dust and distance—and if he was surprised to see her, she couldn't tell, couldn't find words to ask. He was real, and she was in his arms, and they were strong and solid. That was what she knew the moment before she fainted.

When she came to, she was lying on her bedroll in the shade of the wagon, and John was kneeling beside her.

"It's true. You're really here!" She pushed herself up on one elbow. With her other hand she reached out and touched his cheek.

"I'm here," he said. "But you shouldn't be."

"I wasn't about to leave you in this place. I wanted you home . . . where you belong."

Her obvious adoration touched him. "Wh . . . when it's my time, I'll die in bed," he said. "Out here's for the living. For you, and me, and the children. You don't ever have to worry about me."

"Men!" she said scornfully. "You think you're invincible!"

He looked at her a long time before answering. "But I am, Viola," he said. "Believe it. I am."

XVIII

She sat as close to John on the wagon seat as propriety allowed, and once in a while reached out to touch his sleeve, as if to reassure herself. He was alive, and she felt her own life singing in her veins. How different everything looked now! The cottonwoods lush with summer, their leaves in constant, glittering motion, the craggy Huachuca Mountains buttressing sky, the Mule Mountains, softer, the soil under oak and juniper a dark red, indicative of the mineral wealth that lay hidden below the surface.

"Probably not silver like over at Tombstone," John said in answer to her question. "But it won't be long before someone comes along and finds whatever it is. This country's going to bust wide open, mark my words, and I aim to supply all the beef I can."

He frowned, and sensitive to his moods she asked: "What's the matter with that?"

"When they start coming, it'll mean the end of the range. We'll need our own place . . . plenty of grass and water. I've even been thinking about Oregon."

"Oregon!" The very idea of it horrified her. "What's wrong with where we are?" she demanded, then laughed. "Apart from the house."

"The range is already crowded, and new folks are coming every month. Now I've got this herd and the one coming in from Texas this winter. About Oregon . . . it's just a thought."

She hoped he kept it that way, even if she did have to live in what she called to herself "a picket house."

As if he'd read her mind, he said: "About the house . . . before I left I gave orders to have one built. It should be ready before Christmas."

She clasped his arm. "A house? A real one?"

He chuckled. "I say, Vi . . . do you have to repeat everything?"

"Yes," she said. "Just to make sure." Then she threw her arms around him. Be damned to propriety! He was alive, and she loved him down to her toes in her sturdy boots. She'd have a house with solid walls and a roof that didn't threaten to collapse. And, if the gods were good, a cookstove instead of that hated fireplace that threatened her every move.

"A door," she said breathlessly. "Will it have a door we can close?"

He glanced at her out of the corner of his eye and saw her hope imposed on the trials she'd endured for his sake, and he patted her knee. "The door," he said with great satisfaction, "is in Bat's wagon. I bought it myself in Hermosillo. A present for you, my dear, I hope one of many."

True to his word, the house was ready in early December—four rooms with plank floors and the carved door from Mexico to shut out weather and what Viola labeled, in no uncertain terms, "varmints."

This was happiness, she thought, as she went from room to room exclaiming. A home of her own and a ready-made family. The memory of her recent miscarriage brought a moment's pain, but she pushed it away. What was done was done, and the future was bright.

"We'll have a tree," she told the children. "And a real Christmas."

"What's Christmas?" Willie looked doubtful.

Startled, she knelt down beside him. Why, the poor child had no idea of anything, no memories to hold to, pleasurable or otherwise.

"It's a celebration," she said, her arms around him. "It's Christ's birthday, only we all get the presents."

"What's presents?"

How to explain? She sat back on her heels and thought, then said: "A present is something you've wished for with all your heart. And sometimes, on Christmas, your wish comes true."

"I want a pony," he said.

Addie came to stand beside them. "Me, too."

"Ponies," Viola repeated, revising her vision of caps and scarves, sticks of candy, a new dress for Addie. "I see. Well . . . ."

"Why not?" John asked, when she reported the conversation. "We can't be carrying them on our saddles forever. They're old enough. And besides, your brother's got two ponies nearly ready."

Once again, he'd surprised her. "How do you always know what's in people's minds?"

"Better that way," he said. "No surprises for anybody."

And that, she decided, was how he managed to stay alive—with a kind of intuition, an animal sense that read the unspoken, deciphered scents and sounds that rode the air. It was a gift that benefited them all, particularly herself.

With John she had a sense of security she'd found in no one else, certainly not her own family, much as she loved them. With John she was able to relax, to be herself, and the discovery of just who that self was brought her a happiness she'd never known.

"Can I . . . can we afford a shopping trip?" she asked. "To Tombstone? It is almost Christmas."

He couldn't refuse her. "As long as you go easy."

She threw her arms around his neck. "I'll go tomorrow. Just for little things, I promise. But won't it be fun to have Christmas in our first real home?"

"It will. Shall we invite your family? Don't worry. Bat can take over the cooking."

Smiling, she agreed. Now she could entertain and be able to hold up her head.

"And maybe some of the neighbors?" he asked.

Viola's smile was replaced by a frown. "Not if you mean those Clanton boys. I've never seen such a disgusting pair. There's something wrong with both of them, Mister Slaughter. And I won't have them in the house."

He raised his eyebrows. "I say, Vi, isn't that a little harsh?"

"No!" She stamped her foot. "That big brute Billy came by when I was setting out with Tad for Mexico. He was looking for you, and I swear, if I'd given him any encouragement, he'd have come along. And as for his brother. . . ." Her nose twitched. "He *smells*."

John stifled a laugh. What she said was true enough, but he'd come to an agreement with all his disreputable neighbors, some of whom he'd brought into the valley along with his cattle. They left him alone, and he turned his back on their forays outside the law.

"Better let Tad drive you to Tombstone," he said, changing the subject. "God forbid you should run into Billy."

She peered into his eyes. "Are you laughing at me?"

"No, my dear. But I don't think you should travel alone,

and, right now, I can't go with you. Besides, Tombstone's not the place for a lady by herself."

"You think I can't take care of myself."

He shook his head. "I don't think you should have to. Do you?"

Put that way, she had to admit he was right. Billy Clanton had frightened her more than she wanted to admit, and who knew who she would find in town or on the way there?

She hugged him again. "I'll take Tad. And I'll find you a wonderful present. I've been saving my house money."

"You are the best present I've ever had," he said. "I don't need much else."

XIX

Tad dropped her off at the San José House and repeated John's warnings. "When you're ready, send somebody for me. This place is full of riffraff."

As she stood looking around, she realized that the town had more than doubled in size in only a few months. It was like an ant hill, teeming with activity. Ore wagons, freight wagons, strings of mules and burros passed in a steady flowing down the dusty streets, and the wooden sidewalks were crowded with men and women going about their varied chores. It was noisy, colorful, and alive, and she responded to it with that part of her that loved gaiety of any kind, be it parties, dances, or merely good conversation.

"Don't worry about me," she said to Tad with a grin. "I'll be fine."

"Mister Slaughter's orders." He tipped his hat and drove off to the livery, hoping it was all right to leave her.

Viola stepped into the small lobby, blinking at the sudden contrast with the brilliant light from the street, and didn't notice the sharp glance of the woman behind the desk.

"I'll need a room for two nights," she said.

"We're full up." The words were ungracious and unexpectedly harsh, and for a moment Viola was startled.

"Oh, dear. Now where will I go? We always stay here, you know." She gave a tentative smile, and the proprietress leaned across the counter.

"My gracious, Missus Slaughter, is it you?"

"It certainly is."

The woman waved her hands in a placating gesture. "Lordy! I didn't recognize you. Thought you were somebody else. I can't have single women, you know. It leads to trouble, 'specially in this town where we've got all the trouble we can handle and some left over. Sure I have a room. The one at the end of the hall, same as always. But if you don't mind, I'll have your supper sent in. There's a political meeting in the dining room tonight, not the place for you, if you don't mind my saying so."

It appeared that she wasn't safe anywhere in town, Viola thought. The place was worse than the whole of Lincoln County, probably because most of those who had deserved their place on Governor Wallace's list had headed here where they were free to make as much trouble as they wished. And she and John were responsible for bringing some of them. With determination, she forced that idea out of her mind. People did what they had to do as best as they could, and neither she nor John had looked any further into the future than leaving New Mexico. At least she hadn't.

With an effort, she resumed the conversation. "A political meeting? What about?"

The proprietress let indignation spill out. "Town lots, is

what. Folks came here early on and set up businesses, then along comes the mayor and what they call 'The Town Lot Company,' who say we don't own the property we're setting on. Says we got to pay or get out, and there's those of us who don't aim to do either one, seeing as we already paid once."

"It doesn't sound right."

"It doesn't, and it isn't, and there's plenty of hot tempers set to go off. Maybe right in my own dining room. That's why I say, take your supper in your room, and stay out of it."

Viola picked up her bag and took the key. "I'll just have a bath and supper and go to bed early, then. I have shopping to do in the morning."

Regardless of her intentions, she lay awake until long after midnight. Sleep was impossible in the racket that drifted in from the street, the shouting that echoed from the dining room, occasional gunshots that frightened her so that she pulled her pillow over her head and lay waiting for a stray bullet to fly through the window.

John had been right, and Tad, when they called Tombstone no town for a lady.

She was awakened by the shouts of a mob and the screeching of what sounded like metal being dragged over rock. A glance out the window told her nothing. She dressed quickly and went down the hall.

"What on earth?" she said to the proprietress who looked, if possible, even more distraught than she had the night before.

"It's those men I told you about. With the town lots. They're moving poor Mister Reilly's house into the street."

"Whatever for?"

"Eviction. They're kickin' him off his own property." The

woman's mouth snapped shut.

Viola had a vivid picture of a house in ruins. "Is anyone hurt?"

"Nobody's home. Reilly's out of town. If he was here, he'd shoot the cowards." She waved a hand toward the empty dining room. "Best eat some breakfast while you can."

"I will, and thank you," Viola said. "But can't the law do anything about all this?"

The woman laughed. "The law around here is . . . if you can get away with it, it's legal. We're going from bad straight to the devil, and the country with us, and nobody man enough to take charge except maybe one of those Earps."

Viola buttered a piece of toast. "Who are they?"

"Brothers. Come here, like most, hoping to strike it rich, but they're honest at least. Wyatt's deputy sheriff. It was him who put Curly Bill in jail after Marshal White was killed, and over this same problem. Curly said it was an accident, but there's a lot of us that has doubts."

Viola stopped chewing and stared. "Curly!" she exclaimed. "Goodness, I know him."

The woman gave her a hard look. "I wouldn't admit it, if I was you. He runs with a bad crowd. Those Clantons and that Ringo fella. Your neighbors, come to think of it."

"I see," Viola murmured, although she wasn't sure she did. But she did remember her unease when they had left New Mexico, and how some of the men, and Curly in particular, had aroused her dislike. At the mention of the Clantons she remembered only the circumstances of that painful day and the two men staring at her, one with obvious lust, the other as if she was no more to him than an annoyance, an obstacle in his path.

Her little kingdom, that had seemed so secure, had revealed cracks in its structure. Suddenly, irrationally, she longed for home and John, who would put all her worries to rest.

In bed, in the crook of his arm two nights later, Viola brought up the subject of her fears.

"Curly was one of ours," she said. "And Joe Hill. And that . . . that Ringo creature. And now they're outlaws."

His arm tightened beneath her, but all he said was: "Do you expect me to be responsible for men's characters?"

She pushed herself up. "Yes," she said, "if that means we've brought outlaws into the territory. Maybe we'd better be more careful."

"They'd have come with or without us," he said. "Leave well enough alone, my dear, and don't trouble your pretty head." He bent and kissed her, but to his surprise she pulled away.

"But, Mister Slaughter, these men are terrorizing everybody."

"And because they are who they are, you won't kiss me good night?"

"I'm trying to understand. Trying to make sure we don't make the same mistake again."

He sighed and pulled her closer, seeing no way to explain the close-knit network of rustling that went on, and that would continue to go on in the territory, with or without him.

"Will you stop worrying about it?" he whispered against her hair. "Just leave it to me and trust my judgment." And he was relieved when she relaxed against him and opened her mouth for a kiss that, for him, blotted out any necessity to explain the tangled affairs of the soon to be formed county of Cochise.

XX

Willie left the house and went out to the corral where his pony was cropping grass. *His* pony! Excitement and happiness bubbled up in his throat until he felt he was going to burst. Now he could ride out with his father and Aunty Vi like a real man, mounted on his own horse—the gray pony that was a miniature of his father's and that now came over and stood looking at him.

"Hello," Willie whispered, his voice catching in wonder. "Hello, Christmas."

The name slipped out before he thought; a good name, he decided. Every time he said it, he'd remember this astonishing day—the scent of the wild turkeys Bat was roasting in the new iron stove, and how he and Addie and Aunty Vi had made popcorn and threaded it on strings for decoration. And how he'd felt when his father had brought him and Addie outside and helped them get on the two ponies—his gray, Addie's a brown and white pinto.

He wriggled through the fence and put his arms around the sturdy neck and felt the warmth of the animal even through his new jacket—warmth and something like how it was when Aunty Vi hugged him—an explosion of goodness, as if everything that was wrong had come right, and he was safe in a place where hunger and loneliness never came.

"Christmas," he said again, and the horse turned its head and nuzzled his ear, blowing warm, sweet-scented breath.

From the door of the house Viola watched. "Come see," she called to John. "Come see your son."

He stood beside her, one arm around her waist. "He'll make a horseman," he said. "Thanks to you."

"To us, Mister Slaughter," she said. "We've done it to-gether, and that's how it should be."

From overhead came a sudden, wild music, and they looked up to see a formation of cranes flying into the sunset, their motion like a dance to an ancient song.

In the corral, Willie stood, his face turned up to the sky, his mouth open in wonder.

Viola leaned her head against John's shoulder. "I think we've just been blessed," she said.

Three weeks later, huddled next to a campfire made of twigs and cow chips, she remembered her words and wondered if, instead, they had been cursed.

She, John, and Addie had taken the train as far as the Río Grande where they met their third Texas herd—two thousand five hundred longhorns possessed of one thought—to stay on the east bank of the river.

From the opposite side, Viola and Addie had watched as the boys pushed the cattle toward the crossing, only to have them turn off and stampede away in all directions.

"Cattle," she said crossly. "They're dumber than sheep. Why does anybody bother?"

"Because they're gold on the hoof," John answered. "You know it as well as I do." He spurred his horse and rode down to the river edge to confer with John Swain, his black foreman who'd brought the herd from Texas.

When he came back, he was grim-faced. "Swain's got an idea. It's tricky, but it might work."

Her hands tensed on the reins. "What is he going to do?"

John studied the river, a steel-blue ribbon between sandy banks. "Water's low right now. Those cows don't even have to swim, if they only knew it. But they haven't seen a river since the Pecos, so they're spooked. Swain's fixing to drag a couple while the boys try to drive the rest behind. It might work, or it might not. But I want you and Addie back with Bat, out of the way."

"And you?" she asked. "What are you going to do?"

"I'll be right here, pushing them to high ground."

"Be careful."

He studied her face. "Don't worry. It's not my time."

There he went again. So sure of himself. She wished she could be as certain, but she never shared his faith and optimism. Life was too full of danger. She knew it and hated the fact. Obediently, she clucked to the horse and drove the buggy toward the chuck wagon set up in the lee of a brush-covered sandhill.

Bat offered her a cup of coffee from the big enamel pot he kept hot on the fire. "Can't have you freezin' yourself," he said. "Or you, missy." Addie was a favorite. For her he'd brought along a package of the Mexican chocolate she loved.

Viola warmed her hands on the steaming cup and watched the scene across the river. Behind the massed and restless herd, the Organ Mountains, a barrier of crags, turrets, twisted rock, blocked the way to the east and the desert of white sand, while to the north and south the Río Grande wound itself between bare cottonwoods and pink sandhills. In all the wide stretch that she could see, only cattle and riders were moving, a living flood of mottled bodies and flashing horns. Suddenly she closed her eyes. "I can't watch."

Bat patted her shoulder. "Don't you fret. John Swain's nobody's fool. If he says he's gonna do something, it's as good as done, and Mister Slaughter, he's got an angel sits on his shoulder."

Addie giggled. "Where?"

"Why, right there." Bat pointed down to where John sat his big gelding. "I can see him plain as day."

What Addie saw was a spiral of dust rising, caught by the afternoon sun, whirling overhead and shining like flakes of gold.

"I see him, too!" her child's voice rang out. "Aunty Vi, look!"

Bat winked at Viola. "What'd I tell you? You just listen to old Bat who's been with your daddy since before you was born."

Oh, to be a child again, Viola thought. To have such belief. But with love came danger, the insidious fears that at times rendered her helpless. What would become of them all in this empty land with only their wits, their puny strength standing between them and destruction?

"I see," she forced herself to say, then turned and faced away.

With an expertise born of years handling ornery range steers, John Swain roped one of the leaders and urged his horse, a muscled sorrel, toward the river. Simultaneously Tad and Stoney did the same.

"Come on you bone-headed sons-of-bitches!" Swains voice rose above the din as, reluctantly, the steer began to follow.

It was risky as they all knew. A maddened steer could as easily charge a rider as come along tamely, and with the rope tied fast, Texas-style, rider and horse had few choices—run or cut loose and hope you did it before a horn gored your horse and you got thrown and trampled.

Swain went down the low bank and into the water with the steer that, discovering its footing, crossed calmly, reached the opposite shore, and then bawled for company.

Stoney crossed next, and then Tad. Behind them, riders

pushed the herd, forcing them into a narrow opening where their only choice was to follow their leaders and cross the river.

In mid-stream, Tad's steer, pushed from behind, lowered its head and charged horse and rider, but, hampered by the muck of the river bottom, lost its footing, fell, and lay still, a dead weight at the end of Tad's rope. Just like a cow to quit and leave you in a tight spot, Tad thought as his horse struggled for its own footing, while a thousand longhorns hit the water behind them. He reached for the knife he carried in a scabbard, his fingers hampered by the gloves he wore. He'd been in tight spots and lived to tell about them, but a glance over his shoulder told him this was one of the worst.

Fumbling, he sawed at the taut rope, watched it fray too slowly for comfort. "Come on," he muttered, and heard his teeth grinding, heard the cattle sloshing the water close behind. He spurred his horse, and it leaped forward, snapping what was left of the rope and scrambling up the bank a stride ahead of the oncoming herd.

"That was close!" John pulled up alongside.

"Too damn' close." Tad's face was white under his perpetual tan. "Why I ever wanted to be a cowman beats me."

John smiled. "It's a sickness. Can't be cured."

"Except by accident." Tad wiped his face on his sleeve. "Here they come. You want to point them upriver?"

John spun his horse around. "There's good grass up there."

"And the weather's due to change."

"Change or not. They're waiting for us at Fort Bayard. We'll push on tomorrow." Once there, they would have shelter, and he had the women to worry about. Still, it was a comfort to have Viola with him. At that, he squinted up the hill where she and Addie stood watching, probably aghast at Tad's close escape.

"Be back in a minute," he said, and put his big horse into a lope.

XXI

Tad had been right. The morning dawned cold and overcast, and the wind had a bite to it, a taste like cold iron. Above the Organs, the sky was streaked with red, a distant fire that gave no warmth and promised none.

Bat sniffed the air. "Snow comin'," he said. "You can smell it plain. Best keep under that buffalo robe today."

Viola was shivering. Even hot coffee and biscuits weren't enough to warm her. "How soon?" she asked.

He sniffed again. "Weather makes its own rules. If it gets too bad, you and young miss ride in the chuck wagon out of the wind."

Addie was already shivering, but kept quiet. She had pleaded to be able to come along, had sworn she'd not be in the way or ask for special treatment. Now she sipped her chocolate and pretended imperviousness to storm and cold, when all she wanted was to burrow back into her blankets like a little animal safe in its den.

Viola had a sixth sense where Addie was concerned. "I'll drive the buggy," she said to Bat. " But Addie can go with you."

He looked from woman to child and nodded. "Missy, go get your blankets and pile 'em up back of my seat. That way we can talk and maybe even sing, if we feels like it. No storm's gonna bother us." He turned back to Viola. "You be all right?"

"If not, I'll holler."

"Make sure you do." He gave orders with the confidence of familiarity.

"Yes, sir," Viola said, grinning, used to his over-protective ways and enjoying them. With John and Bat she was safe, and the knowledge was comforting.

And she needed that comfort as the day went on and the cold deepened like a chasm, surrounded her, threatened to steal her breath, a white cloud that hung in the air and frosted her eyelashes, numbed the tip of her nose. Behind her, the herd moved slowly, hoofs hitting the hardened ground like the beating of a thousand drums.

"All right?" John rode alongside.

"How much longer?"

"A week. Maybe more if it snows."

She gritted her teeth. "I'm fine."

Except she wasn't. She'd never been so cold with no chance of getting warm, no way to avoid the rising wind that cut like a knife. This was what it must be like to freeze to death. She'd heard the symptoms. How you simply closed your eyes and slept, and your blood changed into ice, and your heart with it. Only pride, the fear that she'd be a nuisance, kept her going throughout the long afternoon.

That night the snow came, burying the hands in their blankets, threatening the coals of Bat's fire that he struggled to keep burning with a pitiable amount of fuel. She and John slept with Addie between them under the buffalo robe, sharing the heat of their bodies while the cold crept up from the ground and through the frail bulwark of their tent, an invisible intruder, harbinger of death.

In the morning, they pushed on through the slush churned up by the hoofs of slow-moving cattle, through the dampness that penetrated their clothes, and, around them, the black mountains, the white plain, all color stripped from earth and sky as if, overnight, the world had lost its vitality and lay wretched and still, marked only by the trudging herd, a chuck wagon, a light buggy, and the steam rising above the cavalcade in a bank of gray fog.

Viola's horse was stumbling. Every mile or two she had to stop and let one of the boys chop the balled ice out of its hoofs, and the other horses were no better. Horses and cattle all had icicles dripping from mouths and chins, yet they moved on, sluggish but recognizing the need to keep moving, to head away from the bitter wind.

How many days and nights passed in the bitter whiteness, Viola never could remember. What she recalled was the cold that tasted like metal in her mouth, that crept into her body and almost succeeded in taking not only her life but the lives of her husband and daughter, and of the men who struggled to keep themselves and the exhausted cattle moving.

They built fires of yucca stalks and cow chips, of brush and of the few branches of mesquite that dotted the desert, and, when they reached what they hoped would be the shelter of the mountains, the storm increased, the snow grew deeper, stunning them all. The men went out then and stripped branches from the pine and oak trees and built fires around the herd, around the wagon and the remuda, and prayed their efforts would see them through to safety. And they worked and prayed in silence, too beaten, too fearful to speak what they were thinking aloud.

Old Bat squinted through the driving snow, wiped his eyes on a frozen sleeve and squinted again, then slapped the reins over the backs of the stumbling mules. "Look there!" he shouted to Addie, huddled behind him. "Look like we made it, missy."

Addie stuck her head out beside him and stared, and

fought back tears. Safe! She was safe, and John, and Viola, and old Bat who'd done the best he could to keep her warm and out of the way of the storm.

"I didn't think we would," she said in a small voice that wobbled, although she tried her best to stop it.

Bat hadn't, either, but refused to admit such a thing to her. "I told you about that angel," he said. "It's watchin' over us all, and don't you never forget it."

But she had. Somewhere on the harrowing, frigid trail, she had forgotten not only about the angel, but about everything except trying to keep warm and not complain. "I won't," she said, still in the same falsetto. "I won't ever again."

Viola had to be carried inside where she sat, wracked by chills and then by pain as feeling returned to her frostbitten feet. Of them all, only Addie, wrapped in her blankets, had escaped frostbite. Bat's right hand had been frozen, and John's ears, but they were alive, all of them.

John knelt beside Viola, rubbing her feet. "Never again," he mumbled. "Never again, you hear? If I lose my ears, will you still love me?" It was a feeble attempt at light-heartedness.

"And if I lose my feet?" she asked, voicing her fright.

"You won't."

"Optimist."

"I forbid it."

In spite of everything, her eyes kept closing. Sleep was what she wanted, what it was now safe to have. "That's good, then."

She was so small! He studied her slender foot and perfect toes, saw the faint flush of pink returning, and sat back on his heels. Lucky. They'd been damned lucky. But he'd be damned if he'd go on like this, risking lives, taking chances, putting his determined wife through hell because of a dream.

Enough was enough.

He'd had his eye on Oregon and the land along the Snake River for a while. With the sale of his cattle they'd have enough to start over, to ranch and farm and be sufficient unto themselves, and be damned to high desert weather that burned one day and froze the next. Be damned to Apaches and *bandidos,* and his renegade neighbors who were running hellbent into trouble and liable to drag him along.

He put another log on the fire, then carefully lay down beside Viola, and pulled up the blanket. They'd survived. This time. For himself he had no fears, but all his instincts urged protection for his wife and children, and logic said that the responsibility was his.

In her sleep, Viola relived the ordeal—Tad struggling in the muddy river; John hunched over a plodding horse, his hat pulled down, icicles in his beard, only his eyes blazing out through falling snow; and herself, on the point of succumbing to cold.

She came awake with a start and lay listening to her heart beating wildly, and to the wind battering the roof. Cautiously she moved a foot, wriggled her toes, and gave a sigh of relief. She was safe. And whole. And John slept soundly beside her, the sleep of exhaustion.

She turned and watched his face in the last of the firelight, memorizing its shape, imprinting each line, the planes of his cheekbones, the faintly arrogant nose, so that, if, by hideous chance, he was taken from her, she would have this, the imprint of his face to carry with her always.

XXII

It would be good to be home again, Viola thought as they drove up the valley of the San Pedro. Home and in one piece, and with the cash from the sale of their cattle in a belt around old Bat's waist.

"They look for me to be carrying it," John had explained. "Who'd believe the cook had it?"

It was a clever ruse, but then he was clever, always planning ahead, never making a move he hadn't thought out.

She smiled up at him. "Won't it be good to get home? Pretty soon I can start my garden."

Now he was in for it. Now he had to shatter her plans. He cleared his throat once, then again. "I say . . . I say," he began, then stroked his beard and was silent.

Under raised brows her eyes were huge and curious. "Is something wrong?"

"We're going to Oregon." He blurted it out, looking straight ahead between his horse's ears.

She gave a gasp of surprise. "You mean walk away from all this? Turn our backs on everything we've done?"

"What have we done except nearly get ourselves killed?"

"Why . . . why. . . ." Her hands went slack on the reins for an instant before she pulled back and brought horse and buggy to a stop.

In the late January sun the valley glittered. Small birds, stirred by their presence, flew up and out of the brush and swept overhead with a flutter of wings, and somewhere a lark was singing its mating song.

It was happening again, she thought miserably. No

sooner settled than she was taken away, forced to move and begin again. The pattern of her life and her mother's before her.

"I . . . we . . . we have a home," she said in a low voice. "We have a life here. And the children. It's not fair to them."

"They'll make do. But we almost lost Addie. Almost died ourselves. I want. . . . I want to make sure that doesn't happen again, Vi. And I intend to make sure it doesn't. The climate's better . . . we can breed our own cattle. Blood stock, not these blasted longhorns. And we won't have to worry about Apaches or the law coming down on us for what our neighbors are doing."

"Neighbors!" She snorted. "We brought them in here."

"A lack of foresight on my part."

"And who will our neighbors be in Oregon?"

Her voice was bitter, and it irritated him. "You sound like it's my fault."

She stared at her hands clenched in her lap. "I'm not blind or foolish, Mister Slaughter. I've seen how our herds increase. I figured out how my father made enough to buy his place. I also know that it's common practice. Everybody does it. But I've heard about how those cowboys are terrorizing the county, and I won't have that affecting us or be in league with them, here or any place else. Do you understand?"

He sighed, then dismounted, and led his horse to the rear of the buggy and tied it before climbing onto the seat beside her. "So you think I'm a cow thief?" he asked. "You think I'm like the others, even after it's been explained to you?"

She sat mute and stubborn, refusing to look at him, and he resisted the urge to shake her.

"Don't you?" His voice was harsh.

She responded wearily, by rote. "An unbranded cow belongs to whoever finds it. I know. But we have thousands of them. Where have they come from? Tell me."

"I can't."

"Why not?"

"Because I don't know. It's as simple as that. Our boys find them and bring them in. *Our boys.* Tad. Even your brother. Are you trying to incriminate him along with me?"

"Stoney? You asked Stoney to steal for us?"

"Stoney's his own man. He's built a herd for himself, too, in case you didn't notice. Also, in case you haven't noticed, I don't change brands like the Clantons and their daddy over in the Animas Valley do. Or like Curly . . . or anybody else I could name. Once and for all, Vi, I do not steal branded cattle. Am I making that clear?"

He was asking for her belief, and she wasn't sure what she believed. In her mind she visualized the herds that grazed in the pastures by the river—several thousand head that had appeared, so it seemed, out of nowhere, but all bearing a single brand, that distinctive Z that had been Amazon's and was now theirs.

She knew how a man clever with a running iron could change a brand, then keep the animals out of sight until the wound healed over. That, too, was common practice—among rustlers. But she'd seen no sign of tampering on their cattle, nor had she seen a running iron anywhere on the place. It was a puzzle, and she solved it the only way she could.

John was her husband whom she had vowed to love, honor, and obey. And he was not a liar. If he swore he was honest, she had to believe him.

She let out a breath. "I understand," she said slowly. Then, because she knew that she belonged with him regardless of circumstances, she said: "And I'll go to Oregon when you do. But I want to settle some place. I want to put down roots and stay. I've been moving all my life, and it's past time to stop. Can *you* understand *that?*"

He supposed it had been hard on her, the constant up-heaval, leaving behind the things she loved and was used to. For himself, he carried with him what was important—cattle, horses, opportunity. But he did have a family, and his duty was to them first and foremost—to his children and to this woman who so unaccountably had fallen in love with him, this woman who had nearly died rather than be separated from him.

He reached over and took one of her hands in his—a small, square hand with strong fingers, a hand that had known hard work, much of it on his behalf. Gently he kissed the palm. "I understand more than you think," he said. "I'll make you a home to be proud of, and that's a promise."

XXIII

"Men are all the same. They have to cross the plains, have to climb the mountains, and then, when they get to the sea, they have to build boats and sail away and leave the women behind to do all the work."

In spite of herself, Viola had to laugh at her mother's dour view. They were at the dépôt in Benson, waiting for the train that would take them to the connection to Colorado and the north, and, as always, Mary Anne was having her say.

"John isn't leaving me, Mama. And he's certainly not go-ing to sail to China. As soon as we're settled, we want you to come and visit."

The June wind was blowing in gusts. Mary Anne held her

hat with one hand, her skirts with the other. "I'm done with traveling, even if this blasted wind does want to blow me to some place else. If you want to see your father and me, you'll have to come back here. But mind you take good care of those dear children. And of your own, when they come."

Her mother, Viola thought, had mellowed, taking Willie and Addie in as if they were her own, and without complaint. "You know I will," she said.

But Mary Anne was determined to have the last word. "I don't know anything for sure. The world's a tricky place, and who's to say what will happen, or if we'll meet again in this life?"

Viola struggled against tears as Mary Anne's doomsaying exaggerated what she herself was feeling. "Don't," she said. "Please, Mama. Let me leave here happy."

"You chose your man," came the harsh response. "Do as best you can, but never say you weren't warned."

There it was. The lack of support, the constant disapproval. Viola straightened her shoulders. "I did choose," she said clearly. "And I'm happy in my choice. It would be nice if you would be happy with me for a change."

She bent then and kissed Mary Anne's cheek, missing contact on purpose, making a gesture for the sake of good manners. Then she turned and threw her arms around Amazon. "Good bye," she whispered. "Good bye, Papa."

"God go with all of you." She was his only daughter—brave, beautiful, adventurous—and he loved her, the girl who should have been a boy, who marched to her own drummer without regret or apologies. Damn but he loved her! And damn if he didn't want to go along—to Oregon, to whatever challenge awaited in a new place, on a different frontier.

"Mind you write," he ordered. "You tell us everything."

"I will," she murmured into his shoulder. "You know I will, always."

In spite of herself, Viola found the trip interesting, pointing out various sights to Addie and Willie who gawked out the window and who, in a matter of hours, captivated the hearts of every passenger in the car.

Yet there was a part of her, kept hidden for fear of dampening John's enthusiasm, that ached at being taken away from the high desert country. All the important events of her life belonged to that empty piece of land labeled Arizona Territory—to its plains, mountains, and long valleys, in one of which what would have been their child was buried.

Who would know in fifty years or a hundred, that beneath the red earth, under the waist-high grama grass, was the end of a scarcely formed life? Who would know of her sorrow, or how so often she stood watching morning lift above the mountains in an exuberant bursting of light?

They left New Mexico behind, stopped for several days in Denver, then headed west for Salt Lake City where they were to board a stage for the long run into Boise.

Her depression deepened as they crossed the heavily forested Rockies, teetered above river gorges, passed mountains whose peaks were white with perpetual snow. She longed for the familiar—the crying of cranes, the rocky face of the Dragoons, the rattle of old Bat's chuck wagon, and the plaintive music of his fiddle winding through the night. Nothing would ever be quite the same. She'd been marked as clearly as if she carried a brand, except the mark was stamped on her senses and on her heart.

Beside her, John was coughing but trying to make light of the cold he'd caught during the storm, and that had never entirely left him.

"Are you sure you're all right?" she asked, more worried than she wanted to admit.

"Positive." He spat into his handkerchief. "I've had worse colds, my dear."

"How much longer?"

"A few days yet to Salt Lake. Rest easy."

She couldn't. Not with the children to entertain and care for, and not with the heaviness of spirit that grew worse with every mile.

"When we get there, I'll make you a mullein tea. That should help." Her herbs and medicines were in the baggage car, and she wished she'd had the foresight to keep them with her.

He leaned back in the seat and closed his eyes. "That will be good. For now, I'll take a nap."

He could sleep anywhere simply by closing his eyes. She envied him that ability. With her own eyes closed, she could still see the country moving past, smell the acrid smoke from the engine, feel the ash and cinders that, even with the windows closed, blew into the car and covered them with grime.

"Where's Christmas?" Willie whined suddenly. "I want Christmas."

Neither Viola nor John had been able to convince the little boy that his beloved pony had been shipped ahead in the care of Tad and John Swain.

She reached across and took him onto her lap. He was still small enough that he fit comfortably. "Christmas will be waiting for you in Boise," she told him. "And just as happy to see you as you will be to see him. He's been on a train, too, you know."

"Tell me." He laid his head on her bosom. "Tell me again, Aunty."

This was what you did as a wife, a mother. You gave comfort when you yourself were in need; you spun tales to soothe anxious children; and you bit down on your own anxieties, covered them up, plastered a smile on a grimy face, put courage into a body that ached from sitting still and from pouring out balm on wounds not your own.

She closed her eyes, began to rock slowly with the motion of the train. "Once upon a time . . . ," she began. "Once upon a time in Arizona Territory. . . ."

XXIV

Viola was wearing John's money belt under her skirt. It was heavy and awkward, and, when she sat, it lay in her lap like a stone, a constant reminder that outside the coach, in the brush, in the folds of barren mountains were men whose only purpose in life was the theft of the hard-earned money of innocent travelers. They had stayed two nights in Salt Lake City, and on the morning of their departure John had insisted that she carry their cash.

"I didn't like the way that fellow was asking questions," he told her, his eyes bright as they always were when he was forming a plan. "We've got a week's travel through hard country, and I'd guess our host out there is the point man for an outlaw gang."

Outlaws! Viola put a hand to her throat. "What if they search me?"

"They won't. They're not about to maul a woman, and, besides, I told him our money was safe in the bank." He coughed, a dry, hacking cough. "But just to make sure, you wear the belt, and, if there's trouble, keep Willie on your lap. Leave the rest to me."

They were four days into their journey, and with the passing of every mile she grew more frightened. Civilization, all that was familiar, lay behind them. They were deep into a country of mountains and gorges, cañons and sagebrush desert, and they had no one to turn to but each other, no family or hired hands to come to their aid.

Her eyes stung from the dust that blew, and her head ached from being constantly alert, watching, waiting for the appearance of masked riders. And all the while she was aware of John's coughing which he did his best to hide. If he died here, in this wilderness? She set her chin. He would not. She wouldn't allow it, and that was final. Perhaps there was a doctor in Boise who could prescribe something other than her own remedies. Before they set out again, she was going to find him, if only to set her mind at ease.

Above the clatter of hoofs, the creak of wheels, and jingle of harness, she said: "When we get to Boise, I want you to consult a doctor."

His mouth twisted in annoyance. "Don't fuss."

"I will, too. I'm your wife."

"More like a setting hen."

"And you're stubborn as a mule. Humor me in this, Mister Slaughter. Please."

"Blast it, Vi . . . ." Coughing shut off the rest of his words. Damnation! Weak lungs were a curse. He could ignore the problem in hopes it would go away, but it was always there, and he knew it better even than his wife.

"All right," he said after a moment. "If it'll make you feel better, I'll go see a sawbones, but he won't tell me anything I haven't heard before."

"He can tell me, then," she said.

He chuckled. "I trust you'll pick his brains for everything he knows, my dear. I've seen you in action."

MRS. SLAUGHTER

★ ★ ★ ★ ★

It had been raining all day when they reached Boise, and Viola shivered as she stood ankle-deep in mud while John gave directions for their luggage to be carried to the hotel.

Willie clung to her neck like a sodden kitten, and Addie clapped her hands to her ears and whimpered when thunder boomed directly overhead.

What was worse, Viola wondered, freezing to death or drowning? Her mouth tilted in a bitter smile. She couldn't recommend either. Life was precious, and she hadn't come this far to give it up.

With her free hand she pulled Addie close. The little girl had been an heroic traveler, amusing Willie and never once uttering a complaint about late hours, indigestible meals, or physical discomfort. Now, however, she had reached the end of her patience—like the rest of them.

"Don't cry, sweetheart," Viola said. "We'll be inside in a minute and get dry and have something to eat."

"I want to go home," Addie wailed. "Please, Aunty Vi."

She knew. Oh, she knew! Standing there in the mud, her hat brim sagging and dripping rain, she summoned her last bit of strength. "Come along, Addie. We'll go to the hotel and wait for your papa where it's warm."

With a look of despair, Addie followed, sloshing through the mud, her eyes fastened on her feet and her new boots, now ruined. She was remembering Amazon and how he'd held her on his knee, and how he'd taken her into the cow barn and taught her how to milk one of the gentle cows. How it had been warm there, and peaceful, the cows munching hay and giving milk, while up in the loft swallows swooped and twittered, their bodies like tiny kites blown by the wind.

Mary Anne had given her a doll made out of a corncob and dressed in a scrap of red calico. She had it with her still in the bottom of her trunk. She wished she'd thought to carry it with her—a thing familiar, a souvenir of the place she'd grown to love and that, for the rest of her life, she'd call home.

Blood spattered the front of John's nightshirt, and, even as Viola watched, stricken into paralysis, he coughed up more. How could there be so much blood? How could she stand frozen while he bled to death? She jerked into frenzied motion.

"You must lie down!"

"And you must get hold of yourself." His words came out in a ragged whisper.

Get hold of herself! And him half dead. But this wasn't the time to vent her anger. As always, practicality took over.

"Lie down and stay still. I'm going to find a doctor." Surely a town like this one had a doctor.

A check into the next room showed Addie and Willie asleep, clutching each other for warmth and security. "Poor babies," Viola said in a low voice. "Poor, sweet children." She shut the door and clattered down the stairs to the small lobby where Tad and John Swain stood up at her approach.

"Miz Slaughter." They held their hats in their hands, and she wanted to tell them that courtesy at this point didn't matter, that who she was, who they thought she was, was irrelevant. But a look at their caring faces brought relief, and she went to them, her hands outstretched.

"We need a doctor," she said. "It's urgent. Mister Slaughter is upstairs in bed and he's hemorrhaging. If one of you will go, I'll stay with him. I think . . . ," her voice broke, "I think I should be there."

"I'll go." Tad slammed his hat on his head. "John"—he turned to the foreman—"you stay and make yourself useful. Do whatever has to get done. All right?"

Swain nodded curtly. "I'm here, and here's where I stay. Miz Slaughter . . . ?" He looked at Viola. "You need anything at all, you just ask. I'll be right outside that door till you tell me otherwise."

"Bless you both." She took their rough hands for an instant, felt the warmth in each. She wasn't alone, after all.

She was pacing up and down the narrow hall outside the room where the doctor had been for what seemed like ten years.

"She gonna wear a hole in the floor," Swain muttered to Tad who had taken up the vigil with him.

"And she'll keep walkin' till she falls through, so forget it," Tad answered.

"Poor little thing's plumb wore out."

Tad knew better. "She's never wore out. Believe it. You 'n' me'll be ready for the bone yard, and she'll still be on her feet givin' orders. That's the goin'est woman I ever saw."

John Swain flashed a wide grin. "Then Mister John picked himself a Thoroughbred."

It was as good a description as any Tad could think of. "Damn' right." He sat up as the door opened and the doctor stepped into the hall.

"Is he all right? Will he be all right?" Viola couldn't control the tremor in her voice.

Doctor Timothy J. MacFarland hadn't been out of medical college long enough to acquire a decent bedside manner. He looked down at the tiny woman clinging to his arm and spoke his mind. "Not if he insists upon continuing this journey, madam. I advise you to go back to the Southwest where his lungs might have a chance. This isn't the climate for a man with your husband's disease."

Viola continued to peer up at him, and, to his astonishment, he thought he saw something like triumph flickering in her dark eyes. "You're certain of this?"

Was she questioning his diagnostic ability? He pulled away from her. "I am, madam. His condition should be apparent, even to you."

She, too, stepped away, annoyed. "It is, sir. But I wanted a learned opinion, and I thank you for your honesty. Now, if I can settle your bill?"

When he had gone, she turned to Tad and John Swain. "You heard what he said?"

They nodded in unison.

"Very well. We're going home as soon as Mister Slaughter can travel. I'll make arrangements for you to start back as soon as possible. I'm sorry you had to come on a fool's errand, but . . . but, oh . . . ." She clasped her hands, and they both saw the happiness on her face. "Oh, boys, we're going home!"

By the next morning John was sitting up in bed, irritated at his own weakness.

"Don't scold, Vi," he said, when she came in. "I've been scolding myself."

She sat down beside him and took his hand. "I won't," she said. "I'm just glad you're alive."

"I'll be up in a few days. Tell the children that, and don't scare them."

A woman could hold in, deny her emotions for only so long. Viola drew a deep breath. "I told them that we're going home, Mister Slaughter. That we're going back where we belong."

He pushed himself higher against the pillows. "Wh . . . what?" he stammered. "What did you just say?"

"You heard me. And I heard what the doctor said last

night. I didn't marry you to become a widow quite so soon, and your children need their father. *I* need you. So we're going back to where we have a chance and forget the dream about Oregon. We had our dream, only we left it, but we can have it again. Except it won't be here. And if you persist, you'll have to do it alone, because I won't be a party to suicide . . . yours, mine, anybody's, and that's final!"

Actually he was quite proud of her, filled with admiration for her ability to take charge and make what she said stick, but all he said was: "And that's your decision?"

"It is for a fact." She was on her feet and moving, her heels striking the floor like castanets. "We don't belong here. We're desert rats. That's obvious. At least to me."

"Why didn't you say so before?" he wanted to know. "Why wait till we burned our bridges?"

She folded her arms under her breasts and faced him, love and anger warring in her dark eyes. "Because you're my husband, and I'm supposed to follow where you go. But I'm not foolish. Or blind. And I know disaster when I see it. We've got a second chance, Mister Slaughter, and I for one intend to take it. And take you back with me, if I have to hog-tie you and throw you on that stage. So, there!"

She had never lost her temper with him, never spoken a harsh word in more than two years. For that, he thought, he should be grateful. Viola in a temper was magnificent. Unfortunately, she also made perfect sense.

He sighed. And coughed. And hated the perfidy of his body. Without opening his eyes he said: "Go down to the stage office and buy our tickets back. I'll sleep for a while, but I'll be ready to leave day after tomorrow."

XXV

Suddenly there it was! The San Pedro Valley with its pink sandhills, the river winding through, and the rock shoulders of the Dragoon Mountains rising out of the brush in the east.

Viola stood on the station platform breathing the high desert air with a relief felt down to her toes. The trip back had seemed interminable. She felt she hadn't slept more than a few hours, always waking to check on John, fearful that she'd see that frightening gush of blood she had no way to prevent or stop.

"Happy?" he asked, coming to stand beside her.

She felt the heat of the sun, the stirring of wind against her face. "Yes," she said. "Here is where we belong."

"You're sure you won't mind living in Tombstone a while?"

She shook her head. Even the idea of town life couldn't shake her optimism, and Addie would be able to go to school, make friends with children her own age. "It won't be forever. Just till we find our own place."

He watched a troop of buffalo soldiers ride down the main street. They were well-armed and well-mounted, and gave credence to the rumors they'd been hearing about trouble on the San Carlos Reservation. If he had his way, his family would stay in town until Geronimo and every one of his warriors was either dead or permanently confined.

"It's true, isn't it?" Viola clutched his arm, her face white. "Geronimo's out and the Apaches are raiding again."

"Now, Vi, don't go getting jumpy before time." He patted her hand. "Let's go over to the stage office and find out what's happening."

He sounded jovial, but she knew. Even the short run from Benson to Tombstone could be perilous. Always, it seemed, there had to be a flaw in paradise, a scimitar hanging over them threatening happiness.

She swept Addie and Willie to her. "We'll make it, won't we?" Her voice trembled.

"Or die trying." He bit off the words that only made the situation worse and tried again. "No need to fear. We're all armed."

Yes, she thought. And much good a few men would be against a horde of murderous Indians. For the sake of the children, she called on her self-control. "Let's just go, then," she said, and headed toward the dépôt, head high.

"No sign of the devils around here, yet." The ticket seller pushed his spectacles high on his nose. "Heard they're south of Globe, but can't say for sure. What's worse is the roads. The summer rains washed out near everything from here to the border. Good for the grass, but hard on travel."

In Silver City, John had contracted to sell beeves to the railroad crews and, cattleman that he was, had already taken into account the lushness of the valley, a sea of moving grass, fodder for the cows he intended to fatten, Apaches or no Apaches, bad lungs or good. Already he felt better. Viola had been right as usual. Here was where they'd make a life, and be damned to anyone, red or white, who attempted to stop him!

The ticket agent had been right about the condition of the road. They hadn't gone ten miles when the heavy coach bogged down.

"Everybody out!" The driver and guard swung down. Seeing Viola's face, the driver added: "Sorry, ma'am. We'll have to dig her out, but it shouldn't take long."

Long enough, she thought as she and the children stood to

one side in the shade of a white-barked sycamore tree. At least the walls of the stage offered some protection. In the open they were defenseless, targets to Apaches or the outlaw gangs who regularly held up the coaches. And she'd been the one who wanted to return!

"Don't go out of sight," she warned Addie and Willie who were picking up stones and tossing them into the brush where, suddenly, a thrasher whistled and was answered by another.

She strained her ears. Was that a bird or could it be an Apache, coming closer? They could all die here, their bones picked over by buzzards, their dreams scattered in the dust. She heard the grunts of the men, the clang of shovels, and one of the horses blew and stamped. She heard the children's voices, a sweet music, and beyond that, nothing. In the whole valley, beneath the dome of blue sky, nothing broke the silence—the hush of the first day of creation before man and his greed came to pass.

She put out her hands clutching at air and space as if they were tangible, and she could hold them, examine them as she might a jewel or a piece of glass. How strange it was to be a part of everything yet separate, with only her own thoughts circling in her head. Fear had no place here—or violence. Only the moment mattered, a moment that stretched out, as the valley stretched out, and the silence, and the small kernel of her intense awareness.

"Aunty Vi!" The peace shattered, her heart jumped.

"What on earth?"

Everything was as it had been—the men struggling to dig the coach out of the mud, the children scampering toward her, faces alight. Where had she been? She didn't know, only that she would cling to her vision, return to it when problems and despair threatened as they inevitably would.

"Gold!" Addie shrieked. "We found gold!"—and held out a piece of quartz that glittered with delicate flakes of mica.

Viola sank to her knees in the sand and examined the rock. Fool's gold, of course, but she hadn't the heart to disappoint. "Goodness," she said. "What will you do with it?"

Addie beamed. "I'll buy us a big house like you and Papa talk about. And we'll have a cook. A real one so you won't have to bother."

"And horses," Willie put in. "Lots of horses."

"That many?"

He nodded solemnly. "Maybe more."

"Well," she said, getting to her feet, "we'll have this assayed in town. But don't be disappointed if it isn't gold."

"It is!" Addie stamped her foot.

"We'll show your papa." A glance toward the road showed the coach out of the mire and the horses impatient.

Once back inside, John took Addie on his lap. "I say, I say, it's a rock that wanted to be gold so badly it painted itself."

She frowned, thinking. "Rocks can't do that," she said finally. "They don't know things like we do."

"You're sure?"

"Yes."

"But the Indians believe that everything has a spirit. Even rocks."

Indians again. Viola peered anxiously out the window but saw nothing except the glittering mesquite leaves and the dust, heavy in the air.

"That's them," Addie said. "We know better."

John chuckled. "Maybe," he said. "Maybe."

Addie's eyes were closing in spite of her excitement. "And we'll buy a house and lots of horses," she mumbled before she fell asleep.

"That we will, eh, Vi?" He looked across at his wife who

seemed as if she, too, needed a nap.

He'd dragged her across half the West to satisfy his own notions, but no more. She'd have her house and her servants as soon as he could manage it. She deserved the best, his Cora Viola.

"I'll just be grateful, if we get to Tombstone without Indian trouble," she said. "Time enough then to think about the future."

"We'll make it all right. We haven't come this far to lose. From here on, things are going our way."

As usual, being John Slaughter, he was planning ahead. And as usual he failed to take into account the world in which he lived.

XXVI

They rented a house at Third and Fremont Streets. John left the furnishing of it to Viola and went off with Tad, John Swain, and old Bat to gather cattle.

"This won't take long, my dear." He kissed her hard. "When I can, I'll be home, but you'll be safe in town, and you're not to worry, you hear?"

He might as well tell her not to breathe. Her fears, however, weren't for herself but for him, out riding the valleys and mountain passes, gathering cattle to be fattened and sold.

Every day came new stories about the Apaches. They were raiding ranches, setting fire to buildings, stealing stock, murdering helpless homesteaders and ranchers. They were in Dragoon Pass, and then in the Sulphur Springs Valley where they swooped down and ran off Frink's horses. They were in the Swisshelms and the Chiricahuas, but no one, not the volunteers from Tombstone or the buffalo soldiers from the fort, found more than beaten trails leading south into Mexico.

In spite of her constant worry, Viola found life in Tombstone pleasant. She was no sooner settled than the ladies called to invite her to church suppers, to join the literary society, to afternoon lunches and teas, and she went to everything with a pleasure that startled her until she recognized that she had been lonely for the company of women.

She had never had a close woman friend, and since her marriage she had spent all her time with John and the children, not realizing the comfort to be had in exchanging ideas, problems, even gossip with others of her sex. From the ladies of Tombstone she learned which dressmaker to patronize, which butcher gave the best value, which tailor took advantage of his customers, and, most important of all, she learned the political complications that slowly but surely were pulling the town apart.

"If you ask me, it's all the fault of that Marcus woman." Mrs. Berry sipped her coffee elegantly, eyeing her audience over the rim of her cup.

"Who?" Viola leaned across the table, curious about the town and its undercurrents, the small truths that men usually overlooked when talking to their wives.

"Josephine Marcus. An actress. She came here to marry our sheriff"—Mrs. Berry allowed herself a sniff of disdain—"but the marriage never took place. And now she's been seeing Wyatt Earp. Oh, he's handsome enough, and worth ten of Sheriff Behan, but . . . ," she lowered her voice to a whisper, "but you know, he's a married man. The whole affair is quite scandalous, and the two men have been at odds ever since she changed her mind. To the detriment of the good of this town, I might add."

Jessica Pridham gave a tinkling laugh. "We don't know for sure that he's married. Only that he lives with that bedraggled Mattie creature. There's no comparing her with Miss Marcus."

"Chasing skirts!" Elizabeth Goodfellow's mouth clamped shut. "He'd do better to pay attention to what's going on."

Mrs. Berry gave her a severe look. "He and his brothers have been chasing those cowboys as well, don't forget."

"So our sheriff can let them out of jail as soon as they're brought in. Isn't that so?" Elizabeth's look challenged them all, even Viola, who was attempting to understand the tangled web.

"Are you saying he's dishonest?" she asked. "The sheriff, I mean."

They laughed in unison, but Elizabeth answered. "The truth is obvious. The sheriff has the cowboys in his pocket. And maybe it's the other way around. All of them . . . Curly Bill, the Clanton boys, that drunken Ringo. It's all about money, of course. Bad men lining their pockets at the expense of decent, hard-working folk. Sometimes I wish we'd never come here."

There were the names again, the names of men she knew, however slightly. Viola shuddered. "The Clantons were our neighbors down on the San Pedro. I thought . . . I thought they were dreadful. They frightened me."

"So they should. They're men without conscience. Of course, the one called Ike isn't interested in the ladies. You needn't be afraid of him." Elizabeth giggled and sat back to wait for the sure-to-follow interrogation.

"What on earth do you mean?"

"How?"

"I eavesdrop in the doctor's surgery," she said with a smug grin. "And sometimes I hear the most interesting things. You should all be careful what you say, my dears."

Startled, her friends straightened in their chairs, forgetting her comments about the Clantons and wondering instead what secrets they might have divulged in the supposed privacy of Dr. Goodfellow's surgery.

"Why Elizabeth Goodfellow," Jessica said. "You should be ashamed!"

"Well, I'm not. It's been very instructive," came the answer. "How else can I expect to learn what's going on? Our husbands never tell us anything and say they're protecting us, and even the newspapers can't agree. We all know that much at least."

Viola listened with private amusement, vowing never to confide anything to the good doctor whom she intended to visit soon. Not that she had any confessions to make. Far from it. But she was almost certain she was with child. The thought brought a smile to her face. John would be so happy. As for herself, she wanted a child of her own more than anything else.

"Are the Clantons part of what you call the cowboys?" she asked, breaking the silence. "I'm sorry to appear ignorant, but the fact is"—she spread her hands—"I am."

With reluctance, Mrs. Berry put her curiosity aside. She had a long neck, like that of a turtle, and she thrust her head forward as she answered. "In this town it doesn't pay to remain ignorant. What's happening is a simple question of morality. Of right versus wrong. And which side you choose . . . the cowboys, and that includes the Clantons, and what is called the County Ring, and our sheriff, or the other, the decent citizens and the Earps. All of those Earps were raised Methodist, by the way," she added, as if that, in itself, constituted righteousness.

"Methodists or not," Elizabeth snapped, "the Earps aren't

saints. They gamble, you know."

"They represent order, and you know that, too. Or you should. But it will come to a showdown one of these days. I feel it in my bones. The situation has gone from bad to worse, and we're sitting on a powder keg about to go off. Mark my words."

Even as she uttered her prophecy, the sound of gunfire reverberated through the room.

XXVII

Viola's first thought in the silence that followed was for Addie who walked home from school every day. She pushed away from the table and stood, and a second burst of gunfire rattled the windows.

The four women looked at each other, cocked their heads toward the street, and listened to the shouting, the thud of running feet.

"I've got to see that Addie's all right." Viola reached for her cloak that was hanging on the coat rack near the door.

"We'll all go," Mrs. Berry said. "Safety in numbers, don't you know."

Outside they found confusion, a crowd surging toward Fremont Street. Mrs. Berry collared a delivery boy. "What is it? What's happened?"

"Big fight. Up by Fly's," he said, and wriggled free.

"Who?"

But he was gone.

"It was the Earps and some of the cowboys." A man with a red beard had stopped beside them. "Maybe you ladies should go back home. Might be dangerous out here."

"Nonsense!" Elizabeth gave him a withering look. "Is anyone hurt?"

"Dunno."

They hurried—as fast as their corsets and narrow skirts would permit—toward the scene. A group of men passed them pulling a cart, and a wagon stopped to let a young woman out on Fremont Street.

"There!" Mrs. Berry nudged Viola. "There's the Marcus chit come to see if she's a widow before the marriage vows."

Viola stared at the young woman and was struck by her beauty and by the yearning of her body as she ran toward the tall figure of Wyatt Earp, who was engaged in what seemed like a bitter argument with John Behan.

"Why, she loves him!" she said to her friends. "The poor thing was probably frightened out of her wits."

"My foot!" Mrs. Berry snapped. "I just got through telling you . . . ." Her words were cut off as the crowd parted and they saw a body lying on the corner of the street.

Elizabeth stood on tiptoe. "Why," she said, "it's Tom McLaury. Dead as a doornail."

Viola's stomach turned. She'd never seen a man shot, never imagined that in death a face froze in agony, or that sightless eyes could carry the remnants of fear and shock. She turned away, wanting the security of her own house, but Mrs. Berry took her elbow.

"There's more than one." She pushed her way through the crowd, dragging Viola with her.

"Billy Clanton. Doesn't look like he's going to make it." The man next to them shook his head. "Bad times," he said. "Bad times and worse ones coming. And you ladies shouldn't be here seeing this."

"Where's Ike?" Mrs. Berry surveyed the onlookers.

The man snorted. "They said he run off. Left his brother in the lurch."

The four women huddled together and watched as Billy was carried into a house. He was clutching his chest with bloody hands and whimpering.

Viola shut her eyes, but Elizabeth stared with obvious interest. "A goner," she announced with satisfaction. "And I guess this means George will be late again for supper tonight. If he gets home at all."

"Who can eat after seeing this?" Viola asked.

Mrs. Berry gave a short laugh. "You'll get used to it. This is Tombstone. After a while you won't pay much attention."

A cold wind blew down Fremont Street, carrying the feel of snow, and a cloud blotted out the sun so that the scene suddenly darkened. The scurrying figures, the wagons bearing the dead and wounded looked, to Viola, like a photograph in a newspaper, black and white and slightly blurry as she stood fighting nausea and dizziness. She would go home and lock her doors, and pull the curtains tight, gather Willie and Addie together for safety, and pray that John would come back soon and put everything in perspective. She swallowed hard. "I'm going to look for Addie."

"We'll go with you," Elizabeth said. "And then we should all go home and stay there. This town won't be safe, day or night, until this is all settled."

"Vengeance is mine saith the Lord," Mrs. Berry quoted. "But it seems the Lord's gone someplace else."

"And left us in hell." Viola forced herself to cross the street.

Mrs. Berry, however, was determined to have the last word. "Stuff! Hell's much worse. We're just a stop on the way, but this is as close as I want to get."

MRS. SLAUGHTER

★ ★ ★ ★ ★

The town seethed, its tension almost visible in the cold October air, and she wished John would come home and dispel her anxiety.

The three dead men had been buried, their funeral attended by a huge crowd, not of mourners, but of the curious who used any excuse to alleviate small town boredom.

None of the ladies had come visiting, all opting to stay at home in safety, and Viola had kept Addie out of school for fear she might become the innocent victim of yet another street fight.

She missed John, she was frustrated at being locked up with only the children for company, and the pain in her side she'd been trying to ignore was growing worse with each passing hour. She couldn't think for the throbbing, and, when at last she fainted, it was on the kitchen floor beside the stove, leaving the two children frightened into immobility.

Tears ran down Willie's face. "Aunty Vi," he sobbed. "Aunty Vi."

With an effort, Addie conquered her fear, although her heart was thumping so hard it threatened to choke her, and her stomach felt like she'd been punched. She crouched down beside her little brother and then, cautiously, reached out and touched Viola's cheek.

"Willie," she whispered, "can you be good and stay right here till I bring the doctor?"

"Stay with Aunty?"

"Yes. Will you do it?"

He nodded. "Is she sick?"

"I think so. But we'll make her better."

Willie moved closer and patted Viola's shoulder. "I love Aunty," he said.

Addie kissed the top of his head. "Me, too. I'll be

back quick as I can."

She slipped out into the street and looked carefully up and down. Then she started toward Dr. Goodfellow's at a trot, careful to stay close to the store fronts for fear she might be shot by a stray bullet, leaving two of the three people she loved best alone and helpless.

John had been edgy for several days for no reason he could put his finger on.

When news of the gunfight reached Tubac, where he'd just finished a purchase of two hundred and fifty head of cattle, he made up his mind without hesitation.

To Tad and John Swain he said: "I'm riding on back. Tonight. You boys bring the cattle, and, if you need extra hands, ask Elias to lend us a couple. I'm worried about Missus Slaughter with what's been going on."

He took off on Old Gray without waiting for their answer, rode under a sliver of moon and tattered clouds, rode until morning when he stopped and rested himself and the horse for an hour before continuing east in a gray light and a wind that carried the scent of snow.

In Tombstone, he left the horse at the livery, giving orders to rub him down, cool him off, and give him a good feed, and learning the particulars of the gunfight in a few words. Then he took off at a run through streets that were quieter than usual, as if the town was waiting for another eruption of violence, sure it would come.

Amazon and Mary Anne met him at his door. Mary Anne was weeping. A haggard Amazon put out his hand and clasped John's.

"Wh . . . what is it? Viola? The ch . . . children? Tell me, man," he stammered.

"It's Viola. She's lost another child, and the doctor . . .

he's afraid we're going to lose her, too." Amazon's voice broke. "He's in with her now, doing what he can."

"He's operating," Mary Anne spoke around her handkerchief. "He said it was the only way."

John felt he himself was bleeding, shot in the gut, and everything that was good and familiar, everything he cherished was being taken away. "Let me by!" He pushed past them and threw open the door to the bedroom.

"For God's sake, shut the damn' door and let me do what I have to!" George Goodfellow didn't look around, simply shouted his orders without raising his head.

The room stank of sweat, blood, and chloroform. Viola was hidden under a stained sheet.

"Is she all right?" John whispered.

"I don't know, and I won't until she wakes up. *If* she does." Goodfellow dropped something into a bowl on the floor. "I went in. Only thing to do. If she makes it, she won't have any more children."

"George . . . damn it! If you've killed her . . . !"

Goodfellow wiped his hands on a towel and spat into the bloody basin. "Damn it, yourself! She was dying and might anyhow. At least this way she's got a chance, so don't fault me for trying. I did what I had to, and there's an end to discussion." He stood up, a tall man, a surgeon with a reputation for brilliance and daring and pulling lives, like a magician, out of his hat.

"It's been one hell of a week around here," he said. "You probably heard."

John sat wearily on the chair beside the bed. "When . . . when did this happen?"

"Probably she was in pain for a few days, but Addie only came for me this morning. I wasn't home. I came as quick as I got word. Elizabeth sent for the Howells and watched the children." He sighed. "I'm sorry, John. We all love her. But there's just so damned much we don't know about these things. I took a chance, but it was better than quitting."

"There's so damned much we'd planned on doing." John turned and looked at Viola who lay still, hardly breathing, her face colorless, her hair a dark, disordered mass.

Goodfellow put a hand on his friend's shoulder. "I'll be outside. I'll stay the night . . . . just in case."

When he had gone, closing the door carefully behind him, John put his head on the pillow beside his wife's and wept.

XXVIII

She had gone far away, into a place without pain or the necessity for speech, and she was floating there, emotionless, wrapped in a gentle light that soothed without sound, that was warm and sweet, and she welcomed it, submitted to it out of a deep weariness. But somewhere, at the periphery of her understanding, a person was crying hopelessly, bitterly, and, with the little energy she had, she responded.

Grief, she knew, was for the living. The dead felt only release, a great freedom, but she was touched with concern that anyone should weep so—and for her who didn't need it. With a great effort, she summoned the extremities of her body, pulled them together, and forced them into motion, forced open the lids of her eyes that were heavy as stone.

The familiar room spun around her—bureau, mirror, her lamp, the light burning low. *Why,* she thought, *I must have been dreaming! But what a strange dream it was!*

And there was John, his face next to hers, the pillow wet with his tears. He wept for her!

She said: "Mister Slaughter," forming the syllables with care for she had almost forgotten how to speak. "Mister Slaughter."

At the faint sound, he raised his head, saw her dark eyes watching him with compassion and what seemed to him to be a kind of curiosity, as if the fact of his emotion was a wonder to her.

"Vi." He took her hand and warmed it in his callused ones.

"I . . . wanted you," she said slowly.

"I know. And I'm here. And I'm not letting you go."

Wherever she had been was receding, vanishing in the shadows where the lamp light couldn't reach.

"Light," she whispered. "Please."

He obeyed, turning the flame up until it dazzled him. Then he came back and knelt again beside the bed.

"I mean it, Vi. We need you. We love you, and that's the truth of it."

"The children?" She raised her eyebrows in question. "Are they all right?"

"Your parents are here. Not to worry. About anything."

"You," she said. "I worry about you." With a rush of longing, she came completely back into the moment, and her face crumpled. "I lost our child. Again. I'm s . . . sorry."

But she was here, and she was alive, and that was what mattered to him.

"The world's full of children, Vi. But there's only one you. Understand?"

She remembered the day she had first met him, at her parents' house—how she had recognized him immediately and had struggled to keep that recognition secret. Looking at him had been like looking into a mirror and finding her own person reflected, even the morass of unvoiced thought, unexamined emotions. Together they made one whole. To be apart, to leave him alone, was unthinkable.

He was, she saw, exhausted, travel-stained, his coat spattered with mud, his eyes red-rimmed. "Now that you're here, I can rest," she said. "And so should you. Everything's going to be all right."

Viola recovered slowly. To all appearances she was happy and healthy, but only she knew that each day she dressed and carefully painted on a mask that disguised her devastation. She had received a life sentence from which there was no reprieve, and with the knowledge of her barrenness she felt increasingly useless, a woman without plan or purpose, save as an ornament.

She did not speak her feelings, even to John, especially not to him who assumed, in his masculine, good-hearted way, that all was well with her, and who strove to please by buying her jewelry and hats and a new riding horse, and who, when he was in town, squired her to parties, dances, the theater, and teased her unmercifully about what he called her "flirtations."

As if, she thought bitterly, anyone would want her if they knew. A man had a right to children, to wholeness in a wife. She could cover herself with feathers and baubles, but all the trimmings in the would could not disguise what she knew to be true—that inside she was empty, and that she ached with that emptiness and mourned a hope that was gone forever.

And around her the town seethed with venom and the accompanying plots and violence.

In December, Virgil Earp was brought down by shadow assassins who shattered his arm rather than killing him, and left him a partial cripple for life. In March, Morgan Earp was shot in the back in Hatch's Billiard Parlor, and the next day the entire Earp clan left Tombstone with the coffin, a line of mounted riders protecting the living family and the remains of the happiest and most insouciant of the brothers.

Viola and Mrs. Berry watched the silent procession as it moved slowly out of town, saw the grim faces of the riders, the even grimmer faces of the women who rode in the wagons.

"Where do you suppose Miss Marcus is?" Viola asked. "It's a wonder she isn't here to say good bye."

Mrs. Berry sniffed, and her mouth pursed as if she'd been handed a sour pickle. "She wouldn't dare show her face. Not now. She's not family, and she's the cause of all this killing. Probably she's home crying. She should be asking forgiveness, but that kind never does. And if you think we've heard the last of the Earps, you have another think coming." With that, she lifted her skirts and stepped into the street. "Come along," she ordered. "Miss Borland has some new dress material. Just the thing for summer."

Within days the proof of her statement drifted back. Frank Stilwell dead at Tucson, Curly Bill at Iron Springs, Indian Charley at South Pass, anyone who had ever given loyalty to the cowboy gang was not going to live to speak of it.

And Viola brooded over responsibility for the deaths, foolish though she tried to tell herself she was.

"We brought some of them here," she said to John at the dinner table.

"We did, and I don't deny it." He looked at her over the rim of his glass, then set it down firmly. "But there's a difference. I hired men who knew one end of a cow from another because I needed them, just like your father did. We never asked about their breeding. If they kept bad company, we're not to blame, and, if I worried about it, why . . . why I'd give up cattle and become a minister like this Peabody fellow you ladies are so fond of." He put his elbows on the table and his chin in his hands.

"We do what we have to Vi, like we had to get out of New Mexico or be put in jail, and we brought our cash with us on the hoof. Thanks to those boys. What they were or made of themselves has nothing to do with us. We can't punish ourselves for the crimes of others. Understand?"

When she met his eyes without a response, he lost his temper. "D . . . damn it, Vi! You think I'm holier than holy? You want to blame me for what's happened here, but you can't. The seeds were sown long before we came. And I won't be any man's confessor any more than your father will. In this country, it's every man for himself, and that's the way it's always been. Now, you either agree or you don't, but I don't want to hear about it again. And I don't want to have you trying to make me feel guilty every time you hear the name of a dead man. It's over. It's done. Or will be when Earp's finished here. And more power to him. He bit off a chunk few men want to handle, but he's handling it. Maybe now we can all go about our business, and maybe you and I can get on with our plans."

She sat silent under what, for him, was a tirade. Silent and taking all the guilt upon herself. She'd been, she thought, a bad wife, questioning, accusing, failing to support him because she'd been preoccupied with herself. In short, she'd failed him in all the ways she knew, and her sorrow struck deep inside.

She toyed with her food, staring at the congealed fat, the soggy potatoes that made her nauseous. Was this where it ended, the love they had, the glorious expectations? In mutual disappointment? Her words stuck in her throat, but she got them out somehow.

"What must I do?"

He burst into laughter. "Do? Do?" Then he reached

across the table and took her hand. "Be yourself. Be my own, sweet Vi, that's all."

And who was that? How did he see her? As a shadow that said what he wanted and nothing more? She shook her head. Never! She'd never be a ghost to him or to herself. She snatched back her hand and made it into a small fist.

"I'm not all sweet, and you know it, Mister Slaughter. I'll speak my mind when I feel it's time. When somebody has to tell you what's what because you aren't God, and that's the way of it. We chose each other, and we'll go on, and you'll not close your ears to what I have to say. I'm as worthy and as smart as anybody to be heard and listened to. You hear me?"

Her eyes flashed for the first time in months, and her cheeks grew pink with indignation. Inwardly, John applauded her—and himself.

"Pack a bag," he said suddenly.

She stared. "Why?"

"We're going to buy a ranch."

Her eyes narrowed. "What ranch? Where? You didn't say anything."

"I didn't know until an hour ago. It's an old Spanish grant in the San Bernardino Valley. Runs both sides of the border. Good grass, water, all we've ever wanted. Are you coming, or do I have to do it alone?" He held his breath and watched her.

It was the dream, wrenched out of nightmare, the offering of the old hope that hadn't, perhaps couldn't, be extinguished.

She said: "You've seen it and didn't tell me?"

"I haven't. But Tad has, and that's good enough for me. Will you come?"

He was pleading as much as he could bring himself to plead, and she felt her anger dissipate. What else, after all, was there? She loved. She had chosen.

She stood up, walked around the table, put her hands on his shoulders. "Of course, I'm coming, Mister Slaughter," she said, bending to kiss the top of his head. "Wild horses wouldn't keep me away."

XXIX

He drove the buggy down Silver Creek where it spilled into the San Bernardino Valley. To the east, the Peloncillo Mountains rose out of a broad plain, and behind them, like an illusion, the peaks of the Animas Range seemed to float against a sky the color of an iris petal.

Looking up the valley, she thought she could see nearly to the end of the world, across infinite space, endless grass interspersed with small hills, relics of fledgling volcanoes from a time so far past no one could remember it. There was distance distorted by dancing waves of heat, and beyond that more distance, and more still, and only a spiraling hawk, the flight of a herd of white-rumped antelope gave perspective to a landscape so large it seemed to have no boundaries at all.

The land called, and she responded with a joyousness she thought she'd lost with her lost children.

They would have a house here, and it would be a happy place, filled with ringing voices and the sound of the wind that blew constantly from the southwest. They would have a house and a life that spun out around them like the moving light, the shadows of rising thunderheads, the mountains whose names she spoke to herself, names that boomed like thunder, whispered with a softness like spring rain—Peloncillo, Pedregosa, Chiricahua, Guadalupe—the Old World and the New come together, the dream and the reality made one.

She blinked away tears. "There it is," she whispered. "There's our future. All that beauty waiting for us."

"We'll have it, Vi," he said, and reached for her hand. "We'll have it here . . . what we planned."

She curled her fingers around his and let her imagination soar. The house would be large, with high windows and a porch to sit on after chores and supper were over. And there would be laughter, lots of it, visitors, neighbors, cattle buyers, and children.

She took a breath, let it out. "Mister Slaughter . . . ," she said slowly, thinking through her vision. "Mister Slaughter . . . there must be children who need a home, who haven't got anybody to care for them. Do you think we could . . . ?" Her voice trailed off, but she looked at him with hope in her eyes.

He understood what she hadn't spoken, caught a glimpse of the desolation she'd tried so hard to disguise, and pity welled up in him, but when he spoke it was jokingly, as if he didn't trust himself. "I say. . . . I say, Vi, I'll bring you all the babies I find and give you the raising of them. How's that, eh?"

After all, she thought, she had chosen wisely, followed her heart and her intuition. Her smile, when she looked at him, was radiant, and her eyes caught and held a reflection of sky.

"I love you, Mister Slaughter," she said. "And I thank you. For my life and for bringing us home."

Author's Note

I have taken a few liberties with dates in this novel, but not with the facts. It is fact that John Slaughter headed New Mexico Governor Lew Wallace's wanted list and that Amazon Howell also appeared on that list. However, it must be taken into consideration that the appropriation of unbranded cattle was a common practice, was, in fact, the foundation of the Texas cattle industry after the Civil War, so that neither John Slaughter, nor his father-in-law, nor any of the other cattle "barons" were any more guilty of "sweeping in" than anyone else.

It is also true that John Slaughter brought into Arizona many of those who became what was known as "The Cowboy Gang"—Curly Bill Brocius, Joe Hill, Billy Grounds, Billy Claiborn, and, possibly, even John Ringo. Again, however, in those days and in those circumstances, one hired men who were capable of sitting a horse and punching cows, regardless of their past records.

I have taken some liberties with Slaughter dates for the purposes of the novel. In 1881, the year of the famous gunfight in Tombstone, the Slaughters were still living on their ranch in the San Pedro Valley. There is, however, no reason to believe that Viola was not in Tombstone at this time as she frequented the town for visits and shopping trips. In addition, the Slaughters went on their ill-fated trip to Idaho in 1882 and were forced to return because of John's health. It was after this trip that they rented their house on Third and Fremont Streets in Tombstone.

Viola had several miscarriages and a life-threatening tubal pregnancy. Whether or not she was operated on by George

Goodfellow is unknown, but, certainly, if that pregnancy occurred in Tombstone, Goodfellow, known for his brilliant surgical procedures, would have been called and would not have hesitated to operate.

John Slaughter was elected sheriff of Cochise County and served two terms, after which he and Viola moved to the San Bernardino Ranch and lived there until a few months before his death in 1922. Viola Slaughter died in Douglas, Arizona in 1941.

Acknowledgments

Without the assistance of Ben T. Traywick, Tombstone town historian, I could not have written "Mrs. Slaughter." Ben provided me with two boot boxes filled with Slaughter material and with much encouragement.

Thanks also to John Tanner, whose overview of the cattle kings clarified their actions and way of life for me.

And to Glenn Boyer, who first took me to the Slaughter Ranch and introduced me to its magic. The ranch is now a National Historic Landmark and a testimony to the lives of two extraordinary Arizona pioneers.

About the Author

Born and raised near Pittsburgh, Pennsylvania, Jane Candia Coleman majored in creative writing at the University of Pittsburgh but stopped writing after graduation in 1960 because she knew she "hadn't lived enough, thought enough, to write anything of interest." Her life changed dramatically when she abandoned the East for the West in 1986, and her creativity came truly into its own. THE VOICES OF DOVES (1988) was written soon after she moved to Tucson. It was followed by a book of poetry, NO ROOF BUT SKY (1990), and by a truly remarkable short story collection that amply repays reading and re-reading, STORIES FROM MESA COUNTRY (1991). Her short story, "Lou" in *Louis L'Amour Western Magazine* (3/94), won the Spur Award from the Western Writers of America as did her later short story, "Are You Coming Back, Phin Montana?" in *Louis L'Amour Magazine* (1/96). She has also won three Western Heritage Awards from the National Cowboy Hall of Fame. DOC HOLLIDAY'S WOMAN (1995) was her first novel and one of vivid and extraordinary power. The highly acclaimed MOVING ON: STORIES OF THE WEST was her first **Five Star Western**, and it contains her two Spur award-winning stories. It was followed in 1998 with the novel, I, PEARL HART. It can be said that a story by Jane Candia Coleman embodies the essence of what is finest in the Western story, intimations of hope, vulnerability, and courage, while she plummets to the depths of her characters, conjuring moods and imagery with the consummate artistry of an accomplished poet. She is currently at work on BORDERLANDS, her next **Five Star Western**.